Lurulu

Tor Books by Jack Vance

JACK VANCE

LURULU

TOR®

A Tom Doherty
Associates Book
New York

LURULU

A Tor Book
Published by Tom Doherty Associates, LLC
175 Fifth Avenue
New York, NY 10010

www.tor.com

Tor® is a registered trademark of Tom Doherty Associates, LLC.

Library of Congress Cataloging-in-Publication Data

Vance, Jack, 1916–
        Lurulu / Jack Vance.
            p. cm.
        "A Tom Doherty Associates book."
        Sequel to: Ports of call.
        ISBN-13: 978-0-312-87279-3
        ISBN-10: 0-312-87279-8
        1. Children of the rich—Fiction. 2. Space flight—Fiction.
    3. Space ships—Fiction. 4. Young men—Fiction. I. Title.

    PS3572.A424L87 2004
    813'.54—dc22

                                                    2004049577

First Hardcover Edition: December 2004
First Trade Paperback Edition: February 2007

Printed in the United States of America

0 9 8 7 6 5 4 3 2 1

To Norma

PREFACE

Several years ago, during work upon *Ports of Call*, I came to a stage where the manuscript had reached book length, but a large amount of material remained that I could not bring myself to jettison. What to do? I solved the problem in the same spirit with which Alexander had dealt with the Gordian Knot: I simply stopped writing, with a note to the effect that the narrative would be continued some time in the future. I then put *Ports of Call* away and started *Lurulu*, which is at last, to my relief, complete.

To bring readers up to speed, Chapter One of *Lurulu* is a reprise of *Ports of Call*. If anyone feels a twitch of déjà vu, it is no hallucination; for expedience, I reused several paragraphs from the first book.

LURULU

ONE

A précis of the first book, *Ports of Call*

As a boy Myron Tany had immersed himself in the lore of space exploration. In his imagination he wandered the far places of the Gaean Reach, thrilling to the exploits of star-dusters and locators; of pirates and slavers; of the IPCC and its brave agents.

By contrast, his home at the bucolic village Lilling, on the pleasant world Vermazen, seemed to encompass everything easy, tranquil, and soporific. Despite Myron's daydreams, his parents persisted in stressing the practicalities. "Most important is your education, if you are to become a financial analyst like your father," Myron was told. "After you finish your course at the Institute, that will be the time to flutter your wings for a bit before taking a post at the Exchange."

Myron, mild and dutiful by temperament, pushed the intoxicating images to the back of his mind, and enrolled at the College of Definable Excellences at the Varley Institute, across the continent at Salou Sain. His parents, who well understood his casual disposition, sent him off with a set of stern injunctions: he must concentrate with full diligence upon his studies; scholastic achievement was highly important when a person prepared for a career.

Myron agreed to do his best, but found himself waylaid by indecision when it came time to propose a schedule of studies. Despite his best intentions, he could not put aside images of majestic space-packets sliding through the void; of cities redolent with strange smells; of taverns open to the warm winds where barefoot maidens served jugs of Mango Slurry and Blue Ruin.

In the end Myron fixed upon a set of courses which, in his opinion, represented a compromise. The list included statistical mathematics, economic patterns of the Gaean Reach, general cosmology, the elementary theory of space propulsion, Gaean anthropology. The program, so he assured his parents, was known as 'Economic Fluxions', and provided a solid foundation upon which a good general education might be based. Myron's parents were not convinced. They knew that Myron's decorous manner, though at times a trifle absent-minded, concealed a streak of irrational intransigence against which no argument could prevail. They would say no more; Myron must discover his mistakes for himself.

Myron could not dismiss the foreboding which his father's glum predictions had induced. As a consequence he attacked his work vigorously. In due course he was matriculated with high honors, and a position at the Exchange was open to him. But now an unforeseen factor disturbed the flow of Myron's life. The disruptive influence was Myron's great-aunt Dame Hester Lajoie, who had inherited great wealth from her first husband. Dame Hester maintained her splendid residence, Sarbiter House, on Dingle Terrace, at the southern edge of Salou Sain. During Myron's last term at Varley Institute, Dame Hester noticed that Myron was no longer a slender stripling with a vague and—as she put it—moony expression, but had become a distinctly good-looking young man, still slender, but of good physical proportions, with sleek blond hair and sea-blue eyes. Dame Hester enjoyed the presence of handsome young men: they acted, so she imagined, as a foil, or perhaps better to say, a setting for the precious gem which was herself. For whatever reason, during Myron's last term, he resided at Sarbiter House with his great-aunt: an education in itself.

Dame Hester fitted no familiar patterns of Gaean woman-hood. She was tall and gaunt, though she insisted upon the word 'slim'. She walked with long strides, head thrust forward like a rapacious animal on the prowl. Her wild mass of mahogany-red hair framed a pale, hollow-cheeked face. Her black eyes were surrounded by small creases and folds of skin, like a parrot's eyes, and her long high-bridged nose terminated in a notable hook. It was a striking face, the mouth jerking and grimacing, parrot-eyes snapping, her expression shifting to the flux of emotions. Her tempestuous moods, quirks and fancies were notorious. One day at a garden party, a gentleman artlessly urged Dame Hester to write her memoirs. The fervor of her response caused him shock and dismay. "Ludicrous! Graceless! Stupid! A beastly idea! How can I write memoirs now when I have scarcely started to live?"

For a fact Dame Hester was not always discreet. She conceived herself a creature of voluptuous charm for whom time had no meaning. Undeniably she made a gorgeous spectacle as she whirled about the haut monde, clad in remarkable garments of magenta, lime green, vermilion and black.

Dame Hester had recently won a judgment of slander against Gower Hatchkey, a wealthy member of the Gadroon Society. In satisfaction of the judgment she had accepted the space-yacht *Glodwyn*.

Initially Dame Hester thought of the *Glodwyn* only as proof that whoever chose to call her 'a bald old harridan in a red fright-wig' must pay well for the privilege. She showed no interest in the vessel, to Myron's astonishment. She told him tartly: "Truly, I have no inclination to go hurtling through space in an oversize coffin. That is sheer lunacy and a mortification of both body and spirit. I shall probably put the vessel up for sale."

Myron groaned and clutched at his sleek blond hair.

Dame Hester watched him closely. "I see that you are perplexed; you think me timid and orthodox! That is incorrect! I pay no heed to convention, and why is this? Because my youthful spirit defies the years! So you dismiss me as an eccentric madcap? What then? It is the price I pay for retaining the verve of youth, and it is the secret of my vivid beauty!"

"Ah yes, of course," said Myron. He added thoughtfully: "Still, it is sad waste of a beautiful ship."

The remark irritated Dame Hester. "Myron, be practical!

Why should I gad about empty space, or trudge through dirty
back alleys in search of strange smells? Preposterous!"

Myron numbly went off to read *Transcendent Lives: The Locators and Their Model 11-B Scudders*.

During a rare moment of repose, Dame Hester chanced upon an
article written by a certain 'Serena', telling of her experiences on
the world Kodaira, where she had undertaken an amazingly effective rejuvenation program. Dame Hester was inspired by the
article. After making inquiries, she altered her views regarding
space travel and resolved to visit Kodaira aboard the *Glodwyn*.

With Dame Hester, to think was to act. She summoned Myron and ordered him to learn the exact location of Kodaira. She
appointed her dear and intimate friend Dauncy Covarth Captain of the *Glodwyn*, but he disgraced himself and Myron was
tendered the position.

The *Glodwyn* departed the Salou Sain spaceport, and Myron
set a course for Naharius, the real name of Kodaira. For a time
the voyage proceeded smoothly. Dame Hester luxuriated in the
tranquility, the absence of stress, the total lack of demands upon
her time. She slept late, dawdled over her meals and read several books. "The voyage," she told Myron, "is a rejuvenation in
itself."

As time passed, Dame Hester's enthusiasm began to wane.
She became ever more restless, and finally she summoned
Myron.

"Yes, Aunt Hester?"

"How far have we come to date?"

"About halfway, I should guess."

"So little? I feel as if we have been traveling forever!"

"Naharius is a long way out, for a fact," Myron admitted.
"Still, there is much to enjoy along the way: untroubled rest,
calm and deep meditation, the sheer joy of easing effortlessly
past the stars."

"Bah!" snapped Dame Hester.

Myron pointed to the observation port. "Observe the stars
drifting past. It is the most romantic spectacle of all!"

"My wish would be to stop by a pleasant way station where
the folk still abide by their ancient customs, where we could

breathe new air, and enjoy the glamour of strange landscapes and quaint villages."

"All very well," said Myron. "No doubt these picturesque places exist, but if we deviate from our planned course we may not so easily return anywhere near our destination, which is Naharius."

Dame Hester seemed not to hear. "I have read of native markets where unique goods can be had: fetishes and masks, emblems of fertility, exotic fabrics. There are true bargains to be found, if one is prepared to haggle a bit."

"Yes, yes, of course! Nevertheless, such worlds are not to be found everywhere."

Dame Hester lurched up from her position on the sofa. "Please! Myron! I have stated my needs! Be good enough to implement them."

Myron spoke with harried patience. "My dear Aunt Hester, if I could produce a world of such gorgeous romance for your pleasure, I would do so on the instant. But I would be performing a miracle!"

Dame Hester spoke icily: "In that case, perform the miracle. Are you finally aware of my mood?"

"Yes," said Myron. "It is clear."

"Good." Dame Hester resumed her supine posture on the sofa.

Myron bowed and went off to consult his references.

Presently he returned to the saloon. "I have studied *Handbook to the Planets* at length," he told Dame Hester. "The most accessible world is Dimmick, in orbit around the white dwarf Maudwell's Star. It would seem queer and odd enough to gratify even the most avid taste.

"The references are somewhat ambiguous, but none seriously emphasize the world's allure. Let me read from the *Handbook*: 'Dimmick is not a world of halcyon charm, although the topography often displays a rugged grandeur. The surface is for the most part covered under harsh mountains and glaciers. A number of small circular plains, depressed below the surface, are in fact meteor craters. In these parts, the air temperature is modified by ground heat to the threshhold of livability. The town Flajaret and the spaceport are located in one of the craters.

"'Dimmick and its people, to say the least, are unusual, though sensitive visitors may not be captivated. The efflux of hot springs creates tunnels through the glaciers, providing shelter for a debased caste of dog-breeders known as 'spockows'. The upper castes keep dogs in their homes, and dress them in fancy suits. There is an undercurrent of hostility between the castes, since one eats the creatures, while the other pampers the animals and feeds them tidbits from their tables.

"'The principal sport is dog-fighting, which is important since it sets the tone for the society. Gambling is obsessive. Even small children crawl to the arena, to bet coins upon their favorite beast. Another vehicle for gambling is the penal system. Near Flajaret is a large lake crusted over with mats of algae. On this surface the penal exercises are conducted, to the great interest of the public at large.

"'Dimmick is not known for its gracious cuisine, since few if any natural foods are consumed. Ordinary victual consists of synthetic gruel, enlivened by artificial flavoring, then fried, baked, boiled, or shirred, to much the same effect.'"

Myron paused. "Shall I go on? The *Handbook* provides several recipes for boiled dog, which may interest you."

"Thank you, no."

Myron looked sidewise at Dame Hester, trying to gauge her mood. Often she could be perverse simply to inject drama into a situation. He risked an opinion: "I suggest that we bypass Dimmick. We are approaching Port Tanjee on Taubry, which surely will be more entertaining."

Dame Hester spoke decisively: "We shall land at Flajaret and briefly explore this benighted world. Then we shall also halt at Port Tanjee. In this way we will be able to compare the good with the bad."

Myron performed a crisp bow. "As you like."

At Flajaret Dame Hester met an off-worlder named Marko Fassig, an engaging young scapegrace with burly shoulders, a bushy mustache, and soft brown eyes. His witticisms and general gallantry impressed Dame Hester to such an extent that she hired him as purser aboard the *Glodwyn*, despite Myron's strenuous objections.

When the *Glodwyn* landed at Port Tanjee, Myron discharged

Fassig from his post, and ordered him off the ship within the hour. But half an hour later it was Myron himself who, in a morose mood, departed the ship carrying his suitcase, with Dame Hester's final remarks still ringing in his ears.

Myron wandered into town and took lodging for the night at the Rambler's Rest rooming house. During the evening he visited the Owlswyck Inn, where he encountered the crew of the freighter *Glicca*, consisting of Captain Adair Maloof, Chief Steward Isel Wingo, Chief Engineer Fay Schwatzendale, and Hilmar Krim, the Supercargo.

Each man contrasted markedly with his fellows, but Krim most of all. He was tall and gaunt, with a high forehead, a curious little mat of black hair, a long chin and hooded black eyes. Krim was given to dogmatic opinions, which his fellows never troubled to contradict. Myron learned that Krim was a dedicated student of jurisprudence, and in fact was composing a three-volume analysis of Gaean law.

On this particular evening, Krim was in good spirits and drank several tankards of Old Gaboon. When the dancing started, he jumped out upon the floor and began to dance an energetic loose-legged strut. A portly well-dressed gentleman, with a fine ginger-colored mustache, also came out upon the floor to perform what was known as 'The Chicken-thief's Trot'—a long loping prance, with body leaning far backwards and legs kicking out high to the front. The two came into contact. During the altercation which followed, Krim committed several offenses against the local law and, when the constable on duty sought to restrain him, aggravated his offenses by kicking the ginger-mustached man in the shins. This gentleman chanced to be the district Magistrate.

The Magistrate hobbled to a chair on the dais and seated himself, while the sergeant of the guard stepped forward and cited the entire list of Krim's infractions. Krim foolishly tried to argue jurisprudence using the terms 'fat lummox' and 'dunderhead': a new transgression of the local antidefamation code. He was arraigned on the spot. The Magistrate put on his judicial hat and took Krim's case under consideration. He now seemed cool and impartial, as befitted his position, and pronounced Krim's sentence in an even voice: "Sir, you have made several interesting legal points, but they fly a bit wide of the mark. My duty is both to better your legal understanding and to shield the innocent folk of this city against acts of mindless violence. Therefore, I sentence you to four months, eleven days and nineteen hours of educational exercises in the rock quarry."

Krim tried to utter further legalities, and to introduce apposite precedents into the case, but was marched from the inn and hustled off to the quarry.

After a decorous interval, Myron applied to Captain Maloof for Krim's position aboard the *Glicca*. Captain Maloof ruminated for a moment. He said: "The job is not simple, and demands all the resources of a competent man."

"I believe that I am that man," declared Myron boldly.

"We shall see," said Captain Maloof. "First, let me ask: are you familiar with the ten primary digits of the numerical scheme?"

"Yes sir. So I am!"

"And you understand their usual employment?"

"Yes, sir."

"You are able to read written documents, and translate them into the spoken tongue?"

"Yes, sir."

"If hired, would you object to balancing your accounts, more or less accurately?"

"No sir; not at all."

Captain Maloof gave a sigh of relief. "Your qualifications seem to be superb. You are hired."

"Thank you, sir."

"Not at all," said Captain Maloof. "While I do not want to bring poor Krim any unnecessary tribulation, it will be something of a relief to have him shifting large rocks, rather than integers in the ledgers. Your main challenge, or so I believe, will be adapting to Krim's intuitive methods of accounting. You may report aboard the *Glicca* tomorrow morning."

In the morning Myron departed the Rambler's Rest, and took his breakfast at an open-air café to the side of the plaza. Then he walked under the cloud-trees to the spaceport, passed through the terminal, and found the *Glicca* a hundred yards out

on the field. It was an ungainly old hulk, carrying freight in
three cargo bays, and a fluctuating number of passengers. The
hull, which at one time had been enamelled blue-gray with dark
red trim, now showed a lusterless gray-white undercoat, along
with daubs of orange primer where it had been thought necessary to seal off scrapes, abrasions and meteor marks. Myron approached, climbed the short gangway and passed through the
open port into the main saloon. He found Captain Maloof and
Schwatzendale lingering over their breakfast.

"Sit down," said Captain Maloof. "Have you had breakfast?"

"I had two fishcakes in a red sauce, and a pot of pepper tea,"
said Myron. "It was, in a sense, breakfast."

Wingo, in the galley, had heard the interchange and immediately brought Myron a bowl of beans with bacon and two
toasted scones. "The food one finds in remote places is often
sub-standard," said Wingo severely. "Aboard the *Glicca* we are
not epicures, but we are never faddists, and we feel no compulsion to explore every intricacy of the local cuisine."

"Wingo acts as our arbiter in these cases," Schwatzendale
told Myron. "If he finds a stuff in the market which intrigues
him, it is served up for our dinner. He watches us carefully, and
if we appear to enjoy the dish he may even sample it himself."

Wingo grinned broadly. "I hear few complaints," he told Myron. "If you care to step this way, I will show you your quarters.
Schwatzendale and I have already taken poor Krim's belongings
to the transit office. The cabin has been well aired, and the linen
is fresh. I think that you will be comfortable."

Myron took his suitcase to the cabin, then returned to the
saloon. Maloof now sat alone.

"Your quarters are suitable, or so I hope?"

"Yes, of course, and I am ready to go to work."

"In that case, I will explain the scope of your duties. They are
more various than you might expect." Maloof looked thoughtfully toward the ceiling. "You may find difficulties taking up
where Krim left off. Despite his many fine qualities, Krim was a
man of the sort known as sui generis."

Myron nodded. "I am not surprised."

"Krim was often a bit short with the passengers, and gener-
ated quite unnecessary friction. In response to a request which

he found irrational, rather than taking five minutes to gratify the passenger's needs, he would explain why the passenger should alter his philosophy. At other times, he might prescribe a holistic remedy for the passenger's indigestion, rather than simply issuing the pastille requested, and the two would debate the case for hours—until the passenger, overcome by cramps, was forced to rush off to the latrine. When I tried to intercede, Krim declared himself a man of principle, and I was made to feel a charlatan."

Myron nodded and spoke as he wrote into a small notebook: "Instruction one: conciliate passengers. Dispense medicine as required."

"Correct. Now then, as to records and accounts, again I must criticize Krim. He was so preoccupied with his monumental compilation of jurisprudence that he avoided the drudgery of keeping accounts. When he was censured, he claimed that he had memorized all pertinent figures, and that they reposed accurately in his mind. One day I asked him: 'What if by some unexpected freak of fortune you are forced off the *Glicca*, as it might be if you were killed by a bandit, or suffered a brainspasm?' 'Nonsense, sheer bullypup!' he told me, quite emphatically. Still, I persisted: 'What if you are taken up by the police and dragged off to jail? Who, then, will interpret your cryptic notes?' At this, Krim became cross. 'The idea,' he stated, 'is farfetched. No police would think to molest a man of my forensic skills.' But Krim was wrong; he was taken off to jail, and his vast store of mental records is lost. The episode, I believe, speaks for itself."

Myron wrote in the notebook: "Instruction two: keep proper records. Avoid police."

"Exactly." Maloof went on to describe Myron's other duties. He would prepare bills of lading, and arrange for import and export licenses when necessary. He would supervise loading, and at each port of call he must verify that the proper parcels were discharged, even if he must carry them out to the dock himself.

Myron wrote: "Instruction three: expedite cargo on and off vessel. Cargo to be recorded in detail."

Maloof continued: "The Supercargo must make sure that freight charges have been paid, before cargo is loaded. Otherwise, chances are good that we will be carrying cargo free of charge, since the consignee will often refuse to pay freight charges—leaving us in possession of the freight, which is often worthless, leading to many difficulties."

Myron wrote: "Instruction four: before all else, collect fees and charges."

"As you can see," said Maloof, "the ideal Supercargo is a man of iron will and a grim disposition. He has a mind like a trap and tolerates no impudence from the warehousemen, no matter how pugnacious they seem."

"I will do my best," said Myron in a subdued voice.

"That should be sufficient," said Maloof. "We travel short-handed aboard the *Glicca*. Everyone is versatile, especially the Supercargo. You are aware of all this?"

"I am now."

Later in the day, eleven pilgrims presented themselves to Captain Maloof, requesting passage to Impy's Landing on the world Kyril, where they would undertake a five-year march around the planet. Captain Maloof explained that the *Glicca* could convey them to Coro-coro on Fluter, but thereafter they must trans-ship to Kyril. After argument, the pilgrims reluctantly agreed to Captain Maloof's stipulations.

There was further contention in regard to the fares. Kalash, the Perrumpter of the group, insisted upon a religious discount. Captain Maloof responded with a sad shake of his head. "If your panel of deities wished you a quick and comfortable transfer to Kyril, it would have been arranged by divine fiat."

Kalash made a final attempt to explain the seeming paradox: "The gods move in mysterious ways."

Maloof nodded sagely. "Agreed! Still, either you or the gods must pay the proper fare."

The Perrumpter had nothing more to say. The pilgrims trooped aboard the ship, and were shown to their quarters by Wingo and Myron.

At sunset the *Glicca* set off on a route which would take it from world to world, through regions obscure and remote, visited only by tramp freighters like the *Glicca*. The pilgrims quickly settled into routines; drinking tea, criticizing the cuisine, performing rites, gambling, and discussing the world Kyril, where they proposed a circumambulation.

Myron adapted quickly to his work, but found some difficulty dealing with Hilmar Krim's extraordinary methods of accounting. Krim had used an abstruse shorthand writing and a system of abbreviations and crabbed hieroglyphics which baffled Myron's understanding. Additionally, Krim had never recorded financial details such as port charges, wages of warehousemen, cash advances to members of the crew, or incidental expenses, preferring to keep a running total in his memory until such a time as he felt inclined to transfer the lump sum to his books. These occasions seemed dictated by caprice, and Krim seldom troubled to identify the numbers.

In the end, Myron devised a method of computation which he called 'creative averaging'. The system was both straightforward and definite, though its basis might be considered intuitive, or even arbitrary. To use the system, Myron replaced Krim's hieroglyphics with more or less imaginary quantities, which he adjusted until they produced a reasonable summation. By this means Myron restored the books to a state of order—though he made no guarantees of precision. Maloof looked over the books, and was well satisfied with Myron's results.

As the days passed, Myron became acquainted with his shipmates. Schwatzendale, so he discovered, was spontaneous and volatile, with a lilting imagination rife with surprises and wonders. In contrast, Wingo was placid, methodical, and a thinker of profound thoughts. Superficially, Schwatzendale seemed a charming rascal of antic habits and slantwise good looks. His heart-shaped face, with its widow's peak and luminous eyes, often prompted strangers to take him for a languid young aesthete, or even a sybarite. Such theories were wildly incorrect. Schwatzendale, in fact, was brash, restless, and extravagant in his moods and attitudes. He skipped and hopped like a child, without perceptible self-consciousness. He attacked his work with disdain, as if it were too contemptible for a person of style and taste to take seriously. In this regard, Schwatzendale was both romantic and vain; he thought of himself as a combination gambler and gentleman-adventurer.

Wingo occasionally spoke of Schwatzendale's exploits in a mixture of awe, grudging admiration, and disapproval. In total contrast to Schwatzendale, Wingo was short, thick, and blue-eyed, with only a few strands of blond hair across his pink scalp. Wingo was mild, amiable, and sympathethic, an avid collector of curios, small trinkets, and interesting oddments, which he prized not for their inherent value, but for the cleverness of their execution. He was also a dedicated photographer, and was engaged in compiling what he called 'mood-impressions', which he hoped ultimately to publish in a portfolio entitled *Pageant of the Gaean Race*.

Wingo was greatly interested in comparative metaphysics. He paid more than casual attention to the sects, superstitions, religions, and transcendental philosophies which he encountered as the *Glicca* travelled from world to world and, whenever he wandered strange places, gave careful attention to local spiritual doctrines—a practice which incurred Schwatzendale's disapproval.

"You are wasting your time! There are a hundred thousand of these creeds; they all talk the same nonsense, and all want your money. Why bother? Religious cant is the greatest nonsense of all!"

"There is much in what you say," Wingo admitted. "Still, is it not possible, that by some odd chance one of these hundred thousand doctrines is correct and precisely defines the Cosmic Way? If we passed it by, we might never encounter Truth again!"

"In theory, yes," grumbled Schwatzendale. "But in practice, your chances are next to nil."

Wingo waved a pink forefinger. "Tut! One can never be sure. Perhaps you have miscalculated the odds."

"I can't answer you properly," growled Schwatzendale. "Odds of zero in a thousand are much the same as zero in a million."

Wingo responded with a wistful smile. "I will check out your formulation. Conceivably you are mistaken."

Schwatzendale agreed that this was possible, and there the matter rested.

For Myron, Schwatzendale was a constant source of wonder and amusement. He was physically beautiful, a fact which Schwatzendale recognized but ignored. In the engine-room, he worked with speed, precision, absolute certainty, and his characteristic panache. Typically he finished each job with a flourish, and a glance of disdainful menace at the repaired part, as if warning it never to repeat its mistake. Myron soon came to see past Schwatzendale's epicene beauty to an inner hardness, which was intensely masculine. He studied Schwatzendale's attributes with covert fascination. They manifested themselves in many tricks and habits, sardonic jokes, and oblique ideas, in the tilt of his head and the angle of his elbows; in his quick, loping strides. Myron sometimes fantasized that Schwatzendale's parts were all askew, so that they necessarily fitted together on the bias and all was asymmetric, quirky, 'slantwise'. Schwatzendale was like a knight on the chessboard, which could move only by eccentric hops and bounds.

The *Glicca* cruised from world to world, controlled by bills of lading and cargo destinations. At Girandole on the world Fiametta, the *Glicca* landed beside the *Fontenoy*—a large space-yacht almost as grand as the *Glodwyn*. The master of the *Fontenoy* was Joss Garwig, Director of Acquisitions for the Pan-Arts Museum at Duvray on the world Alcydon. Garwig was accompanied by his wife Vermyra, his son Mirl, and daughter Tibbet.

At Sweetfleur, the crew of the *Glicca* joined Garwig and his family for the 'Lalapalooza', a carnival of many dimensions. They watched while Moncrief the Mouse-rider and his troupe bamboozled the public with zeal and finesse. Schwatzendale took particular interest, as this was the selfsame Moncrief who had at one time taken almost fifty sols from him at a game of Cagliostro. Schwatzendale had never ceased to yearn for revenge.

Myron and Tibbet slipped away to visit 'The Tunnel of Love', and were not seen again until late in the evening. Their parting was sad-sweet, for the Gaean Reach was long and wide, and they could not guess when they would meet again. "You can write to me care of the Pan-Arts Museum at Duvray," said Tibbet. "If I don't hear from you, I'll know that you have forgotten me."

At the end of the day's business Moncrief took Captain Maloof aside, and arranged transport for himself and his troupe to Cax on the world Blenkinsop. On the following morning the newcomers boarded the *Glicca*: a party of six, including Flook, Pook, and Snook, three enchanting young maidens of lively disposition; the Klutes, Siglaf and Hunzel, a pair of truculent warrior-women from the Bleary Hills of Numoy; and Mon-crief himself—all in all, a picturesque company.

The *Glicca* continued along its route. Leaving behind the four dreary spaceports of Mariah, the *Glicca* began the long run to Fluter, and fabled Coro-coro.

TWO

1

Excerpt from *Handbook to the Planets*: Fluter, World of Glamour

There is nothing to be gained by describing the climate of Fluter: it is perfect, and as such it is taken for granted, as are most of the other aspects of this magnificent world. The landscapes are as sunny and verdant as a view across lost Arcady.

The people of Fluter share the attributes of their wonderful world. They seem to dance through life to the measures of music they alone can hear: women of many talents, noble philosophers, solitary vagabonds wandering the lonely places. In general they are friendly and gay, and anxious to appear beautiful in the eyes of the off-worlders, whom they revere perhaps unreasonably. In the main they are addicted to the joys of feasting, music, star-naming, sailing the wild seas, and love-making in a style known as 'ingesting the perfumed flowers'.

The intelligent reader will quickly observe that the article quoted above (from the periodical *Touristic Topics*) is a masterpiece of hyperbole; doubtless the writer was never any closer to Fluter than his local amusement park. Only the most naive of readers, upon exposure to the article, will set off pell-mell for Fluter hoping to find 'ineffable glamour and daily episodes of erotic hi-jinks'.

The following facts should be noted. The scenery of Fluter is very pleasant. The best hotel in Coro-coro is the O-Shar-Shan, but there is no running hot water. The girls are neither seductive, nor particularly amiable. Arrivals at the spaceport are allowed visitor's permits of thirty days' duration.

2

The *Glicca* drifted through space, unsubstantial as a puff of magic smoke. Far astern, Pfitz was a dying white spark, which presently faded. Ahead, golden Frametta could not yet be seen.

In the pilot-house of the *Glicca*, Captain Maloof turned from the observation window and stepped aft into the main saloon. He waited until the cheerful voices quieted, then spoke.

"Before long we will be arriving at the Coro-coro spaceport on Fluter, and you should know something of local conditions, which at times are ambiguous, if not extraordinary.

"In general, Fluter is a tranquil world with beautiful landscapes in every direction, and a near-total lack of natural hazards. On Fluter time seems to move at a languid pace, possibly because there are twenty-eight hours to the Fluter day.

"Coro-coro is the only settlement of consequence. Aside from the tourist facilities, there is nothing much to the town. A boulevard runs from the spaceport to the O-Shar-Shan Hotel, with more hotels along the way; also agencies, shops, and taverns. Residences are scattered in the gardens to either side of the boulevard. These are the homes of the folk native to Coro-coro, who are different from the Flauts who live in the back-country villages. The folk of the town regard themselves as sophisticated aristocrats, with wealth derived from the tourist trade—which on Fluter is highly developed, and very lucrative.

"Permanent residence is forbidden to off-worlders. Tourists are allowed entry permits of thirty days; then they are required to leave the planet, although in practice, the entry permit can be extended.

"If you should visit a village, remain unobtrusive; express no opinions, and drink with temperance. No one worries for the drunken tourist who has been tossed into the sump! Do not haggle or complain, and above all else, ignore the girls. The Flauts observe an exact sexual morality, and if you wonder why suddenly you have been emasculated, it is probably because you have committed an immoral act, such as looking under a girl's skirt. The village may seem a placid place where nothing ever happens, but it is almost certainly the scene of a thousand grisly events.

"The first settlers arrived from the congested world Ergard. At their first conclave, they vowed that pressure of population should never again become distressful. The number they fixed upon was ninety-nine thousand, and by great effort across the ages the limit has been maintained. The population of Fluter is now at equilibrium, but bitter events of the past still rankle and gnaw at the Flaut soul. They display a peculiar personality, a kind of sullen grandiosity. Today, the Flauts are a dour, suspicious folk, by reason of their grim history, which I will not touch further upon now.

"I think I have covered everything important. Are there any questions?"

Kalash, Perrumpter of the pilgrims, raised his hand. "What of our cases? They contain valuable materials. Will you relinquish them to us?"

"Certainly, as soon as you pay off the freight charges."

"Ah, bah!" cried Kalash. "Can you not take the long view? If you recall, we gambled with Schwatzendale; now we lack funds."

"That was your mistake, not mine."

Kalash grimaced. "We are quite at a loss. Ours is a pilgrimage of immense importance, but Schwatzendale avoids all talk of restitution! Our needs are urgent; think, if you will—we must pay our fares to Kyril, return fares home to Komard—not to mention our expenses during the march around Kyril. How can we obtain this necessary money?"

"Simply enough: through the process of work."

Kalash made a face. "That is easier said than done."

"Not altogether, as there is a labor shortage at Coro-coro. You should have no trouble."

"And the cases?"

"I will leave them in the transit warehouse. To redeem them, pay off storage and freight charges, and they are yours. Have you any further questions?"

"Bah," grumbled Kalash. "What good are questions when the answers are all non-sequiturs?"

Maloof nodded in agreement. "There is something in what you say."

Kalash was not yet done. "We had hoped for an easy generosity on your part, but reasoning with you is like gnawing on a stone."

Maloof turned away from Kalash. "Any other questions?"

Cooner stepped forward, frowning thoughtfully, to indicate that he might have a question, possibly of a recondite nature. Maloof looked past him and addressed the group.

"I have an announcement to make. The crew of this ship needs both bodily rest and nervous regeneration, and the *Glicca* itself is in need of maintenance. Therefore we shall sojourn upon Fluter for perhaps a week or two. The pilgrims will debark and prepare to trans-ship to Kyril. We shall miss their wise counsel and happy songs, but after Coro-coro we must fare onward to Cax. Thereafter, who knows? I can make no prediction; we are like the romantic vagabonds of old, each searching for lurulu."

Cooner called out: "The place is unknown to me! What or where, pray, is 'lurulu'?"

" 'Lurulu' is a special word from the language of myth. It is as much of a mystery to me now as when I first yearned for something which seemed forever lost. But one day I shall glance over my shoulder, and there it will be, wondering why I had not come sooner. For now, it is on to Coro-coro. Here I feel an imminence; something important will happen, of this I feel certain. What? I do not know; it is a mystery."

Cooner's puzzlement had not yet been assuaged. "And 'lurulu' is part of this mystery?"

Maloof gave a non-committal shrug. "Perhaps. I may not be happy with what I find, if and when I find it."

"But what is it you seek?"

Maloof smiled. "I can tell you this much: if I am lucky—or perhaps unlucky—I will find it on Fluter."

"Interesting," declared Cooner. He turned to Moncrief. "And you, sir—are you also in pursuit of 'lurulu'?"

"I am sidling in its direction," Moncrief admitted. "I see a glimmer every time I take some of Schwatzendale's money. In the main, I hope that the Mouse-riders will resurge in all their glory! That would be lurulu of the purest water!"

Cooner looked to Wingo. "How about you, Brother Wingo? Where do you seek lurulu?"

"I cannot put it aptly into words," said Wingo. "It is what I hope to capture in my *Pageant of the Gaean Race*. There is also an elemental equation which describes Truth; but in this regard I am reluctant to say more."

Myron called out: "I am not so diffident; the object of my quest is named Dame Hester Lajoie, and when I catch her I hope that a jail is near, since gallantry would not allow me to do what I would like."

Cooner turned to Captain Maloof. "Do you, sir, care to tell us a bit more of your own quest?"

Captain Maloof smiled sadly. "I will say only that I am anxious to arrive on Fluter. Out among the back-lands mysteries still abide. In any case: good luck to us all."

Cooner started to ask a cogent new question, but Captain Maloof turned back into the pilot-house, and went to look again from the observation window. The star Frametta still could not be seen. He muttered to himself, "How will it be, if it happens at all? I must take care not to commit myself absolutely." He stared out the window. "Whatever happens, life will go on."

For several moments he stood gazing out the window. At last, far across the void, he thought to see the small gleam which would be the star Frametta.

THREE

1

The geography of Fluter as seen from space was extraordinary, and perhaps unique—certainly within the bounds of the Gaean Reach. In cooling from its primal melt the world had shrunk, squeezing up the crust into nine enormous anticlines, running north and south across all of one hemisphere, leaving the opposite hemisphere a flat peneplain. In the course of time, the sea rose, and the rock-folds became nine narrow continents running north and south, with shallow seas between. The opposite hemisphere was drowned beneath the waters of a vast, featureless ocean. The climate was benign; life came to Fluter, and clothed the land in verdure of innumerable varieties.

In time, a band of Gaean pioneers arrived from the crowded world Ergard, to settle all nine continents. Five years later, at the First Conclave, they bound themselves to a set of strict covenants by which to control their population, so that never should Fluter become the congested jungle of concrete towers, underground warrens, smells, stinks, and pollution, crowded streets, and cramped space which they had left behind. Time might pass—a hundred years, a thousand years—but never, so they swore, would they allow their wonderful new world to be so desecrated. The Flauts, as they called themselves, surveyed the nine continents and divided the arable land into sections, with each section rated for a population which might never be exceeded. A thousand years later, the population of Fluter occupied one hundred and forty-seven villages scattered at random across all nine continents, along with a special node surrounding the Coro-coro spaceport on Continent Five. A population of ninety-nine thousand Flauts had long since been reached.

The native flora co-existed amiably with dozens of exotic imports, from Old Earth and elsewhere. The ubiquitous coconut palm* leaned across a thousand beaches; exotic hardwoods, softwoods, flowering shrubs, and vines grew in the Fluter forests and along the mountain slopes. The fauna consisted of a few lizards and insects on land and a variety of marine life, which made the waters fascinating but dangerous.

At Coro-coro was the famous O-Shar-Shan Hotel, as well as a dozen other tourist hotels more or less fashionable. Although the calculations were complicated, Coro-coro was subject to the same population controls as the rest of Fluter, and would never grow larger than an oversized village.

2

The *Glicca* landed at the Coro-coro spaceport and was boarded by a team of local officials. Their routines were unusually careful; a pair of medics tested ship, crew, and passengers for noxious diseases, while another technician filtered samples of air in search of undesirable viruses, pollen, spores, or proteins. Finding nothing of interest, the team departed the ship.

Meanwhile, an immigration officer noted name, age, world of origin, reason for visit, and criminal record, if any, for each member of the ship's complement, issuing entry permits as he did so.

---

* The coconut palm, native to Old Earth, had been transferred across the Gaean Reach to wherever climate and saltwater provided a habitat, and now seemed native to the entire universe.

He then addressed the company. "Please listen with care! I am Civil Agent Uther Taun. I represent the administration of Coro-coro, and effectually of all Fluter.

"Civil Agents are charged with many responsibilities, but most importantly, we guard the beauty of our beloved world. Severe penalties are visited upon anyone so depraved as to distribute litter, or cause any other defilement.

"I need not enlarge upon these laws, except to state that they are enforced with diligence by a corps of special Civil Agents, and equally vigilant Land Agents, and—if appropriate—penalties of all three orders are inflicted. Neither the Land Agents nor the Civil Agents accept excuses. Wastes must be deposited in certified receptacles!

"Random micturition or defecation at large is never encouraged, for reasons which need not be particularized. Nevertheless, rather than frowning and wincing, you should think yourselves privileged to enjoy the delights of Fluter!

"I remind you that vistor's permits are valid for thirty days but may be renewed upon timely application. I will also mention that for persons desiring temporary employment, a labor exchange is situated nearby, along Pomare Boulevard.

"A final word. If, during your excursions, you should come upon a village, you would be prudent to turn away and go elsewhere. But should you ignore my advice and enter the village, be absolutely discreet—the typical Flaut may not impress you as a graceful host; to the contrary, he may appear both unfeeling and surly. If you visit a village tavern, use total decorum; if you encounter a female, abstain from familiarity, since the Flauts have no qualms about thrashing an obnoxious tourist.

"In the end, if you are careful, and pay with a willing hand, you will encounter no trouble on Fluter.

"Now then: are there questions?"

The ineffable Cooner stepped forward, his plump face alight with eager innocence. He raised his hand on high, fingers fluttering. The Civil Agent looked down at him. "You have a question?"

"Yes, sir! Why are there both Civil Agents and Land Agents?"

The Agent frowned coldly. "The differences are real, but sometimes unclear to the public. In general, the Civil Agents patrol Coro-coro, while the Land Agents keep a vigilant surveillance over the conduct of campers and excursionists."

"And which is the more severe?"

"Neither is severe. Both enforce the law of the land to the exact jot and tittle."

"Ha!" cried Cooner, with unbecoming joviality. "And what, may I ask, is the nature of the three orders of punishment? What, exactly, do they designate?"

The Agent, not happy with Cooner's flippant demeanor, answered tersely. "These matters are considered indelicate; ladies and gentlemen prefer to ignore them."

"Aha," chuckled Cooner, "but you misread your audience—aboard the *Glicca* we are all philosophers, not a lady or a gentleman in the group! You may speak on, with an easy mind."

The Agent's voice became even more terse than before. "Just as you like. Listen, then. Punishment of the first order is public chastisement. Punishment of the second order includes disgrace, confiscation of all property, and expulsion from Fluter dressed only in a bramble! Punishment of the third order involves death, by subaqueation in Sharler's Pond."

"Hm," said Cooner, more soberly than before. "I see that you take your litigation seriously. Perhaps it is wise to stay within the law."

"That is ever the case," said the official.

"How might I detect a Civil Agent, or a Land Agent, when one is in the vicinity? How are they different?"

"The questions are nuncupatory. The most prudent conduct is to assume that you are being watched by one or the other at all times.

"To answer your question more circumspectly: the Civil Agent is never conspicuous, even though he wears a neat uniform. He is polite even when he is taking you into custody. Tradition ordains that he wear a short, square beard; he is mature but never infirm, and is notable for his punctilio. The Land Agent wears a green sash and carries a ceremonial whangee; Otherwise he is much like a Civil Agent.

"Now: to other business." From his pouch Uther Taun brought pamphlets entitled: *Legal Code, Ordinary Regulations, Duties of the Visitor,* and *Advice From a Civil Agent.*

"Everyone must study this compendium with care!" declared the Agent. "There can then be no excuses for misconduct."

Cooner muttered: "Never fear, we shall creep about our affairs on tiptoe."

The Agent pretended not to hear. He distributed the pamphlets, then departed the ship.

3

Perrumpter Kalash made a final attempt to soften the resolve of Captain Maloof. He approached, face wreathed in a tremulous smile. "Sir, in talking with my colleagues, I find that we are united in admiration for the clarity of your wisdom!"

"Thank you," said Maloof. "That is good to hear."

"But we also feel that certain of your views are so abstract as to insulate you from the woes of humanity. It is our sincere hope that you have reconsidered our unhappy situation, that perhaps you have reached a better understanding and now feel a surge of sympathy for our plight. Am I right?"

"You could not be more wrong. My recommendation is as before."

Kalash threw up his arms in defeat and turned away. The pilgrims gathered to confer, and decided to ask Schwatzendale to return his winnings. Wingo overheard their muttered plans and assured them that Schwatzendale "would rather drain blood from his leg than relinquish money, once it had come into his possession."

Schwatzendale himself joined the conversation. He asked Perrumpter Kalash: "Would you have returned my losses, had you depredated my wealth? Remember, if you will, that I too have feelings!"

The pilgrims murmured resentfully, then left the ship and straggled off toward the labor exchange.

Captain Maloof and Myron went off to the warehouse to arrange for the discharge of cargo. Moncrief, along with Flook, Pook, and Snook, set off toward the center of town, with Hunzel and Siglaf hunching behind.

Wingo and Schwatzendale changed into shoreside clothes before leaving the ship. Wingo donned dust-brown breeches, a gray-pink shirt with a black string cravat, a loose brown cloak, and his brown planter's hat with the sweeping brim—a costume harking back to those gallant artists who swaggered with such élan across the early romantic eras. His sensitive feet were at ease in the fine boots of soft leather by which he set great store. Schwatzendale wore black breeches, a shirt patterned in a black and green diaper, and a soft black cap, pulled askew over his black locks.

They set off along the Pomare Boulevard, walking under a rustling canopy of overhanging foliage and sweet-smelling flowers. The trees were of many varieties: some indigenous, others brought from far worlds. Certain of the trees towered grandly on high, while others crouched, contorted with heavy limbs, spreading fans of foliage over the roadway. Silurian elms displayed fronds of pale blue and sea-green; dendrons released lobes of gas-filled membrane, which floated off down the boulevard. Quake-trees shuddered in the breeze, dropping pods loaded with spores. Nectarcups hanging on corkscrew tendrils bobbed and bounced, spilling perfume into the air.

Schwatzendale trotted along in jaunty high spirits. He danced first ahead of Wingo's staunch and steady gait, then off to the side, to pluck a flower, which a moment later he flung over his shoulder, in flamboyant disregard for the law. Wingo watched benignly and paused to pick up Schwatzendale's litter, which he tucked into his pocket.

The two passed the Labor Exchange: a long, open-sided shed overhung by talisman trees. Behind the counter, a single clerk attended to the needs of a stout woman wearing black boots and wide orange pantaloons. The pilgrims stood in a glum huddle reading notices on a bulletin board, striking from time to time at flying insects.

Wingo and Schwatzendale continued along the way. Wingo was inclined to commiserate with the pilgrims, citing the inconveniences of their present plight. Schwatzendale was more detached. "They were not compelled to march off on this fateful expedition! Had they stayed at home, they might have slept in their own beds, or performed religious rites whenever the notion took them, each to his heart's content."

"They are driven by something called 'afflatus'," Wingo told him. "It is an all-consuming force, which cannot be explained."

Schwatzendale nodded his comprehension. They proceeded, passing the premises of the Tarquin Transit Agency, which offered rental vehicles of all kinds. Three- and four-wheeled vehicles were known locally as 'skitters', some fanciful and ostentatious, others built for speed, low in front with two tall spindly wheels behind. There were flitters so fragile and light that it seemed as if the wind might carry them away. At the back of the lot, several lordly way-cars were ranked, awaiting the pleasure of those who wished to roam the wilderness in comfort, if not luxury. The firm also announced itself as agent for the rental of houseboats moored in every river and waterway of Fluter.

Taking in the sights along the way, Schwatzendale and Wingo went on, dodging the occasional skitter which trundled along the boulevard. They noticed several bungalows, almost hidden in the foliage, then came upon a rambling structure built of old boards and panels of compressed grass, under a high-peaked roof of palm thatch. A sagging porch ran along the front, with three wooden steps connecting the porch to the ground. Above the porch hung a sign: PINGIS TAVERN.

Wingo and Schwatzendale stopped short. They appraised the raffish structure with practiced eyes, then with one accord turned aside, mounted the steps and entered the tavern.

They were met by a familiar odor: the scent of old wood permeated by generations of spilled beer, along with the must of dry palm. At this time of day, business was slow; the interior was dim and quiet. At the back of the tavern, a pair of stout ladies gossiped earnestly over small beers. A gentleman of evident respectability leaned against the bar, clasping a goblet of pale liquor in his right hand. He wore a smart blue tunic, breeches of black whipcord, and black ankle-boots of good quality. His face was long and sober, under a neatly ordered ruff of crisp brown hair. A short, square beard emphasized the sobriety of his features. He nodded politely as Wingo and Schwatzendale seated themselves at a scarred wooden table.

On the wall behind the bar, a board listed a dozen special drinks in an illegible scrawl. The brown-bearded gentleman watched tolerantly as Wingo and Schwatzendale studied the board, then volunteered advice: "Balrob, our host, is a man of good reputation, and I can vouch for his bitter ale."

Balrob bowed in gratification. "Thank you, Sir Agent! Your commendation carries weight."

The gentleman straightened to an erect posture. "Allow me to introduce myself; I am Efram Shant, Land Agent, at your service."

Wingo and Schwatzendale mentioned their own names, and the Land Agent continued his remarks.

"If you are partial to toddies, the Tingletown, the Importunata, and the Old Reliable are all well regarded. Balrob, however, feels that his first speciality is Pooncho Punch, and I am inclined to agree."

"Hm," mused Wingo. "I am not familiar with this drink."

Schwatzendale gave his head a doubtful shake. "I have tested many formulations, but never Pooncho Punch."

"I am not surprised," said Balrob. "There are four versions of Pooncho; all have been developed locally, using local ingredients only. The recipe is, of course, a guarded family secret."

Agent Shant said: "My own preference is Pooncho Number Three. It is bracing and flavorful, yet never sits heavy on the tongue."

Wingo looked at Schwatzendale. "Shall we attempt this storied tipple?"

"The opportunity should not be wasted!" declared Schwatzendale without hesitation.

"My feelings exactly," said Wingo. He signalled to Balrob. "Two orders of the Number Three Pooncho, if you please."

"With pleasure, sir."

The 'Pooncho' was served in distinctive earthenware mugs, glazed dark green. Agent Shant watched as the two raised the mugs and tested the contents.

"Well, then? What is your verdict?"

Wingo coughed and cleared his throat. "This is a drink of several dimensions. It should not be judged in haste."

Schwatzendale said: "I find the drink stimulating, well balanced, and rife with a distinctive panache."

Wingo sipped again from the mug. "Most refreshing! Might there be a Number Four Pooncho?"

Agent Shant pulled soberly at his beard. "I have no personal

experience with the drink. However, I understand that it is
sometimes known as the 'Pingis Rejuvenator' and is occasionally administered to the dead, or unconscious."

"Indeed!" marvelled Wingo. "To what effect?"

"I have not witnessed the cure myself. Still, I have had a
broad experience of life, and I have seen some startling events,
so that I no longer make absolute assertions."

"You would seem a man to be trusted," said Schwatzendale.
"I would value your advice on another topic altogether."

"Speak! I shall answer to my best ability."

"We are new arrivals upon this remarkable world. How best
might we entertain ourselves, at modest expense, and within
the limits of the law?"

"Hm." Agent Shant again pulled at his beard. "That is like
asking how to dive into water, without getting wet. But let me
reflect. If you are keen botanists, you will enjoy examining
the flowers in the public parks, or you may go on nature walks
about the countryside. At slightly larger expense, you may hire a
way-car, which affords you more latitude. Or you might rent a
houseboat and cruise our incomparable waterways." The Land
Agent squared his shoulders, drained his goblet, and glanced
around the room. "I must be off about my business."

Schwatzendale, never diffident, asked: "With full respect, I
wonder what might be your business?"

The Land Agent turned Schwatzendale a brief, rather severe
look. "I am a member of the Land Committee. I supervise thirty
Land Agents, and as many sub-Agents, often known as the 'Land
Rovers', all of whom seek illicit rubbish and bring culprits to justice. It is a taxing job, and not without danger."

Wingo asked innocently: "Do you yourself search out litter?"

Agent Shant stood erect, with shoulders thrown back. "I
never shrink from my duty, at all times and in all places. I must
set an example for my men!"

Agent Shant glanced idly down at the floor, then frowned
and stared more fixedly. Wingo, sensing a change in the Agent's
demeanor, followed his gaze to the floor, where, to his alarm, he
found that one of the dead flowers he had picked up from the
road had fallen from his pocket and now lay blatantly in full
view.

Wingo hastily reached down and retrieved the illicit object.
The Land Agent gave a grim shrug, then turned away and departed.

Wingo and Schwatzendale discussed the episode in low
tones for a moment, then decided to attempt another Number
Three Pooncho Punch. They gave the order, and were served.

4

Aboard the *Glicca* Myron saw to the discharge of cargo, then
retired to his office to deal with paperwork. After a time Captain Maloof appeared in the doorway.

Myron looked up. "Something, sir?"

Maloof waved his hand. "Nothing of consequence. Proceed
with your work."

"I am almost finished. It won't be more than a minute."

Maloof came into the office, seated himself, and watched
while Myron made a few final entries.

Myron closed his ledger and looked toward Maloof, wondering what was in the wind.

Maloof asked: "Is there outbound cargo to interest us?"

Myron nodded. "A good bit—all transshipment. About half
a bay for Blenkinsop."

"I see." Maloof showed no great interest; Myron thought
that he seemed preoccupied.

Presently Maloof said: "A few days ago I mentioned that I
might have some private business here at Coro-coro."

"So you did," said Myron. "As I recall, you used the word
'lurulu' in this connection."

Maloof nodded. "I am inclined to think that I spoke care-
lessly. My quest is more prosaic; I want to resolve a mystery,
which has been troubling me a long time."

"What sort of mystery?"

Maloof hesitated. "I'll explain, if you have the patience to
listen."

"I'll listen, of course. In fact, I'll be happy to help you in any
way that I can."

"That is a kind offer, which I am tempted to accept. But
first, I should mention the very real possibility of danger."

Myron shrugged. "There will be two of us, and if nothing else, I can guard your back."

"Perhaps it won't come to that," said Maloof, without conviction. "In any case, I am pleased for the help, especially since your temperament seems suitable for this sort of undertaking. Wingo and Schwatzendale are excellent fellows, no doubt, but for this particular work neither would be at his best. Wingo is too artless, and Schwatzendale too flamboyant. What is needed is someone quiet, subtle, and unobtrusive, or who will adapt himself to such a role; in short, a person like yourself, with a cap pulled down to hide your blond hair—which is rather conspicuous."

Myron decided to take the remark as a compliment. It could be worse, he reflected.

For a time Maloof sat deep in thought. At last he stirred. "I will explain the background to the case; it is not simple, but I will try to be succinct. I must start many years ago—at Traven on the world Morlock, in Argo Navis.

"I was born into the patrician caste and spent a privileged childhood, which now seems unthinkably far away. My father was a banker, and wealthy. I remember him as a tall, erect gentleman, fastidious, humorless, and definite in his views. My mother was altogether different: she was pretty, frivolous, impulsive, and always ready to try a new fad. We lived in a grand house overlooking Faurency Weald, the countryside spread out before us all the way to Leyland Forest.

"My father and I were never on the best of terms—my fault more than his, so I understand now. When I was eighteen, I left home to become an IPCC cadet, which further estranged both my father and mother, who wanted me to become a banker.

"In those days I was wild and reckless and thought very well of myself. Six years of IPCC training ground away the worst of my rough edges and brought discipline into my life. In the end, I was commissioned a junior officer, Level Eight, and I thought that my parents might even be pleased with me.

"I was allowed a short leave of absence, which I spent at Traven. My father had become more opinionated than ever, or so it seemed; now I understand that I had never appreciated his regard for me, and that my leaving home had left him forlorn and lonely. My mother, on the other hand, seemed more frivolous and foolish than before. She fluttered and flitted about in girlish frocks, more fluffy-minded than ever. I felt concern for both of them and was sorry to return to duty.

"I was sent out on a tour of service which took me here and there across the Reach. After a promotion to Level Six, I was posted to Olfane on Sigil 92; then I was promoted Lieutenant Grade Five and posted to the town Wanne on the hard little world Dusa—at the very brink of Beyond.

"Wanne was reputedly the meanest posting on this side of the Reach, but I survived, and learned what there was to be learned. Finally, I was promoted again, to a grade just short of Captain. But by this time I was ready for something new; there was talk of transfer to a new posting, but an event occurred which changed the course of my life.

"From the town Serafim, out in the Beyond, came a dilapidated old Model 9-B Locator with a crew of four ruffians. They attacked the *Creach*, a freighter which happened to be in port, killed the master and crew, then took the ship aloft and away—presumably back into the Beyond, where our authority was nil and the law barred our presence.

"At the time there were only three agents posted to the Wanne office. We were all outraged by the contemptuous act of the pirates; it was an insult to our dignity and demanded a reaction, legal or not.

"The commanding officer was Captain Wistelrod. He promoted me to full Captain, then put me on indefinite leave and decommissioned me, so that I was temporarily a civilian and could go where I saw fit—without arousing an uproar from do-gooders and pussy-footers. I took the Model 9-B up from the Wanne spaceport and flew across the edge into the Beyond, and made for the town Serafim, where we thought the pirates would take their prize.

"When I arrived at Serafim, I put down at night, in the wilderness which surrounded the town, and ran through the moonlight to the spaceport. Sure enough, there was the *Creach*!

"To make a long story short, I killed the pirates and took the *Creach* back into Gaean space. Along the way back to Wanne, a constructive idea came to me. The previous owner of the vessel was dead. De facto title had passed to the pirates, once they had gone Beyond. By salvaging the ship from the pirates, title had devolved upon me; and since I was now a civilian, I need not surrender the ship to the IPCC. I fell in love with the ship, which was sound, secure, and competent. I renamed it the *'Glicca'*.

"At Wanne I reported briefly to Captain Wistelrod and told him of my decision, which was to remain on indefinite leave. He was sorry to lose me but wished me well. I assembled a crew and at once began to transport cargo.

"Three years passed before I put into Traven. My father had been killed in a boating accident at the lake. After a few days of mourning, my foolish mother had gone off with a man whom my aunt and cousin described as an out-and-out adventurer, who had beguiled her with romantic nonsense. Their present whereabouts was uncertain.

"The big house on Telmany Heights had been sold and was now inhabited by strangers. It was a depressing situation, with a single spark of comfort: my father, knowing my mother's impulsive disposition, had placed his assets into a trust fund from which my mother should be paid an adequate but not lavish annuity; a wise precaution, which could only frustrate her new consort.

"My father had drowned when his small sailboat capsized on a calm day. I had come to revere if not love my father; I was troubled by the circumstances of his death.

"I spoke with my aunt and my cousin; they knew very little of the man involved with my mother. She had brought him to their house only once, for a visit of half an hour. He had given his name as 'Loy Tremaine', and seemed considerably younger than my mother; she clearly doted upon him, and acted like a moonstruck girl. Tremaine made no effort to hide his boredom.

"Neither my aunt nor my cousin found him agreeable, though they admitted that he was personable, even magnetically so. His hair was short, thick, and black and clasped his head like a casque. His eyes were black and intense, close together beside a high-bridged nose. It was a face which, in the opinion of both my aunt and my cousin, indicated a self-centered willfulness, or even cruelty. Both noticed a small tattoo on his neck, just under the turn of his jaw, a cross inside two concentric circles, in a distinctive black-purple ink.

"Tremaine had spoken little, responding to questions in monosyllables. Only when asked as to his world of origin did he respond at length, and then in an excited and exalted manner, walking back and forth, flourishing his hands for emphasis. But he gave little real information. 'It is a far world,' he said. 'Its name would mean nothing to you; in fact, it is known only to discriminating and wealthy tourists, who are allowed to make limited stays—despite their reluctance to leave! But we cannot relax, and money means nothing to us. The world must be protected; it is entrancing for its serenity, and we cannot allow it to be defiled by vulgar hordes.'

"My mother proudly amplified the statement. 'Loy claims that it is the most beautiful world in all the Reach—so beautiful that it compels the return of anyone who has lived there. I am anxious to know this wonderful place!'

"At that time, according to my aunt, Tremaine rose to his feet and said: 'It is time that we were leaving,' and a moment later they were gone.

"I made inquiries at the bank. I learned that a few months before, my mother had come to the bank in the company of a surly gentleman. She had stated her intention to travel and had requested that the trust be broken so that she might realize the full value of the fund at once. The bank officials had decisively denied the request, eliciting sharp comments from the gentleman. This troubled them not at all; they tendered my mother a set of dated coupons, which she might cash at any local bank at the beginning of each year. After a set of formalities to prove her identity, the coupons would be referred to the bank at Traven, and the value of the coupon returned to my mother. She complained that the process seemed cumbersome and was told that it was the only means to ensure that her money was paid to her, and not some clever swindler, and that she should not complain.

"I asked if they as yet had paid off any of the coupons, but none had been presented for payment. The bank had no clue as to my mother's whereabouts.

"At the spaceport, I tried to discover when Loy Tremaine had arrived on Morlock, when he and my mother had departed, and what had been their destination? I learned nothing.

"There was urgent cargo aboard the *Glicca*; I could delay no longer and departed Morlock.

"Sometime later the *Glicca* put into Lorca on the world Sansevere. I went to the Aetna University and sought out Doctor Tessing, a savant in the field of social anthropology. I described Tremaine to the best of my ability, and mentioned that he was native to what he felt was the most beautiful world of the Gaean Reach—which no one could leave without yearning to return.

"I asked if he could identify this world, and Doctor Tessing said that the chances were good. He worked the controls of his information processor, studied the output, and told me: 'The problem is relatively simple. Both man and world have well-defined characteristics, and together they indicate that the man is a Flaut, native to the world Fluter—which is famed for the charm of its landscapes.' He told me also that Flauts are obsessional in regard to their world and under ordinary circumstances would not be likely to leave.

"I asked: 'What do you make of the tattoo on his neck?'

" 'It is either a status symbol, or it identifies his place of origin.'

"There was nothing more he could tell me. I expressed my thanks and returned to the *Glicca*.

"I now had a good idea where my mother could be found, and reasoned that her money would keep her safe. Tremaine could not get at her capital, but her annuity nevertheless was a substantial sum and was, in effect, her insurance policy.

"For a time the transport business kept us across the Reach and far away from Fluter. We drifted here and there, but one day settled upon the Coro-coro spaceport.

"We had three days to spend at Coro-coro. I spent the first day with the senior official in the Office of Entry Formalities. Together we searched the files, but there was no record of either the man who called himself 'Tremaine' or my mother. The official was not altogether surprised; he told me—rather reluctantly—that certain rogues and blackguards avoided the immigration laws by arranging to be set down in the wilderness, then walking into town. This was a serious offense, he told me, and if apprehended the perpetrators were liable to penalties of the third order since they were violating the basic canon of Flaut law—namely, the statutes controlling the population.

Without valid entry permits, they were in constant danger of being taken up by a Civil Agent, and this would be the case if they tried to book into a hotel.

"I asked: 'What if they use forged documents?'

" 'Possible,' he admitted, 'but such documents must be renewed monthly, which would soon arouse attention. After two or three such renewals the permit would be voided, and the guilty person would suffer appropriate penalties.' "

Myron grimaced. "It all seems rather extreme."

"Not when you know Flaut history. During their 'Terrible Times', they learned to accept death as the all-purpose punishment for any mistake whatsoever. It was easy, and there was no quibbling.

"On the second day, I went to the IPCC office. The commanding officer was Captain Harms, a crusty old veteran who had been sent out to rusticate at Coro-coro—a post considered a safe and comfortable sinecure, where the agent in charge could do no great damage. His assistant was an innocuous young lieutenant who had learned to exert no twitch of initiative, for fear of Captain Harms's displeasure.

"I found Captain Harms sitting at his desk. He was, in fact, a man of formidable aspect, with the broad chest and thin legs of a pouter pigeon. His face had been weathered pinkish-brown, against which jutting white eyebrows, ferocious blue eyes, an ungovernable tuft of white hair, and a bristling white mustache made a fine contrast.

"I introduced myself and explained my problem. As I expected, he produced a dozen reasons why the IPCC could not stir its majestic bulk to interfere in the local jurisdiction.

"I told him that Tremaine almost certainly had killed my father and that the safety of my mother was at risk. Harms declared that these factors were extraneous to the case, and that I should report my suspicions to the Civil Agents. I explained that, by so doing, I would be exposing my mother to a penalty of the third order. He shrugged, implying that she should have foreseen the eventuality before she indulged in a criminal act.

"I mentioned Tremaine's tattoo. Harms said that it identified his native village, but beyond that he could not help, as he had no list or compendium of the Flaut tattoos. For such information I might apply to the Office of Civil Dispositions, or the

Bureau of Vital Statistics, or the Population Registry. I bade
Captain Harms farewell and left the agency.

"On the third day I followed Captain Harms's suggestion and
presented myself to the Office of Civil Dispositions. After two
hours they referred me to the Population Registry, where, after
another two hours, I was told that the information could most
easily be had at the Bureau of Vital Statistics. After another wait,
I learned that the clerk who might have this information had
gone off to a houseboat for a two-week vacation, and nothing
could be done until her return. They suggested that I make inquiries at the Bureau for Archaeological Research.

"But by this time I was certain that they were playing a game
with me. I returned to the *Glicca* in a very bad mood. On the
next day we departed Fluter.

"The *Glicca* has returned to Fluter. I now plan to resume
where I left off."

Maloof surveyed Myron. "There you have it. Now that you
understand the program, do you still care to participate?"

"Certainly, but how do you plan to proceed?"

Maloof shrugged. "I wish I had a clever strategy, but I expect that I will do as before—which means trudging around and
asking questions until someone decides to answer. The clerk at
Vital Statistics may now, at least, be back from her houseboat
vacation."

"We have one advantage," said Myron. "Tremaine will not
know that we are looking for him."

"True."

"And if we find him—what then?"

"Much depends upon circumstances."

Myron rose to his feet. "I'm ready when you are."

Maloof also stood erect. "Wear a dark jacket. We are an-
thropologists from Aetna University on Sansevere. And don't
forget your hat."

Four

1

Excerpt from *Handbook to the Planets*:
Fluter: The Terrible Times

Visitors to this most beautiful of worlds are ordinarily ignorant of a dark episode in Fluter's past. When they learn the facts, more often than not the information is received with polite incredulity, or more intelligently, as just another scar on the body of Gaean history. Nevertheless, here is an outline of what happened across the pleasant landscapes of Fluter during those dark events.

The original settlers came in reaction to the insufferable overcrowding of their native world-city, Coreon on Ergard. They made population control the first and most stringent law of the land. As the centuries passed the strictures gradually relaxed, and memories of Coreon became dim. The spectre of overcrowding once again cast a dreary shadow over the land, and fervor for reviving the old statutes increased—rather hysterically, so it seems now. At the first Conclave for Population Readjustment, the old laws were emphatically renewed. Zealots ruled the day; proposals for gradual retrenchment were shouted down in favor of immediacy.

Each village was assigned an index indicating how far its population must be reduced to stay within the norms; killing became an ordinary affair. First to go were the aged and the infirm, along with the feeble-minded or any-one considered deficient in some regard. Family feuded with family; the elderly and even the middle-aged walked abroad at their peril. Ambush became a fine art, but the elderly suffered most until they organized themselves into fearsome gangs: the 'Silver Ghosts', who skulked through shadows seeking children and wailing babies, whose brains they dashed out against a rock. When at last the roster of the village declined below the index, and the need for slaughter was gone, furtive killing persisted, from habit and engendered hatred.

Eventually equilibrium returned. Population control was everywhere rigidly enforced through regulation of procreation, fertility, elimination of abnormal children, and abortion, producing more or less the same condi-tions we find in the Flaut villages today.

The question is often asked: where was the IPCC dur-ing these times? It has been asserted that the IPCC was in-different, but such was not the case. In sheer point of fact, the IPCC could function effectively only if it occupied each of the Flaut villages and Coro-coro. A force of at least fifty thousand field agents would have been needed for the operation, resulting in a program so complex as to be unacceptable. When the Flauts became surfeited with killing, they would stop of their own accord; and so it happened.

2

The IPCC at Coro-coro kept a low profile, and in the main there was little need for a strong presence, the influence of the Civil Agents generally sufficient to maintain order and disci-pline among the folk of Fluter.

On several occasions the Civil Agents demanded that the IPCC remove its office from Coro-coro; the IPCC eventually responded by constructing a new headquarters of obvious permanence, situated near the O-Shar-Shan circus.

Maloof and Myron set off along the tree-shaded Pomare Boulevard, under dangling white blossoms from which drifted a barely perceptible perfume. They might have jumped aboard one of the picturesque open-sided omnibuses which plied the boulevard—long, high-wheeled charabancs carrying tourists and Flauts alike between the spaceport and the O-Shar-Shan circus— but instead chose to walk.

They passed the Labor Exchange, where business was conducted under a long, open-sided shed thatched with tawny palm fronds. Lined up at the counter were the pilgrims, now receiving referrals to potential employers. None showed enthusiasm toward the prospect of employment. Cooner, dissatisfied with his referral, stood leaning over the counter angrily waving his referral in the air, half-prancing with indignation. The clerk gave him a glance of mild wonder before turning back to his work.

At the Tarquin Transit Agency, Maloof and Myron stopped to inspect the vehicles in the yard, intrigued—like Wingo and Schwatzendale before them—by the idiosyncratic constructions. Bamboo and membrane flitters, resembling disheveled winged insects, appeared to be of local manufacture except for the imported power units; each was unique, built to the dictates of possibly amateur designers. Like the flitters, the skitters were of ad hoc construction, with struts, frames, and braces installed where the builder thought they would do the most good. Controls were different from one to the next, as if a standard system were an affront to the skill and brio of the driver. The three-wheelers, appealing to persons of feckless disposition, were in a separate area; in some of these the driver rode high behind the two after-wheels, with the third wheel on a boom thrust forward like an instrument of attack. Vanities were raised aloft, on struts clamped to the forward boom: a peacock's fan; a winged cherub blowing a clarion; a grotesque head, with features articulated to contort in hideous grimaces as the vehicle moved along.

Similar vehicles coursed up and down the boulevard, high wheels whirring and thumping, the driver sitting proudly aloft, regarding other drivers with disdain as if questioning their competence.

Maloof and Myron walked on, almost brushed by the white dangling blossoms which trailed over the boulevard. They came to the Pingis Tavern and stopped short to appraise the rustic structure. Maloof mused: "It is early, of course, but I wonder if Wingo and Schwatzendale might have paused here to test the local ale."

"The idea would certainly occur to them," said Myron.

Without further words the two climbed the steps to the porch and entered the tavern. Halting, they surveyed the dim interior. Behind the bar was a bartender of middle age; in a corner two old women sat engrossed in a game of some sort.

Maloof asked the bartender: "Have our friends looked in this morning? One is plump, round-faced, with a rather pink complexion, and going bald. He would be wearing a pale brown cloak. The other is dark-haired and nervous, wearing a shirt of striking green-and-black diaper pattern, so that he seems a harlequin."

The bartender placed both hands on the bar and frowned toward the old women; then his face cleared into remembrance. "Two gentlemen stepped in this morning. One was sturdy, with a kind pink face. The other was all elbows and knees, with eyes that looked in two directions at once." He shook his head, caught up by some marvelous recollection.

"Now I recall everything. They drank three tankards each of Number Three Pooncho Punch, then, despite my earnest advice, called for a fourth tankard, which they also consumed. They are now resting in the back room. I could have given them a gill each of the Number Four Pooncho, but I thought better of it, as the Four Pooncho sometimes has startling effects. While you wait, will you each take a Pooncho, to foster your own vigor?"

"At this moment, no," said Maloof. "Perhaps the next time we pass. You say that our friends are resting in comfort?"

"Just so. They are as limp as dead eels."

Thus reassured, Maloof and Myron left the tavern.

Not far ahead, the boulevard entered the O-Shar-Shan circus, across from the wonderful O-Shar-Shan terrace, where
tourists wearing their most splendid regalia sat under gay para-
sols, drinking fizzes, punches, and toddies from tall bamboo
mugs. They were on hand early, to see and be seen; in modes of
feigned languor and sophisticated indifference they covertly
studied the folk at nearby tables, speculating as to their places of
origin, social status, and moral standards.

From time to time, charabancs stopped before the terrace.
Passengers disembarked, others were loaded aboard, and the
charabanc set off on a new sortie into the wilderness. Around the
circus, skitters of a dozen sorts rolled on high, spindly wheels,
some decorated with arrays of banderoles, others with bouquets
of artificial flowers. The drivers in the main were sportive types,
sitting high and erect in the approved posture; they tended to be
critical of other drivers and easily became outraged by faulty or
intemperate techniques. Calling out advice, whirring and veering
in and out of the traffic patterns, they waved their arms to indicate the nature of the other's mistake—which usually evoked responsive comments and significant gestures, while the skitters
careened from lane to lane.

A few yards short of the circus a walkway led off under tall
yew trees to an impressive stone structure. A vertical arrangement of bronze characters beside the door read: IPCC. At the approach of Maloof and Myron, the door slid aside, and after they
had entered, slid softly shut.

The two stood in a large, high-ceilinged chamber, which, like
the exterior, conveyed a sense of uncompromising certitude. The
floor was paved with pale gray tile, and the walls were washed severely white, unadorned except for the IPCC starburst emblem
high on the back wall.

Behind a desk sat a man who might have been purposely
selected for the office itself. He was in his early maturity, with
dark golden hair and intelligent blue eyes. A plaque on his
desk identified him as 'Captain Skahy Serle'. He rose to his
feet and waited as Maloof and Myron approached, then indicated chairs. "Good morning, gentlemen; be seated, if you
will."

When Maloof and Myron had seated themselves, Serle

resumed his own place behind the desk. "Now then, introduce yourselves, and tell me how I can be of service."

"Very well. I am Adair Maloof, master of the ship *Glicca*, now at the spaceport; this is Myron Tany, my first assistant. To begin with, we need information; after that, much depends upon what you can tell us."

"Please continue."

"We are trying to locate a certain Loy Tremaine, who may now be on Fluter. Do you care to hear the background details? They are a trifle sordid."

Serle smiled. "I am not easily disturbed! I have nothing better to do than make out the monthly reports, which I can easily assign to Jervis, my subaltern."

Maloof collected his thoughts. "About a year ago I took the *Glicca* to Traven, on the world Morlock, for two reasons. The *Glicca* needed modifications and an overhaul, and I wanted to visit my father and mother, who resided there.

"My father had substantial wealth, and I expected to find my parents in comfortable retirement in their home on Telmany Heights—but instead, I discovered that my father had died, under suspicious circumstances, and that my mother had left Morlock in the company of a man much younger than she, for destinations unknown.

"Ill health had overtaken my father, and he had lost most of his initiative, demanding no more from life than quiet and the solace of his books. My mother, on the other hand, had thrown herself into a whirl of social activities, giddy and a bit senile, desperately seeking to recapture the fervor of youth. Despite my father's complaints, she opened the house to eccentric semi-scandalous masques, and wild midnight revels.

"My father was forced to take refuge in his country home on Lake Cristel, and this allowed my mother more scope than ever. He finally became disgusted with her extravagances and put the whole of his wealth into a trust fund, from which she would be paid a moderate annuity. When notified of the changes, my mother was outraged, but was careful to keep quiet her altered circumstances, since the news would surely excite the furtive amusement of her cronies. By one means or another she managed to sustain the illusion of grandiose wealth.

"My mother became fascinated by a swashbuckling young rogue named Loy Tremaine. His appearance was striking—his hair was lustrous black, his features aquiline. His eyes burned with a black intensity, and his manners were flamboyant. The old ladies could not take their eyes from him; they were universally smitten with this picaresque rogue and hung on his every word, each trying to outdo the others in girlish verve, preening and simpering when he spoke to them, though he gave my mother—known to control a notable family fortune—the most earnest attention.

"On one occasion, Tremaine drank much wine and became vainglorious. He told of escapades and dangerous ventures Beyond—all no doubt fictitious, but which held the old ladies spellbound. He mentioned his home world, which he declared to be the most beautiful planet of the Reach! He spoke with a curious passion, more than a simple yearning for home; one day, so he declared, he would return—as soon as a small misunderstanding with the civil authorities could be adjusted.

"My mother was much affected. She said that she also longed to wander among the exotic worlds, but her husband considered such off-world travel dangerous, and a waste of money. She complained that it was his penury which prevented her from enjoying the full amplitude of the family fortune, which was her due. Tremaine listened sympathetically, making no comment; still, two days later, my father drowned when his boat mysteriously capsized—on a calm day—in Lake Cristel.

"My mother appeared at the funeral in company with Loy Tremaine. A few days later he apparently induced her to go off with him, for romantic adventures among the fabulous far worlds of the Reach; at least this was the thrust of a hurried note my mother left for a friend. They departed incognito and left no hints as to their destination.

"Tremaine's background was never clear. But he had a curious tattoo on his neck, a slantwise cross inside two concentric circles. The location and style of this mark, I understand, are typically Flaut."

Maloof paused, and after a moment continued, with delicate precision. "That, by and large, is the situation. Tremaine would seem to be a native of Fluter. He may be here—now—with my mother. It is only fitting that I make inquiries, and if the IPCC can be of assistance, so much the better."

"What do you have in mind for Tremaine?"

"There is much about Tremaine which we do not know," replied Maloof carefully. "A great deal will depend upon the way he conducts himself."

Serle sat for a moment in thought. "My instructions are not to interfere with the activities of the Agents, unless they put too many tourists—or Flauts, for that matter—to punishments of the third order. At this moment, if I were to act as they think proper, I would refer you to the local office of the Civil Agents." He leaned back in his chair. "But I will naturally do what I can for you, given the strictures under which I work.

"The tattoo on Tremaine's neck indicates his place of origin. He is not from Coro-coro—if so, the tattoo would be a sunburst. Still, it should be easy to identify. I will put Jervis on the job." He pressed a button on his desk.

A door in the back wall opened, and a young man in the blue and black IPCC uniform appeared. He was slender, dark-haired, and carried himself with almost military punctilio. "Sir, you have need of me?"

"So I do. This is Captain Maloof and his shipmate Myron Tany. Gentlemen, this is my assistant Ian Jervis."

Maloof and Myron acknowledged the introductions. Serle turned to Jervis. "Do you know where to find the artist Florio?"

"Yes, his shop is across the boulevard."

Serle drew on a card, then tucked the card into an envelope, which he handed to Jervis. "I have drawn the pattern of a tattoo on the card. Please ask Florio to identify the tattoo." Jervis took the envelope and departed.

A few minutes passed; then Jervis returned in company with a thin, white-haired man. Jervis said apologetically: "I showed the card to Master Florio, and he insisted on speaking to you in person."

"Just so," said Florio. "I must confer with you privately. Certain of my affairs may not be circulated in the public forum."

"As you wish." Serle led Florio into a side room and

closed the door. Jervis bowed politely and returned to his own
office.

Maloof and Myron waited in silence; the implications of
Florio's conduct were too recondite to prompt speculation.

After a prolonged interval, Florio and Serle returned to
the chamber. Florio gave Maloof and Myron nods of impersonal courtesy and departed the office, while Serle resumed
his seat.

For a moment, Serle sat considering the two off-worlders, his
face a study. Finally he roused himself and straightened in his
chair. "You will wonder at Florio's insistence upon privacy. Need-
less to say, any information or hints of enlightenment you hear
now must never be revealed, especially to the Civil Agents—
toward whom Florio feels total contempt.

"To begin with, Florio identified Tremaine's tattoo as the
emblem of the village Krenke, which indicates that Krenke
was his place of origin. In itself this is not significant. More
important is that two months ago a man answering Tremaine's
description came to Florio's studio; for a large cash payment,
Florio altered the man's Krenke tattoo to a Coro-coro sunburst, and also applied a sunburst tattoo to the neck of an old
woman who was Tremaine's companion. Here is evidence
that Tremaine and your mother have established themselves
somewhere on Fluter; precisely where, it is impossible to
surmise."

Maloof reflected. "If Krenke were his native village, this is
where he might feel most secure from the Civil Agents."

Serle shrugged. "Possibly so. For a fact he would be conspicuous in Coro-coro."

Maloof considered further. "Where is Krenke? What kind
of a village is it?"

Again Serle summoned Jervis, and instructed him to discover what there was to be learned about Krenke. After a period, Jervis returned to report that Krenke was a village of
moderate size, adequately prosperous, where the Three Feathers Inn provided decent lodging for tourists.

Serle provided Maloof a map indicating the location of
Krenke. "It is remote, but not too remote. If you leave now, you
should arrive by this evening."

3

Maloof and Myron returned to the *Glicca* to find themselves
alone aboard, with the rest of the ship's company occupied elsewhere. Maloof left a note on the galley table. "That should
soothe their anxieties, if any exist."

To Myron's comment that he would have been comforted
by the support of Wingo and Schwatzendale, Maloof replied,
"We can deal adequately with the situation, and we are far less
conspicuous alone." Myron accepted Maloof's program without protest, but checked that his hand-weapons were in good
working order.

The two unshipped the flitter and stowed a few items of
equipment aboard. Once aloft, they set off over the arcadian
landscapes of Fluter, toward the village Krenke. As the sun tra-
versed the sky, the continents and seas passed below.

With the sun close to the horizon, Krenke appeared below,
dozing in the golden light of late afternoon. Maloof put the flitter into a slow circle over the village. A road from the east
crossed a tranquil river by an iron bridge, to become the high
street of the village. After passing the Three Feathers Inn, the
road proceeded a hundred yards to give upon a public square,
then angled away and was lost under the foliage of tall trees.
Across the bridge from the inn was an area of open land, occupied by a variety of vehicles: farm equipment, drays, power-carts,
a few skitters badly in need of maintenance, and a pair of antique
flitters, fragile as moth-wings. Maloof found an empty bay at the
back of the area and landed the flitter just as the last sliver of sun
dropped below the horizon, leaving behind a tumble of clouds
glowing vermilion, amber, and gold.

Dusk was gathering as Maloof and Myron made their way
to the bridge and crossed the river. Ahead loomed the Three
Feathers Inn, a massive structure of timber and stone with
a high-peaked roof. Over the entrance hung a sign depicting
three iron feathers splayed out into a fan, constrained within a
heavy iron frame in the traditional style. Maloof and Myron
pushed open the heavy door and entered the common room of
the inn.

They found themselves in a large chamber, almost majestic
in its scale. Timber posts supported gnarled cross-room

baulks, on which rested ceiling joists, and the age-darkened planks of the ceiling proper. A line of tables ranged the wall to the left; a long bar flanked the wall to the right. The tables were occupied by diners: men, women, and a few children dressed in their best. They were served by a gaunt, middle-aged woman with lank arms and legs, who loped with long bent-kneed strides back and forth between tables and kitchen. She wore a loose gown striped brown and green, so long that it almost swept the floor. Her hair was piled into a pyramid, with a blue flower thrust in demurely at the apex. The diners constantly importuned her as she strode back and forth: "Dinka! More sauce is needed!" "Dinka! Bring more batrachies, with fresh vinegar!" "Dinka! The bread is musty; we need more savoury paste."

A doorway into the kitchen allowed occasional glimpses of a short, squat woman with a perspiring red face, who glared out toward the tables in what seemed a state of chronic fury.

Along the bar a dozen men in working-class garments, or the somewhat more pretentious costumes of tradesmen, sat hunched over tall wooden tankards of beer talking in gruff mutters. Behind the bar a moon-faced bartender danced nimbly back and forth, his great paunch pressed against the counter, refilling tankards, wiping up spills, and chaffing the drinkers, who stared at him blankly.

Maloof and Myron seated themselves at the end of the bar and waited.

Jodel, the bartender, noticing the newcomers, sidled down the length of the bar. He spoke: "Gentlemen, what is your pleasure?"

"We have just arrived from Coro-coro," said Maloof. "We want lodging for the night, supper, and breakfast in the morning."

"No problem whatever!" declared Jodel. "Here is the registry; you need only sign, and formalities are over."

"So it might be, providing that we can afford your rates."

Jodel made an indulgent gesture. "Fear nothing; our rates are considered moderate."

"And the specific numbers?"

Jodel shrugged. "If you like. Let us say four sols for the room and fifty dinkets for each meal, to a total of six sols."

"The charges are tolerable," said Maloof, "provided that you add on no unexpected extras, let us say, for clean linen or hot water."

"Our rates are all-inclusive," said Jodel. "However, we prefer that the score be paid in advance, for practical reasons. Certain of our clientele will rise early, take a special deluxe breakfast, then decamp before settling the account."

"That is not our habit," said Maloof. "Still, one must be on guard against scoundrels. In Coro-coro we encountered a certain 'Loy Tremaine' who thought to swindle us. By an odd coincidence, he stated that he made his home in Krenke."

Jodel gave his head a dubious shake. "Somewhere there is a mistake. Tremaines have never resided in Krenke. You misheard the name of his village."

"Probably so," said Maloof.

"More likely, he was an impostor," mused Jodel. "Only last month, a huckster of wild currants arrived in Krenke. While folk were inspecting his merchandise, he laid hold of a girl and took her behind his dray, where he lifted her skirt a full five inches! Her cries brought help on the run. The hawker was dragged away to the rollers, where he danced among the coils for two days. He was also fined the contents of his dray. It was a woebegone wretch who finally took his empty dray back to Lilancx!

"But now you will wish to visit your accommodations. You may take your supper when you come down." He placed his hands on the bar and, leaning forward, searched the chamber. Dissatisfied, he threw back his head and shouted: "Buntje! Buntje! Come at the double! Where are you, Buntje?" He listened, then called again, in a louder voice: "Buntje! Do you not hear me? Come at once! Buntje! I am calling you!"

Into the room burst a girl of about fourteen, running at speed, arms pumping and skirt flapping, so that a lascivious eye might have glimpsed at least an inch of ankle. Maloof and Myron modestly averted their eyes. She wore a tight pink blouse over a near-flat chest, and a voluminous black skirt, which barely cleared the floor. Like Dinka, she had gathered her hair up into a tall pyramid, with a flower precariously thrust into the apex. Halting in front of Jodel, she panted: "Roar no further; I am here!"

"You were slow. Can you move no faster? What kept you so long?"

The girl cried out in a passion: "Must I explain every detail of my personal conduct? If I am forced to particularize, I will state that I was occupied in the retreat! When you called I could not jump up and run through the chamber, without creating a scandal; is this what you wish?"

"Bah," muttered Jodel. "You should accomplish these acts in your spare time. While you were luxuriating, these gentlemen have been awaiting your help. Now then: escort them to their quarters at once. Make sure that all is in order."

Buntje surveyed Maloof and Myron with mouth primly downturned. "I take them to be off-worlders, and the young one has a queer look."

"No matter," said Jodel. "It is all one. Take them to Chamber Six, and see to their needs."

Buntje grimaced and composed herself. She asked Maloof, "Where is your luggage?"

"We have only these small travel bags, and we will carry them ourselves."

Buntje's face became a frozen mask. "As you like! However, please know that I am not the thief you take me for. Your precious belongings are safe from me."

Maloof stuttered an apology, which Buntje ignored. "Come; I will take you to your chamber."

"Hold hard!" cried Jodel, slapping the bar. "I want to see six sols shining in a row, before events move another inch."

Maloof paid over the required sum. Buntje led them to a narrow staircase. Maloof and Myron politely waited for Buntje to precede them, but she indignantly jerked aside. "Do you take me for a raw innocent? I know your off-world tricks! The ruse has failed; you may go first."

"As you wish," sighed Maloof. The two climbed the stairs, with Buntje several steps behind. At the landing she slipped past, giving Myron a wide berth. She opened the door with the numeral '6', and, after looking warily at Maloof and Myron, glanced into the room, then stepped quickly back out.

"You may enter; the room is in order."

"Just a moment," said Maloof. "You were supposed to check the room carefully. Are the beds fresh?"

"And what about towels and soap?" Myron asked. "You should at least look into the bathroom."

"Everything is as it should be. If you find any rodents, chase them into the hall."

Buntje retreated and clattered down the stairs. Maloof and Myron inspected the room, and found no cause for complaint. The furniture was massive, durable, and obviously of great age. A door led into a rather quaint bathroom.

For a moment the two stood by the window, looking out over the village. A few wavering street-lights came on, casting islands of wan illumination. In the public square a number of young men were preparing for a social event of a sort not immediately clear. The two turned from the window and went down to the common room. They seated themselves at a vacant table, and waited for attention.

Dinka loped past, back and forth, and eventually halted. When Maloof requested a menu, she seemed puzzled; when he explained, she said with the ghost of a prim smile: "Sir, we have no such documents on hand."

"Then what is available for our supper?"

"That depends upon the decision of Wilkin."

"Indeed." Looking toward the kitchen, Maloof and Myron saw the squat, red-faced cook glaring at them through the doorway, brandishing a wooden spoon.

Dinka said: "She is in a bit of a tantrum. Buntje has reported that the young one tried to lure her into the bathroom, planning a lewd antic, which she took heroic measures to avoid."

"Absurd!" declared Maloof. "Ask Wilkin to step out here, and we will explain the situation in detail. We cannot let such slander go unchallenged."

Dinka shook her head. "I will talk to Wilkin and put matters right. Buntje is subject to adolescent fits; this is known, and perhaps Wilkin will see reason. If not, I can bring you some dried fish, and some dried bread with suet."

Dinka went off to the kitchen, closing the door behind her. After a time she emerged carrying a tureen of pungent soup, which she placed before Maloof and Myron. She glanced toward the kitchen and said: "Wilkin has herself in control now. It seems that tonight there is a romp; Buntje has never before dared to attend, for fear that she might fall sprawling, with legs in the air. In any case, your supper is secure."

Following the soup, Dinka brought a platter of fish stewed with ramp and small tubers, which might have been acorns, and finally dumplings in fruit sauce.

The supper was over. The two sat over mugs of herbal tea. The night was still young, and it was too early to retire to their room. For a time they watched the coming and going of patrons at the bar, but there was no entertainment here. All conducted themselves with somber restraint, and spoke in mutters to each other. Jodel darted back and forth, his great paunch pressed against the counter, his moon-face fixed in the semblance of smiling cordiality. No one took notice of the offworlders.

After a time, Maloof and Myron rose from the table and went to the door. They pushed through and passed out into the evening.

4

For a moment they stood in front of the inn, the sign swinging gently over their heads to vagrant puffs of wind. Dusk had not yet left the sky; up and down the high street the roofs of cottages were black outlines against the gray murk.

The two set off up the high street, keeping to the shadows. Where the street entered the square, they halted to watch what seemed to be the early stages of a social event involving the adolescent population of Krenke. On one side of the square a group of boys had gathered, in the main striplings of about sixteen to perhaps eighteen. Opposite was a group of girls of similar age, perhaps a year or so younger. They chattered, laughed, made extravagant gestures, and ran a few steps back and forth, creating a spectacle of gay spontaneity, meanwhile turning covert glances toward the boys, who for the most part were quiet, gazing shamelessly toward the girls.

Maloof and Myron, beguiled by the situation, seated themselves on a bench under a tall plumeria tree and waited to discover how the event would develop. As they watched, teams of young men using ground-marking equipment laid down sets of parallel lines to create a system of lanes about five feet wide running from side to side across the square.

When the work was finished, the boys and girls at once spread out, each selecting a lane, sometimes backing away and going to another lane when they did not particularly approve of the person at the other end, running quickly back and forth. At the far end of the square a group of young men, apparently musicians, climbed onto a low platform and busied themselves setting up their instruments. They wore special costumes of odd style and color: tight open-midriff shirts of fluorescent blue; expansive breeches, vermilion, lime green, and black, ballooning out over the hips and tied at the knees, and long pointed white shoes. Now they all donned grotesque vulpine masks and were suddenly transformed into a cabal of minor devils.

Tension increased; the air seemed to tingle. The boys and girls began to jig and caper, tentatively at first but with ever more abandon. They jabbed the air with their fingers, jerked their thumbs to the side. On the far platform the tympanist arranged a battery of chimes over the great bass drum, tested a hollow wood-block with a bamboo whisk, then stood at the ready and waited while profound silence came to the square. He raised his arm dramatically high, then struck down at his cylindrical gong. The other musicians were off and away, producing a sudden din of wails, quavers, and random arpeggios, paced by a fateful booming of the great drum.

The effect took Maloof and Myron by surprise; for some reason they had expected music more structured and melodic than what they now heard. They listened carefully.

"I have the answer," said Myron. "We do not understand this music because it is too subtle for us."

Maloof agreed. "No doubt you are right."

The boys and girls at the open ends of lanes were reacting to the music with enthusiasm, and stood jerking to the beat of the big drum, the most exuberant squirming and twisting, kicking forward, knees bent, then thrusting out with pointed toes. Myron noted that the girls had tied their skirts more or less tightly to their shoes, so as not to flaunt too much ankle, though the most audacious allowed a few provocative inches to flash in and out of sight.

The drum became more urgent; the kicking and prancing grew vehement, and the energies reached a critical level. At each end of a lane a boy and a girl broke free, and advanced to meet, kicking and jigging, hands thrusting at hips. They arrived at the center and jerked to a halt, shoulders squirming, hips twisting; then, wheeling and bending so that they bumped buttocks, each returned jigging and jerking in triumph along the way they had come.

The music continued as before, the great drum maintaining its thundering beat. Another pair broke free and repeated the routine, followed by two others.

Myron suddenly leaned forward and pointed. "Look yonder—the fourth girl along the line!"

"It is Buntje, cavorting with the best of them!"

"There she goes!" cried Myron, as Buntje set off along the lane, performing with no less energy than the others.

The lanes were suddenly active, the participants each demonstrating his or her particular style: some ponderous and meaningful, others lightsome and frivolous, like careening insects. At times a boy or a girl would start out in a lane, jigging and twitching in notable display, only to find that no one was advancing from the opposite end of the lane. It was a humiliating experience. The person so slighted might halt, then return crestfallen to the starting point, or if sufficiently angry might proceed to the middle and there perform a grotesque travesty of the usual postures, hoping to shame the offender.

After a time the function came to an end. There was a crescendo of chimes, a wild glissando from the belp-horn, a final fateful thump of the drum, then silence. The musicians removed their masks, packed their instruments, jumped down from the platform, and disappeared into the night. The boys and girls, now ignoring each other, formed chattering little groups discussing the evening's events. Some were elated and celebrated their successes. Others were more subdued, and wondered about themselves.

"So there you have it," said Maloof. "That is how life goes at Krenke. We witnessed a hundred small triumphs and gratified hopes, and as many small tragedies."

Myron nodded soberly. "I wonder what happens next," he said. "They can't be ready to go home."

Myron's speculations were soon put to rest. The boys moved to the high street, where they dispersed to their various destinations. From the shadows beside the square, men and women materialized as if by magic, and one by one the girls were whisked unceremoniously out to the high street and away to home.

A few minutes later the square was deserted and dark, except for a light in one of the offices across the square.

"Someone is working late," said Myron. He rose to his feet and studied the office more closely; beside the door he saw a rack which offered journals for sale.

"It might be the local news agency," he told Maloof, "assuming that such an enterprise exists at Krenke."

The two men crossed the square. As they approached the office, they noticed a sign above the door. Gold script on a black background read:

THE KRENKE OBSERVER
ULWYN FARRO, PURVEYOR

Maloof tapped at the door. A calm voice said: "Come!"

The two entered a small, neat office, furnished sparsely. One wall was completely covered by hundreds of photographs, depicting men, women, and children of all ages and conditions, for the most part staring blankly into the camera. The other walls were washed starkly white, and lacked all decoration.

Behind a desk sat a pale young man of unimpressive physique. A few strands of ash-blond hair fringed his forehead; his long, thin face was unremarkable, except for luminous gray eyes. He said: "I am Ulwyn Farro, as you may have guessed. Do you have business with me?"

"Nothing of consequence," said Maloof. "We happened to notice your sign and looked in out of sheer curiosity."

Farro surveyed his two visitors with curiosity of his own. "I assume that you are the off-worlders who arrived this afternoon and are lodging at the Three Feathers."

"Quite correct," said Maloof.

Myron added with a sardonic grin: "Rumor travels fast across Krenke."

Farro gave an indifferent shrug. "One way or another, I am grateful—it brings me most of my material. Do you care to sit?"

"Thank you." The two settled themselves upon straight-backed chairs. "I am Adair Maloof, master of the spaceship *Glicca*. This is my first officer, Myron Tany."

Farro acknowledged the introductions with a nod. "What brings you to this rather remote village? Are you tourists, or do you have other business in mind?"

Maloof said: "If you are hoping to develop an interesting article for the *Observer*, put the idea aside. We are ordinary tourists, wandering the far places of Fluter as the mood takes us."

"As you say." Farro leaned back in his chair and subjected his visitors to a moment of contemplation. "If I were to risk an offhand comment, I might say that neither of you fits the mold of the ordinary tourist. Still, what other conceivable purpose could bring you to a somnolent backwater such as Krenke? You are truly something of a puzzle. My speculations, I hasten to say, are no more than whimsical fancy, in no way relevant to the *Observer*."

Maloof reflected before responding. He said, rather ponderously: "You seem a sensitive man, with an agile mind. Let me float another 'whimsical fancy', to the effect that we are, for a fact, pursuing a topic regarding which we need information, but only if the topic were totally isolated from any form of publicity."

Farro leaned forward. "Let us bring the matter into closer focus. I gather that you want me to supply information, and thereafter keep the discussion hermetically secret. Is this correct?"

"Precisely so. If the reason for our presence became known, our function would be compromised."

"Very well," said Farro. "I agree to your conditions, unless your revelations are so dire and disastrous that I am forced to make them known."

Maloof smiled grimly. "You shall hear neither of disasters nor cataclysms. Shall I proceed?"

"Yes," said Farro. "Proceed."

"A year ago at Traven, on the world Morlock, I encountered a young man who called himself 'Loy Tremaine'. He occupied himself charming old women and defrauding them of their wealth. He had a magnetic presence and carried himself with incredible arrogance. On his neck he wore a tattoo, which we have identified as the Krenke insignia. During this time at Traven, he stated that he desperately wished to return to Fluter but must make an adjustment with the Civil Agents. In the end he committed a murder and induced a wealthy widow to leave Morlock so that the two could pursue wonderful adventures among the far worlds, but he had Fluter in mind.

"Two days ago the *Glicca* landed at the Coro-coro spaceport. We discovered that Tremaine was resident on Fluter. We could not find him in Coro-coro and theorized that he might have taken refuge in Krenke, which is why we are here."

Farro shook his head. "Something is wrong. There have never been 'Tremaines' at Krenke; perhaps you misread the tattoo."

"Definitely not. It was seen and certified by an expert, who had altered it to a Coro-coro sunburst."

"In that case, there is no doubt about it—your man is using a false name. What did he look like?"

Maloof gave a short harsh laugh. "Once seen, he can never be mistaken. He is tall and strong. He moves with dramatic pride—like a cavalier of old dancing the shebardigan. Dark curls fall over his forehead; his eyes burn with black intensity, close beside a lordly nose. He likes to act the rakehelly damn-your-eyes bravo, and uses flamboyant gestures."

"Hold," cried Farro, his voice husky with excitement. "I know this man. His name is Orlo Cavke! I can assure you that he is not at Krenke."

"Why is that?"

"He would not dare show his face where it might be recognized! He committed abominable crimes here but escaped punishment.

"His deeds were sickening. He took three girls, one after the other, and led them by night up the Mellamy Steeps. It was a terrible time at Krenke, with every man looking askance at every other. Orlo Cavke violated the girls in every conceivable manner, and perhaps in other ways not immediately conceivable. He vented a mad rage upon these poor children, punishing them for the beauty which they had withheld from him. He was captured and dragged back to the village in chains, but he escaped, and it

was learned that he had left Fluter. I am shocked to learn of his
return!"

Maloof muttered: "This casts a new light upon Loy
Tremaine." He grunted. "I suppose that now we must call him
'Orlo Cavke'."

Farro regarded them thoughtfully. "What will you do
now?"

"We have no choice," said Maloof. "We will look for him
elsewhere. If he is on Fluter, we shall find him."

"Then what will you do?"

"I don't know. Much will depend upon circumstances."

Farro said earnestly: "If you find him, I hope that you will
return him to Krenke. He has dealt us a foul wound that only
he can make better."

Maloof shook his head sadly. "We can promise nothing. He
has my mother in his custody, and we must be guided by what
we find." He stopped to consider. "Can you provide us a picture
of Orlo Cavke?"

Farro hesitated, then reached into a drawer and brought out
a pair of photographs, which he pushed across the desk to
Maloof.

"Thank you."

Maloof studied the two poses a moment, then passed them
to Myron.

In the first photo Myron saw a tall, dark-haired man of striking appearance, standing manacled before a stone wall. Cavke
glared at the camera, projecting a near-tangible fury. In the second, Cavke had swung aside, showing a profile which might
have been that of an ancient demonic hero. His posture conveyed only defiance and contempt.

Farro asked: "When will you be leaving Krenke?"

"In the morning; there is nothing to keep us in Krenke any
longer."

Maloof and Myron rose to their feet and gave Farro their
thanks. They departed into the night leaving Farro at his desk,
staring disconsolately after them.

Arriving at the Three Feathers Inn, the two entered the
common room. A pair of beer-drinkers sat in colloquy with
Jodel. Along the line of empty tables, Dinka stood looking out

the window, engrossed in private reverie. The door into the kitchen was closed, concealing the irascible Wilkin, if indeed she were still striding about among her pots and pans, gesticulating with her spoon.

The two gave Dinka a polite good night as they passed, but she barely noticed. They climbed the stairs to their room, made preparations for the night, sought their beds, and were soon asleep.

5

In the morning, a dismal overcast had drifted down from the hills to the north, and from the window the village seemed more dank, cheerless, and worn by the passage of time than ever.

The two men dressed in silence, depressed by what they had learned, and descended the stairs to the common room. Dinka met them and took them to what she called "the breakfast saloon"—a long, dim chamber smelling of mold and wet stone. A small window in the back wall admitted a watery gray light, barely sufficient to illuminate their table.

"Wilkin is in a good mood," Dinka told them. "She has allowed you her best porridge, and also dishes of fruit."

The two were served crusty bread and marmalade, thick porridge flavored with fragments of salt fish, and dishes of boiled figs in a syrup of spiced honey. They gnawed at the bread and drank as much herbal tea as they could tolerate, then returned to the common room.

At the bar three men of middle years sat hunched over tankards of beer.

Jodel called out a jovial greeting and said: "The time is early; are you leaving so soon?"

Maloof paused. "Our visit to Krenke has been pleasant, but it is time we were returning to Coro-coro."

"Just so," said Jodel. "You must do as you think best. But perhaps you will delay your departure a few moments; these gentlemen wish to make your acquaintance."

"Indeed!" said Maloof. He muttered to Myron: "It seems

that Farro found the news too dire and terrible to be kept secret."

"I am not surprised," said Myron. "In truth, he had no choice."

Jodel, looking from one to the other, said anxiously: "There is no need for diffidence. These are gentlemen of reputation; I vouch for them myself."

The Krenks stepped down from their stools and turned to face the off-worlders. They were much alike: dour, hard-featured men with sturdy torsos, heavy shoulders, and dark hair pulled back and tied with leather thongs. They wore long black coats flaring at the hip, black pantaloons tied at the knee, black stockings, and long pointed shoes.

Jodel spoke with careful deference. "Allow me to make introductions." He tapped each Krenk on the shoulder in turn. "This is Derl Mone. This is Avern Glister. This is Madrig Cargus." With a sheepish grin he looked sidewise at Maloof. "I fear that I have forgotten your names."

"No matter. I am Adair Maloof; this is Myron Tany. We both serve aboard the *Glicca*, now at the Coro-coro spaceport. What do you wish of us?"

Derl Mone spoke, his voice rasping with the effort to maintain civility. "You have taken an unusual interest in a certain Orlo Cavke. As you may have discovered, he is a criminal who escaped our justice. We are anxious to repair our mistake."

"I understand your concern," said Maloof. "Last night we learned more about Orlo Cavke—Loy Tremaine, as we knew him—than we had ever suspected."

As before, Mone controlled his voice with an effort. "Why do you seek Cavke?"

"He killed my father, and now controls my mother, living on her income."

Mone made an ambiguous sound, then asked: "What do you intend to do now?"

"At the moment, we have no idea of his whereabouts. Still, we will find him, probably by tracing my mother's annuity. If she were not receiving this money, he would have abandoned her. The foolish old lady certainly cannot be an exciting companion."

Mone made a grim sound. "Orlo's inclinations take him

differently—toward innocent pretty little creatures, hardly more than children. First he took Lally Glister and led her to a forest den, where he did incredible things to her. When she died, he buried her under the mold. After a time, he stole my girl Murs, and followed the same procedure. By this time the village was wild with horror, and no one raged more wildly than Orlo Cavke! After a time, he lay in wait for Salu Cargus, and what he did to her is beyond belief. But he had become careless. The farmboy Tinnoc, who worked a plot close by Orlo's planting, noticed Orlo's absences when he should have been tending his crops. There was no sign of tillage, and the weeds were rampant. Tinnoc told us of his suspicions, and we put a tracer button in Orlo's shoe and tracked him to his den.

"We unearthed the things from under the mold which once had been our daughters, and looked to Orlo for explanation. He merely smiled and shrugged.

"We dragged him back to the village and loaded him with chains. While we pondered the best way to deal with him, he squirmed free and fled into the forest; we fell to the ground and chewed stones. Five days of mourning were decreed: one day for the lost girls, three days for the loss of Orlo, and a final day to curse the great and only god for his apathy, whom we now reject as a turncoat. You will understand why we have questioned you in such detail."

Maloof assented. "You have our total sympathy."

Cargus broke his silence. "That is not enough—you claim that you will capture Orlo Cavke, and so it may be; when you have him in your custody, you must return him to Krenke, where we will provide him a suitable home-coming."

Maloof shook his head apologetically. "We cannot make such a commitment, which might be impossible for us to implement. I can only say that if we capture him and it is practical, we will turn him over to you. Any other promise I could make would be meaningless."

The three Krenks turned back to the bar. They drained the beer from their tankards, then turned toward the door and departed the inn.

Maloof and Myron paused long enough to give Jodel a polite farewell, then also departed the inn. For a moment they stood before the Three Feathers. They looked a last time up the high street, then marched over the iron bridge and crossed the parking yard to their flitter.

The flitter rose through the low overcast and broke out into sunlight. With the autopilot set, Maloof and Myron flew back over the landscapes of Fluter toward Coro-coro.

FIVE

1

The flitter arrived at the Coro-coro spaceport during the soft Fluter dusk. Aboard the *Glicca*, Wingo and Schwatzendale sat at the galley table making a meal of bread, sardines, and onions. Maloof and Myron joined the repast and told of their visit to Krenke.

Wingo and Schwatzendale were suitably impressed. "Strange," mused Wingo, "one would think that, after so many years, they might have evolved a cuisine more subtle than what you have described."

Schwatzendale pointed out that Wingo's theories were ad hoc and relativistic, since Wingo had no information as to the gastronomical standards of two thousand years previously. "For all we know, they subsisted on grass."

Wingo ignored the remark. "Conceivably each village of Fluter has developed a unique cuisine." He pondered a moment. "Hmm. A student of anthropology might find here scope for an interesting monograph." He brought a pot of tea and a plate of fruit tarts to the table; then he and Schwatzendale recounted their own exploits of the day. They had passed the afternoon on the O-Shar-Shan terrace, where Wingo had captured a number of vivid mood-impressions for his monumental *Pageant of the Gaean Race*.

"The terrace is a vast reservoir of material," said Wingo. "I give special attention to the ladies! Each has gone to great lengths to make herself supreme. Gentlemen are also on hand, naturally, but in general they lack a certain éclat.

"The terrace has become an avenue of almost transcendental mystique. Tourists are permeated by this extraordinary afflatus, and come to think of themselves as a privileged elite—free to indulge in whatever extravagance occurs to them." Wingo gave a rueful laugh. "It is ironic that when I encountered a truly startling circumstance, I failed to record the event, and I will regret the lapse forever." Wingo paused for reflection.

Maloof became impatient. "Please be more explicit! We sit here on tenterhooks, while you reminisce."

"Sorry," said Wingo. "I shall be more direct. When we arrived at the terrace, Schwatzendale went off on affairs of his own, while I found a table beside an ornamental planting and for a time was busy capturing mood-impressions. Then I put my equipment aside and sat at my ease drinking rum punch.

"Suddenly, at a nearby table, half hidden by the planting, I noticed what I had unaccountably missed before: a pair of young ladies, both exceedingly beautiful. Most notable was their resemblance to each other, so that I felt that they must be twins. They wore their honey-yellow curls in the same style; their features were identical, and they wore identical white blouses decorated with blue and red embroidery. The planting concealed their nether garments, but I was sure that they were the same.

"There was, however, a difference between the two. One was happy; her face glowed with excitement, humor, and ardent vitality, while the other sat steeped in despair and defeat, with mouth drooping and eyes downcast.

"I sat staring in wonder: what had caused such a disparity of emotion?"

Schwatzendale leaned forward. "I have the answer. They noticed you staring at them; one was amused; the other was angry, and about to shake her fist!"

"Nonsense!" scoffed Wingo. "The facts are quite different; neither so much as glanced in my direction."

"Belatedly I thought to capture the two faces for the *Pageant*," continued Wingo. "I reached for my gear, which I had tucked under the table. The other table was just across the planter, and I knew that I must be unobtrusive. I pretended ennui, and finally was ready to record the remarkable scene. But when I turned to look, the table was vacant; while I had been occupied, the girls had departed.

"I jumped to my feet and searched along the passages, up and down the aisles among the surge of tourists, and at last I saw them! They were walking away from me, so I saw only their backs. One was of ordinary height and walked with an easy athletic grace, while the other was half her height, and scuttled along on grotesquely deformed legs.

"I finally remembered my camera, but when I made ready, they were gone, and I saw no more of them."

"Hmm," said Maloof. "There is a lesson to be learned here, but I find it hard to quantify. Where was Schwatzendale during this episode?"

Wingo gave his head a dubious shake. "For a time, at least, he sat at a table on the level above me, in company with a woman of a most unusual type. She was tall, thin, and sinuous, with long white arms and long pale fingers. Her hair was white, and surrounded her head like a nimbus of dandelion fluff. Her face was long and gaunt, with eyebrows and mouth marked with black—like the face of a pierrette. She wore a number of white ribbons dangling from epaulets—when she moved the ribbons shifted, allowing glimpses of the anatomy below—and carried a fan of lavish white plumes. When she spoke, she flourished the fan to hide their faces, evidently to ensure privacy. I asked Schwatzendale what went on behind the fan, but he refused to describe the conversation."

"Surely no surprise," said Myron. "Schwatzendale is a man of honor; he does not care to betray the secrets of a lady."

Schwatzendale gave his head a puzzled shake. "There were no secrets. The lady revealed herself to be an addict of long walks in the countryside; she wanted to know if I cared to join her on a ramble across the Maudlen Moors. I explained that I lacked a proper costume for the sport and therefore must decline. And that was the way of it."

"All is explained," said Wingo. "Still, why did the conversation take place behind her fan?"

"For no particular reason," said Schwatzendale. "It was as good a place as any."

Wingo accepted the explanation, and the conversation came to a close.

2

The following morning Maloof and Myron breakfasted in the galley, then rode the omnibus along Pomare Boulevard to the IPCC office. They found Serle at his desk, occupied with the paperwork which, because of Civil Agent sensitivity, comprised most of his official duties. He greeted the two spacemen politely and indicated chairs.

Leaning back, Serle surveyed the two with dispassionate curiosity. "You seem to have avoided serious damage. How did you fare?"

"Well enough, all taken with all," replied Maloof. "We watched the young folk of the town engage in what seemed to be an energetic courtship rite in the public square. We dined at the Three Feathers Inn and took our breakfast in a special breakfast saloon. A serving girl named Buntje accused Myron of peering at her ankles and reported his conduct to the cook.

"More importantly, we learned that Loy Tremaine is in fact a man named Orlo Cavke, who killed three children. The folk of Krenke captured him, but he broke free and fled to Coro-coro, then escaped off-world. The Krenks were surprised to learn that he had returned to Fluter. They want him badly."

"Amazing!" said Serle. "I marvel at his audacity."

"So long as he avoids the Civil Agents he is in no great danger—until we find him."

"So it would seem," Serle agreed.

"The presence of Lady Maloof reduces his options," continued Serle. "It would not be practical for him to take a house in Coro-coro; too much paperwork is involved, and the lady would surely want to make sorties to the O-Shar-Shan and other places of high fashion. After a month, the Agents would wonder about her entry papers, whereupon both she and Cavke would be in serious trouble. Cavke could set up a romantic camp in the wilderness, but Lady Maloof might not enjoy cold water, bad food, insects, or crouching over a hole in the ground when the need becomes urgent."

"This option may be dismissed," said Maloof.

"Another possibility exists, which is more probable. I refer to the use of a houseboat. They come in all sizes, configurations, and degrees of luxury, and can be taken to where scenery is most appealing and anchored without restriction. Supplies can be obtained at waterside villages; from Cavke's point of view, a houseboat would seem the optimum solution to his problems."

"Perhaps so," mused Myron. "What then? Fluter is a world with a hundred rivers, and probably hundreds of houseboats. Once Cavke is anchored on some lonely river he is lost to us."

"Not necessarily," said Serle. "There is a way to check out every houseboat on Fluter, without leaving Coro-coro."

"That sounds useful. How is it done?"

"In a most logical fashion," said Serle. "Suppose that you owned a fleet of rental houseboats. What would be your greatest fear?"

Myron reflected, then said: "I would be afraid that a drunken tourist would run my best boat onto a reef, then leave my boat to rot. By the time I learned what had happened, the tourist would be back on his home-world."

Serle nodded. "Exactly. To guard against this event, the renter installs a tracer button aboard each of his houseboats. On a map in his office, the position of each houseboat is plotted. You need only learn which vessel Orlo Cavke has rented, obtain the coordinates, and proceed to this position. Board the houseboat and apprehend Cavke, and the job is done."

"Simple enough," said Maloof, "especially if Cavke makes no objection."

"That is the only dubious link in the chain," Serle agreed. "I am sorry to say that I am restricted by IPCC protocol with the Agency; otherwise Jervis and I, wearing field uniforms, could board the houseboat and put Cavke under arrest—which would finalize the matter very neatly."

"No matter," said Maloof. "One way or another, we will get the job done, even if we have to set fire to the houseboat and make the capture as Cavke jumps overboard."

3

The *Tourist Guide to Fluter* listed two concerns from which houseboats might be rented or leased.

The Tarquin Transit Agency maintained premises on Pomare Boulevard, next to the Pingis Tavern. Maloof and Myron sought out the yardmaster, a debonair young man with a fine set of silky yellow side-whiskers. When Maloof put his initial questions, the yardmaster looked at him a trifle askance. "Are the Civil Agents concerned in this matter?"

"Absolutely not—it is the IPCC which has become interested in Loy Tremaine, and the rather haughty old lady with whom he is travelling. There is no wish to involve the Civil Agents."

"Ah, well!" said the yardmaster. "That puts a new face on the matter. For your information, then, Tarquin Transit has never, within the span of my employment, rented to a couple such as that which you have described. For the most part we serve groups of three or four tourists, often with children." He consulted his listings but was only confirmed in his statements.

Maloof and Myron went on to the Zangwill Agency, situated on a side street behind the O-Shar-Shan Hotel. The proprietor, Urban Zangwill, unlike the Tarquin yardmaster, showed no inclination whatever to cooperate, and responded to Maloof's initial inquiry with disdain. "I have an enviable reputation for discretion. Am I likely to risk this priceless asset at the behest of a pair of off-worlders?"

As Serle had predicted, Zangwill became cooperative as soon as the IPCC was mentioned. Grudgingly, he looked into his ledger and presently announced that the *Maijaro*—a luxury vessel of excellent characteristics—had been let on a long-term basis to a distinguished gentleman named Loy Tremaine, and his ailing mother, who displayed a testy temperament.

Zangwill brought out plans which depicted a fine vessel, forty-eight feet long, with a fifteen-foot beam. The plans showed a forward pilot station, a large main saloon, a galley with a pantry, two staterooms each with a bath, and forward and aft decks six feet wide.

"Where is the *Maijaro* anchored?" Maloof asked.

Zangwill took them into his inner office. A table supported a large-scale map of Fluter embossed on a surface of matte black glass, with pale tinted continents in relief, the waterways spangled here and there by white sparks.

In a voice without accent, as if detaching himself from all association with Maloof and Myron, Zangwill said: "The sparks represent Agency houseboats. There are fifty-one vessels, of four classes."

"And which is the *Maijaro*?"

Still impassive, Zangwill looked into a ledger, then touched buttons on a panel beside the map. One of the white sparks became a bright green glitter.

"That is the *Maijaro*. It is anchored on the Suametta River, to the west of the second continent."

Maloof studied the map with care, and noted the geographical coordinates which defined the exact position of the *Maijaro*.

Zangwill spoke, still in the same uninterested voice: "This is an especially fine anchorage. The scenery is excellent, there is adequate privacy, and supplies are available at a village a few miles upstream."

"The information is important," said Maloof. "You should know that Tremaine is a criminal. I tell you this so that you will feel no compulsion to warn him of our interest—by any means whatever. If you do so, you become an accessory to his crimes, which are serious. You will incur the same penalties that will be visited upon Tremaine. The IPCC penitential colonies are cold, wet, miserable, and long-term. The food is bad. Your fellow prisoners are vicious. Are these facts well understood?"

Zangwill grimaced. "You have made them clear. The Zangwill Agency operates in total accord with the law."

"Good," said Maloof. "We are reassured."

4

Maloof and Myron returned to the IPCC office. Serle looked up from his work in surprise. "You are back earlier than I had expected. Is this a positive sign?"

Maloof assented. "Our affairs seem to be moving forward." He described the events of the morning.

"Zangwill was cooperative, but he would seem a man of flexible principles. For this reason, I warned him that he would incur severe punishment if he should communicate with Orlo Cavke—Loy Tremaine, as he knows him."

"Good," said Serle. He pondered. "But not good enough." He spoke into his telephone.

The screen brightened to reveal a somber, black-browed face.

"Urban Zangwill here."

"I am Commander Skahy Serle, at the IPCC office."

Zangwill studied Serle's image. "I have not had the pleasure of meeting you before. How may I be of service?"

Serle smiled. "I am about to inform you of something which you may find unusual, but I am sure that in your lifetime you have adapted to many odd circumstances."

Zangwill responded cautiously: "I suppose that this is true."

"Then you will have no difficulty with the following fact. This morning, as you sat relaxing in your office, you drifted into what is called a fugue, a kind of day-dream. At this time you may have a vague recollection that two IPCC operatives spoke to you, in relation to a certain houseboat. Am I right?"

Zangwill's eyes narrowed in puzzlement. "I do not quite understand the thrust of your remarks."

"It is no mystery. During your day-dream, you fabricated a hallucinatory event. I now assure you that no such operatives appeared at your yard, and that for the sake of your mental health you should totally dismiss such peculiar dream-figments from your mind. Even as we speak, I am sure that these notions have disappeared—especially if someone should ask a foolish question. Am I clear on this?"

Zangwill's heavy mouth twitched. "In short, if someone asks about your operatives, I am to forget that they ever existed."

"How can you forget a fact which has never existed?"

Zangwill licked his lips. "I see that it would not be possible."

"Correct." Serle examined Zangwill's face with attention. "In general, how is your memory?"

Zangwill took time to consider. "I believe that it is good."

"Excellent. Therefore, if you do not recall a visit by anyone this morning, such event never occurred."

"That would be my conclusion; yes, indeed!"

"And you do not recall any such event?"

Zangwill grimaced. "No; I fear not."

"If anyone shows an interest in this hypothetical occasion, communicate with me immediately, and I will put matters right. I may say that your cooperation has established you in the good graces of the IPCC."

Zangwill showed a wry smile. "That is good news."

The screen went blank. Serle, frowning at some unwelcome thought, asked Maloof: "I assume that you learned the exact location of the *Maijaro*?"

Maloof responded without emphasis. "I took the coordinates from Zangwill's map." He recited numbers.

Serle brought out a map of the second continent and spread it upon his desk. Maloof repeated the numbers; Serle traced the coordinates and marked the intersection. "The *Maijaro* is here, where the river passes close under the Sumberlin Ridge." He studied the map.

"Upstream about eight miles is a small village. Its name is 'Pengelly'; it seems of no great importance." He reached into a drawer, brought out a reference book, found relevant information, and read: "Pengelly: a village of considerable antiquity on the Suametta River, with a population of about four hundred, occupied principally with fishing and agriculture. Pengelly figures to a small extent in historical lore, and at one time was the lair of the bandit Rasselbane. The single structure of importance is the 'Iron Crow Inn'." Serle put the book aside. "And there you have it. The *Maijaro* lies at anchor on the Suametta, with your mother and Cavke drowsing away the hours. Cavke will not surrender gracefully. Apart from setting the houseboat on fire, how will you proceed?"

"There is no lack of options," said Maloof. "We may dress

as fisherman and try to sell Cavke some fish, or we may present ourselves as river police, looking for a stolen houseboat. During the night we could transfer the anchor line to a tree on the shore; the current would swing the houseboat up on the beach, and when Cavke waded ashore we could apprehend him. In any case, we will bring my mother back to Coro-coro, and return her to Morlock." Maloof rose to his feet. "We will keep in touch with you."

Serle also rose. "If you leave now, you will arrive at the Suametta by late afternoon. I suggest that you put down somewhere for the night and reconnoiter in the morning."

"No doubt that is what we shall do."

5

Returning to the *Glicca*, Maloof and Myron found no one aboard. They left a note on the galley table, then set off once again in the flitter across the pleasant landscapes of Fluter, holding to a north-westerly course.

Early in the afternoon they passed over a long line of cliffs and set out over the blue ocean beyond, reaching the white beach which fringed the second continent as the sun approached the noon meridian. They flew on, over forests, rolling hills, mountains, cultivated lands, and tracts of wilderness.

Late in the day the River Suametta appeared ahead. In the failing light of afternoon, the village Pengelly could be seen on the opposite shore, half-hidden under tall trees.

Several miles downstream, a houseboat was visible lying quietly at anchor.

The Iron Crow Inn was immediately noticeable: a massive two-story structure built of antique timber and stone under a crotchety slate roof, with ghost-chasers protecting the ridges. The single street of the village led away under the trees, past weathered stone houses. Tendrils of somnolent smoke rose from chimneys; Pengelly had succumbed to the torpor of age.

Maloof and Myron surveyed the village from above, then dropped to a landing upon a strip of wasteland beside the inn. Alighting, they stood watching and listening, but heard neither voices nor running footsteps; their arrival apparently had gone unnoticed.

They set off along a path which led to the front of the building. The sign over the door depicted a black iron crow four feet tall, in an attitude of intrepid defiance. The frame hung by iron chains from an overhead gallows. Under the sign, a pair of heavy doors opened into the inn.

Maloof and Myron pushed through the doors, and entered a large, high-ceilinged common room. Windows in the left wall overlooked the Suametta, admitting a tide of dim light. A glossy wooden bar occupied the front half of the right-hand wall, with a dining area to the rear. Alone in the room, at a table to the back, sat two children busily writing in exercise books. The boy was about eleven, the girl somewhat younger.

Entering the chamber, Maloof and Myron came forward, then stopped short, staring in fascination at the wall behind the bar. An artist of long ago had painted a remarkable mural four feet high and extending the length of the bar. In meticulous detail, and with absolute preciosity the artist had simulated a long mirror reflecting the images of the patrons, who sat studying their simulated reflections in the mirror. A representative group of villagers were present on that long-past occasion: young, old, men and women, a few laughing, others grave, wearing clothes of archaic style, all concerned with the exigencies of their now forgotten lives. The bar was untenanted, except perhaps for the ghosts of those who sat reflected in the mirror.

The children had become aware of the newcomers. Both were clean, alert, and self-assured. The boy jumped to his feet, ran to a door in the back wall, called through a message, then trotted back to his place at the table. In the doorway a grizzled old man showed himself. He was small, bony, and dour, wearing a white apron. Muttering an objurgation, he sidled down behind the bar to where Maloof and Myron waited. Halting, he subjected them to a brief inspection, then spoke.

"Gentlemen, what are your needs?"

"They are quite ordinary," said Maloof. "We want lodging for the night, supper, and breakfast in the morning."

The bartender reflected at length, nodding in slow cogitation, until Maloof became impatient. "Surely this is the Iron

Crow Inn? Am I addressing the proper official? If not, please direct us to someone in authority."

The bartender surveyed Maloof with disapproval. He responded carefully, using precise diction, so as not to confuse Maloof. "Be calm—you have certainly arrived at the historic Iron Crow Inn. I am Ugo Teybald, the proprietor. I am obliged to notify you that our clientele is select, and we cannot indulge the habits of off-worlders, except at premium rates."

Maloof smiled grimly. "Your preconceptions are wrong. We are savants touring Fluter like vagabonds, and we are accustomed to the hospitality of Fluter inns. Nothing surprises us, and we will make do with your standard accommodation. Put away all thought of premium rates, since we have agreed to report all instances of over-charging to the District Control."

"Bah," muttered Teybald. "Our rates are graven in stone. If the goddess Hyrcania came up from her cave and wanted lodging, she would find that our rates were immutable."

"Very well, then; we shall be content with the best you can offer, at the immutable rate."

Teybald deliberated, then said gruffly: "The season is slack; we can allow you a first-class chamber, which includes fine furniture and a splendid view of the river. An adjacent lavatory is offered as an extra."

"Oh? How much extra? And what will be the immutable total?"

The two eventually agreed upon an all-inclusive price for room, lavatory, supper, breakfast, service, and view for a rate which Maloof found acceptable.

Teybald looked here and there. "And where is your luggage?"

"Still aboard the flitter."

Teybald slapped his hand upon the bar and cried out: "Berard! Sonssi! Be quick—these rich off-worlders want service! Smartly now, if you hope for a noble gratuity!"

Almost before he had finished speaking, the children had dashed from the inn, and around the building to the flitter. Myron hurried after them and reached the flitter in time to extricate the luggage before Berard and Sonssi swarmed aboard to do the work themselves. Myron passed out the luggage; the children seized the cases and carried them triumphantly back to the inn, up the stairs, and into the room which had been assigned to the spacemen.

Maloof and Myron followed more sedately, and were ushered by the children into a large room smelling of wax and old wood. The room lacked ornament, but was furnished with massive pieces clearly of great age. Maloof went to look from the window, which, as advertised, commanded a view of the river. A path led from the inn down to a dock, where several boats bobbed at their moorings.

Maloof signalled Sonssi, who sprang forward, quivering with eagerness. Maloof said: "I notice boats at the dock yonder. Are they to be used by guests of the inn?"

"Indeed they are, sir, and they provide truly fine sport or—if you prefer—calm and gentle rest. You are assured of a pleasant evening on the water."

"Not tonight," said Maloof. "Perhaps tomorrow morning."

"Still, you should reserve now. In the morning the fishermen come early and take out the best boats until nothing remains but the scow."

Berard stepped forward. "May I ask what sort of boat you require?"

Maloof considered. "Something not too large, but it should move well through the water, and be very quiet."

"Perhaps you should come down to the dock while the light still holds, and make your own selection."

"A good idea," said Maloof. "We will come down in five minutes."

"We will be ready."

Berard and Sonssi marched to the door, where they turned to stand in postures of formal decorum. Maloof and Myron paid them no heed, and began to arrange their belongings.

Berard spoke. "Sirs, we have done our best to serve you. If we have failed, then we deserve no gratuity."

"Aha!" said Maloof. "All is now clear." He gave five dinkets to each, which the children accepted, politely but without enthusiasm, then departed.

Ten minutes later Maloof and Myron walked down to the dock, with Berard and Sonssi running ahead. Four boats were moored to the dock. In the end they selected the *Lulio*, an unpretentious work-boat about twenty feet long, with a small cuddy.

Sonssi endorsed the choice. "All are good boats; they float without hesitation, and the engine propels them in a direction of your choice. The *Lulio* has a small cabin which will deflect the rain, should this occur."

Berard demonstrated the controls and certified that the boat was capable of at least adequate speed. Sonssi told them confidently: "Naturally, you will need a skillful pilot, and here I am superior to Berard—who is somewhat reckless, and likes to try sidewise swashes. He is also absent-minded and is apt to run you aground. If you trust Berard, you are likely to come back bedraggled and wet. As for me, I know all the secret places of the river and the fine streams."

Berard said scornfully: "Pay no heed to Sonssi; she is a bit of a braggart. I am by far the superior pilot! I take it for granted that you will hire me in this capacity."

Maloof explained that no pilot whatever would be needed, while the two listened glumly. The four returned up the path. Berard and Sonssi raced ahead, and stationed themselves by the door to the inn.

Maloof looked from one to the other. "So what is it now?"

"Nothing of consequence, sir," said Berard. "We were waiting in case other services might be needed."

Sonssi added: "Also, if you planned gratuities, we wanted to be ready at hand, to cause you the least inconvenience."

Maloof gave a rueful laugh and distributed five-dinket coins to each; then he and Myron entered the inn.

They went to sit at the bar, where four villagers were already present, drinking beer from tall tankards. They darted sidelong glances toward Maloof and Myron, then turned back to their beer, to mutter in undertones.

Teybald approached, now wearing a white smock and a small white cap. "What, sirs, is your pleasure?"

"You may serve us a bitter ale, if it is readily available," said Maloof.

Without comment Teybald produced two tankards of foaming ale.

"Further," said Maloof, "we want to cruise the river for a few hours tomorrow. For preference we will use the *Lulio*. I expect that this is a service that you offer to guests at the inn without charge?"

"Wrong! We rent the *Lulio* out at a rate of seven sols per day."

Maloof raised his eyebrows in shock. "That is a large sum! We can swim the river free of charge."

"True, and you will lose your private parts to the glass-fish within the minute. Swimming is a poor economy."

In the end Maloof secured the *Lulio* for five sols, payment to be made in advance. Maloof agreed to the provision, and paid on the spot.

The two were presently called to supper, which consisted of a dish of sharp greens, fried fish with sour fritters, goulash with seasoned barley, a compote of fresh fruit, and a pot of tea. Berard and Sonssi, wearing white aprons, served them deftly and again received gratuities.

After supper Maloof and Myron resisted a second visit to the bar, and went upstairs to their beds. The evening was quiet; there were no sounds from the village. After half an hour of desultory conversation, they slept.

6

Maloof and Myron arose early and descended to the common room, where they were served a substantial breakfast of porridge, griddlecakes with marmalade, and fried sausages.

In the pre-dawn stillness, they walked down to the dock. The day was clear and crisp, without so much as a breeze to ruffle the face of the river. The two boarded the *Lulio*, loosed the mooring, and set off downstream with the first glimmer of dawn light reflecting on the water. Under different conditions, the two men would have enjoyed the peace of the river and the idyllic scenery along the shores.

The *Lulio* moved quietly at ten miles per hour, according to the meter on the console. Maloof kept the boat close to the right-hand shore, where they should be less conspicuous to anyone watching from the *Maijaro*, although it seemed unlikely that either Cavke or Lady Maloof would be vigilant at this early hour.

Half an hour passed, and the two began to search the water ahead for a glimpse of the *Maijaro*, but there was no sign of the houseboat. Another ten minutes went by while Maloof and Myron became increasingly tense; at last the *Maijaro* came into view, anchored beside a small island, the bow pointing downstream.

Maloof idled the engine. The *Lulio* drifted toward the *Maijaro*, close under the trees which shaded the water, and at last drew alongside. They watched and listened, but detected neither sound nor movement from within.

With the utmost delicacy, Myron transferred himself to the front deck, where he made the painter fast to a stanchion. Maloof joined him, and they let the boat swing past, to lie downstream, where it could not bump into the houseboat.

For a moment they stood listening, wary that someone within had noticed movement of the houseboat when they climbed aboard. But all remained silent.

Maloof tested the door into the front cabin, and eased it ajar. Across the cabin a doorway opened into the main saloon. From where they stood, only a section of the far wall was visible, but clearly through the open doorway came the chink of porcelain, and a faint sipping sound. Maloof shifted cautiously forward, and brought most of the saloon into view.

In a high-backed wicker chair sat Lady Maloof. At her side, an octagonal tabouret of split bamboo supported a tray with a pot of tea, a plate of small pastries, and a saucer of what might have been honey. In her bony hand she held a fluted yellow teacup.

She wore a voluminous peignoir of pale blue silk, decorated with a fantastic array of flamboyant birds sitting on perches. Their dangling tails spread into extravagant fans, creating patterns of vivid color: tangerine-red, phosphorescent green, acrid blue. The garment was wildly unsuitable to the circumstances, and would seem to represent Lady Maloof's brave but futile attempts to deny the remorseless passage of time. Apparently she had undergone surgical techniques to the same ends, and the results were not at all happy; the skin adjacent to her eyelids had been gathered, causing her eyes to tilt upward as if in querulous inquiry. The wattles under her chin were gone, leaving a long, pointed chin. Myron saw Maloof wince and shake his head.

The two searched the saloon. Lady Maloof was alone, thinking her dismal thoughts.

Holding his hand-gun at the ready, Maloof stole step by step into the saloon. Myron silently followed. Lady Maloof became fretful and raised her head, as if to call out. Maloof and Myron froze in their tracks, but she changed her mind, and drank more tea.

Maloof eased silently forward, slow step by slow step. Lady Maloof sat nodding over her tea until, warned by some small sound, she looked over her shoulder. At the sight of the intruders, her eyes went wide and her mouth sagged open; she started to scream.

Maloof was upon her, clamping her mouth before she could utter more than a terrified squeak. Her eyes bulged as she stared at her still-strange assailant. As for Maloof, this haggard old woman was only barely recognizable as his mother; Orlo Cavke had lavished little loving care upon the source of his income.

At last Lady Maloof's shoulders sagged, as Maloof's identity penetrated her consciousness. She clawed his hand away from her mouth. "You are Adair," she croaked. "Adair!"

"Yes, I am Adair. I am taking you back to Traven."

Lady Maloof's eyes filled with tears, which trickled down her addled old cheeks.

Maloof said: "Your friend Cavke"—he corrected himself—"Loy Tremaine; where is he now?"

Lady Maloof looked toward the hall which led to the after-cabins. Maloof followed her gaze, to find Cavke standing in the doorway, naked to the waist and barefoot.

"Here I am," said Cavke. He peered at Maloof, then at Myron. "What do you want of me?"

"I have come for my mother. I am taking her home to Traven."

Cavke took note of the hand-gun which Maloof held at the ready. "Not a good idea," said Cavke easily, apparently relaxed in the doorway.

With two sudden long strides, Cavke stood behind Lady Maloof. He seized her scrawny neck; with the other hand he swept up a knife from the galley counter and thrust the point against Lady Maloof's corded gray neck.

"You are a fine and noble son, but why should I be inconvenienced on that account? She will not go with you, or anyone else!"

Maloof studied the dark aquiline face. Remembering the Krenke photographs, Maloof saw that Cavke had become indefinably coarse. The lips had thickened; there was a puffiness under the eyes, and a slack rotundity at the abdomen marked the beginnings of a paunch. His black trousers were almost indecently tight around the hips, flaring at the knees. His naked chest was hairless, and glistened as if oiled. A gold ring hung from his left ear; the sunburst tattoo was visible under his jaw.

Cavke asked suddenly: "How did you know where to find your mother?"

"It was simple enough. You gave out the information yourself."

"Oh? How so?"

"At my aunt's house on Traven you said that you intended to return to the most beautiful world in the Reach. I took you at your word. At Coro-coro the IPCC agent suggested that you would rent a houseboat. Zangwill Transit told us where to find the *Maijaro*, and here we are."

Cavke grinned wolfishly. "I see."

"I suggest that you leave the houseboat and return to Coro-coro. But do not try to interfere with my plans."

"A good idea, if a trifle droll," said Cavke. "I have an even better idea. In a month or so I will drop this old woman off at the O-Shar-Shan, and you can do what you like with her."

"No!" squeaked Lady Maloof. "He wants to cash my annuity. To this I say no! Not another dinket for this brute!"

Maloof said to Cavke: "That seems definite enough."

Lady Maloof continued: "I cannot tell you how he has abused me. His insults have been beyond belief!"

Cavke gave her a half-amused jostle. "Quiet, you old mudlark—have you no dignity? These men are not interested in your complaints."

Lady Maloof only raised her voice. "His insults were cruel! He called me a bony old sandpiper with the molt! He said that I smelled like pickled herring, and that I must bathe—and he suggested that I use the river, since the glass-fish would give me one look, then rush off to find something edible!"

"Not at all nice," said Maloof.

"Just a bit of jocularity," said Cavke, grinning.

"He has slandered me in a hundred ways," wailed Lady Maloof. "I want to go home!"

"Not so fast," said Cavke. "Find me some clean clothes." He started for the hallway, dragging Lady Maloof along in front of him.

Myron instantly bounded across the room, and stationed himself in the opening, holding his gun at the ready. He grinned at Cavke. "You have a gun in your room. You don't need it at the moment."

Cavke saw that if he moved toward the hall, he would be putting himself between Myron and Maloof, which would not be to his advantage, since he could not watch both at once. With a sulky expression, he backed into a corner, dragging Lady Maloof stumbling and hopping. He spoke in a sibilant voice: "This stalemate must be resolved. If you behave reasonably, in three weeks, or a month, you may take custody of this woman and go your way, and I shall not interfere—unless you attempt some act of mindless vengeance upon me. Otherwise this lady shall be dead."

From somewhere came a soft thud. Myron looked toward Maloof, and the act nearly cost him his life. Cavke hurled his knife at Myron's neck. Maloof shouted; Myron saw the flicker of steel and slumped over backward, almost to the floor. Cavke then spun; in a single unbroken motion he snatched up a cleaver, which he slung with great force at Myron's head.

The cleaver spun through the air and struck Myron's shoulder, handle-first. Myron's arm went numb instantly; his gun clattered to the floor. Cavke took advantage of the occasion. Lunging forward, he scooped up the gun and lurched for the hallway, dragging Lady Maloof behind him. He gained the opening and turned back triumphantly.

"Now I will shoot you both dead. If you retreat to your boat, I will shoot you from the deck! You gambled with your lives, and you have lost at the great game; prepare to meet the judgment of your—"

Behind Cavke a heavy form appeared. A hand reached over

his shoulder, twisted, and wrenched. Cavke screamed; his weapons fell to the deck. Lady Maloof fell in a whimpering heap of scarlet birds and sprawling limbs.

Cavke screamed again, as his arm was wrenched into an unnatural position; he was thrust stumbling into the saloon.

Three men entered from the rear cabin. Myron and Maloof recognized Derl Mone, Avern Glister, and Madrig Cargus, who had come up from behind Cavke, in the rear passage.

Mone and Glister advanced upon Cavke; they shackled his arms behind his back, then tied a lead-rope around his neck. Cavke stood limp, his features sagging, stricken by the disaster which had so suddenly overtaken him.

The men from Krenke, standing back, surveyed Cavke with cold satisfaction.

Mone spoke: "Orlo! Do you know me? I am Derl Mone. My daughter was Murs Mone. Do you remember her?"

Glister spoke: "Orlo, do you remember me? I am Avern Glister. My daughter was Lally Glister. She had brown hair and a tip-tilted nose."

Cargus spoke. "Orlo—do you know me? I am Madrig Cargus. My daughter was Salu; surely you remember Salu."

Cavke grinned a ghastly grin. "I know you all well, and the three girls also. The brain is a wonderful instrument, that it remembers so well." Then he added, in a voice suddenly husky: "How did you find me, so far from Krenke?"

Mone showed a small cold grin: "You have these off-worlders to thank. They flew their flitter out to Krenke and asked questions about you. We put a tracer button on their flitter and followed wherever they led. As we expected, they brought us to you."

"Be assured that you will not escape us again," said Glister. "We shall watch you with care, as if you were our ailing child!"

"Your return to Krenke will be a great sensation," said Cargus. "The homecoming celebration will be remembered down the ages. The entire village will be in a froth of excitement!"

"Just so," said Mone. "We plan a festival of seven days, at which you shall be the dance-master. But we must not keep all of your old acquaintances waiting! Now, it is back to Krenke, in grand style!"

"You will want to make an impressive entry," said Cargus. "I will get you a shirt, a coat, and shoes."

Maloof asked Mone: "Will you be able to rise from the roof, with so much of a load?"

"Feel no concern; we came in our working flitter. It will carry double the weight, and fly like a bird."

7

The Flauts with their wretched prisoner were gone. Lady Maloof changed her costume and packed a few of her belongings into a travelling bag; then the three boarded the *Lulio* and returned upstream to dock at Pengelly.

Lady Maloof was placed aboard the flitter; there were final gratuities for Berard and Sonssi, and then the flitter rose above the village and set off back toward Coro-coro.

Maloof told Lady Maloof, "There is a final critical moment when we transfer you from the flitter to the *Glicca*. We must be as inconspicuous as possible, so as not to attract the notice of the Civil Agents."

Lady Maloof made a querulous sound. "Surely they will recognize me for what I am, and not molest me in any way."

Maloof chuckled sadly. "Unlikely. In any case, we will take as few risks as possible."

"I cannot concern myself with such affairs," said Lady Maloof. "I am anxious only for a bath, fresh garments, and a proper meal."

Maloof served her bread, cheese, and a cold meat pie, at which she nibbled with condescension, with an occasional sniff. Lady Maloof thereupon arranged herself on a bench and fell asleep.

The flitter arrived at Coro-coro during the middle evening. Maloof made sure that no Civil Agents were in evidence, then took Lady Maloof trotting and hopping at best speed to the gangway and up into the saloon.

Lady Maloof at once began to complain. "Really, Adair, have you lost all respect for propriety? You jerk me about as if I were a wayward animal. This sort of thing must not be repeated, and I shall be firm on this."

"You were not moving fast enough," said Maloof. "I wanted to evade attention."

Lady Maloof said querulously: "I felt as if I were hurtling through the air like a sack of chaff, all to no sensible purpose. But now I am tired and hungry."

Maloof served her a bowl of soup, an omelet, hot buttered scones, and a cream tart, then bedded her down in his own quarters, where she quickly fell asleep.

SIX

1

Once secure aboard the *Glicca*, Lady Maloof dismissed the *Maijaro* from her mind as if it had been a bad dream. Once again she became the grande dame of Traven society, with prestige so exalted as to insulate her from petty official annoyances.

Maloof patiently tried to explain the functioning of the Civil Authority. "The Agents interpret the Protocols rigidly; in their view you are a lawbreaker and subject to penalties of at least the second order."

Lady Maloof only shook her head and smiled. "Come now, Adair, they would not concern themselves over a trifling peccadillo, especially after they understand who I am."

"Who you are means nothing! They prosecute the act, not the person."

"Hmmf," sniffed Lady Maloof. "In my experience, all officials are flexible—especially if you show them a ten-sol certificate."

Maloof managed a painful grin. "The subject is moot, since you will not be leaving the *Glicca*."

Lady Maloof gave a gurgle of amusement. "Truly, Adair, you must cultivate a more sophisticated outlook; I do not intend to be immured as if I were a pariah! Be reasonable, Adair!"

"I plan to ship you back to Morlock at the first opportunity," said Maloof. "That is realism. Until that time, you must keep a low profile aboard the *Glicca*."

"This is quite impractical," said Lady Maloof haughtily. "I am planning to order a carriage and visit the O-Shar-Shan terrace, where I can enjoy the civilized intercourse to which I am entitled."

"I think not," said Maloof. "The Agents would pick you up before you left the spaceport."

Lady Maloof daubed at her brow with a handkerchief. "I cannot understand why you have to be so brutally dogmatic! As a boy, you were most gallant, at all times—the change is most unsettling!"

She rose to her feet and threw the handkerchief down to the deck. "You may take me to my stateroom."

2

An hour later, leaving Myron on guard, Maloof visited the passengers' lounge in the spaceport administration building, where he checked the posting of schedules for ships arriving at Coro-coro. He was delighted to find that the tourist packet *Farway Rambler* would depart Coro-coro at midnight and in due course would touch into Port Pallas on Tran, which served as a transfer depot for a dozen shipping lines and where a connection to Morlock could be arranged without difficulty.

Maloof departed the lounge and crossed the field to the great blue and silver packet. He went aboard and was conducted to the office of Captain Brevet Fane, with whom he had some previous acquaintance.

Maloof was cordially received and installed in a comfortable chair. After a few minutes of casual conversation, Maloof mentioned his mother, her difficulties, and his efforts to extricate her from own foolishness.

Fane listened sympathetically and assured Maloof that he need only bring his mother aboard the *Farway Rambler*; he and his staff would take care of any remaining problems. Maloof provided such information as was needed; then Fane pressed a button to summon his steward, who arrived carrying a tray on which rested a heavy bottle and two goblets.

Fane reverently lifted the bottle and poured three inches of a tawny liquor into each of the glasses, one of which he slid across to Maloof.

"In the ancient language, the word 'uisquebaugh' means 'water of life'," said Fane. "According to legend, the liquor is created from sunshine, rain, and soft turf smoke."

He raised his glass. "Slanche."

"Slanche," said Maloof.

3

Maloof returned to the *Glicca*, where he found Myron sitting alone at the galley table, reading a list of various cargoes awaiting transfer. Maloof looked into the saloon, which was empty. He asked: "Where is she?"

"Still in her cabin," said Myron. "She has not so much as stirred—I assume she is asleep."

Maloof went to the cabin which had been assigned to Lady Maloof. He knocked at the door and listened but heard nothing. He knocked again. This time Lady Maloof responded, in a fluting voice: "Who is it?"

Maloof pushed open the door and stepped into the cabin. He stopped short, eyebrows lofting in wonder.

Lady Maloof sat before the mirror of the dressing table, applying a mask of white cosmetic to her sagging features. She had accented her eye sockets with splotches of brown-purple pigment, so that she resembled an old white raccoon. Her hair, now dyed jet black, was drawn up into a tuft and was constrained by a binding of white beads. She wore a spectacular gown of lambent green, split down the legs to reveal a pale blue lining and glimpses of match-stick legs. She noticed Maloof's presence and turned upon him a glance of disapproval.

"Have you forgotten even the rudiments of decorum? You are intruding upon my privacy."

"Sorry," said Maloof. "I came to tell you that I have obtained

passage for you back to Morlock. The ship leaves tonight, so
pack your bags."

Lady Maloof turned her attention back to the mirror. "This
arrangement must be postponed; it does not accord with my
plans. I am ordering a carriage for the O-Shar-Shan. If I find
the circumstances amusing, I may well book a suite for a week
or two."

Maloof wasted neither time nor breath in recriminations.
He called in Myron, and ignoring Lady Maloof's shrill protests,
they crammed her belongings into her travel bags.

Maloof stepped down from the *Glicca* and surveyed the
field, now obscured by the coming of dusk. Tourists in groups
were returning to their ships. Maloof went back into the *Glicca*.

"Now is as good a time as any," he told his mother. "Are you
ready?"

"Naturally not! This is a farrago of utter nonsense—it is
tragic!"

"Very sad," said Maloof, bringing out a long black cloak
which had been discarded by one of the pilgrims. "Your costume is a bit conspicuous; cover yourself in this cloak."

"What? It seethes with dirt!"

"Nevertheless, it must serve." Maloof wrapped the cloak
about Lady Maloof's shrinking form and jammed a broad-
brimmed hat down over her head. "We are as ready as we ever
will be. Let's be away."

"This is a great fiasco," declared Lady Maloof. "I do not intend to walk a single step."

"Either you walk, or we take you in a wheelbarrow," said
Maloof. "Are you ready?"

"It seems that I have no choice!" cried Lady Maloof
piteously. "If I must, I must. I shall never forget this indignity."
With Maloof at her side, she set forth, and at her best speed
made for the *Farway Rambler* with Myron coming behind, carrying the bags.

Without incident they reached the comforting bulk of the
packet. Mounting the embarcation ramp, they passed through a
vestibule and entered the main saloon. The purser was not at
hand; Myron went off to find him.

Maloof surveyed the chamber, which was panelled in golden-
brown wood and carpeted with soft green plush, creating an

ambience of understated elegance. He glanced sidewise at Lady Maloof, to find her looking about with a supercilious droop to her mouth.

"It seems comfortable enough," said Maloof cautiously. "You should have a pleasant voyage."

Lady Maloof gave a critical sniff. A group of passengers at a nearby table were drinking from frosted glasses and holding an animated conversation. They took note of Lady Maloof, and the conversation trailed off. A discreet chuckle or two could be heard, then the conversation resumed.

Lady Maloof made a hissing sound between her teeth. She wrenched her arms back and let the black cloak fall to the deck. For good measure she snatched the hat from her head and threw it aside.

Maloof watched gravely but made no attempt to interfere.

At that moment, Myron returned with the purser, who welcomed Lady Maloof aboard with punctilious formality. Using a rich baritone voice he exclaimed: "I admit to surprise! I had expected someone considerably older than yourself, and definitely lacking your evident panache!"

Lady Maloof muttered: "I feel that in many ways I am distinctly remarkable. I have never renounced my yearning to live by the precepts of romance!"

"A remarkable trait," declared the purser.

"Now I must conduct you to your cabin, where you will undoubtedly wish to rest before the gala following departure."

Maloof patted his mother's shoulder. "I am sure that you will enjoy your voyage. Soon you will be home."

"I shall do well enough, or so I suppose," said Lady Maloof distantly.

Myron also made his farewells, to which Lady Maloof vouchsafed only a curt nod, then the purser led her away. A porter followed, carrying her bags.

Maloof and Myron waited until the purser returned. Maloof asked: "I assume that you still depart at midnight?"

"There have been no changes; the ship will depart according to schedule."

"I must warn you that my mother is often headstrong, if not unreasonable—even to her own detriment."

The purser smiled politely. "We accommodate passengers

of many temperaments. I doubt if Lady Maloof can show us anything novel."

"It is of utmost importance that she not be allowed to leave the ship before departure. She has no legal papers, and the Civil Agents will be sure to pick her up and subject her to the second order. If necessary, lock her in her stateroom, or even sedate her. Do not relax your vigilance! She uses an animal cunning to get her own way."

"We will take special precautions," said the purser. "In fact, I will go at once to lock her door. You need not concern yourselves, she will not be allowed to leave the ship."

"Thank you, I am reassured," said Maloof. Taking their leave, the two returned across the field to the *Glicca*.

Hours passed. Dusk deepened through evening into night, and the *Farway Rambler* prepared for departure.

Midnight approached. Aboard the *Glicca*, Maloof and Myron went out upon the small staging deck at the head of the gangway. At three minutes to the hour the packet's embarcation ramp was drawn up into the ship, and the entry port sealed; at midnight the farewell horn sounded, rising from a mournful moan up the scale to an eerie soprano wail, then dropping again to fade below the threshold of perception.

The *Farway Rambler* eased up from the field to an altitude of five hundred feet, then slid off into the night, rising and gathering speed to become a glimmer and disappear among the stars.

4

Aboard the *Glicca*, Maloof and Myron lingered in the dark, each with his own thoughts. After a time Maloof went to the galley and returned with a bottle of soft yellow wine.

He poured and they sat as before, although the wine, by some subtle process, had altered their mood.

Maloof spoke, half to himself. "The venture is over. There is nothing more to do, and I feel empty. It is a most curious sensation; what next? Perhaps nothing. Perhaps I shall try to rest; it is as if I have entered another phase of existence."

After a pause, Myron replied. "It seems natural enough,

with so much less tension in your life. You might even ease into something like 'lurulu'."

Maloof laughed softly. "Lurulu is something different, and far more elusive. It cannot be precisely defined, but seems to come when yearnings are being gratified—not necessarily from the fact, which is too close to an inert tranquillity." He mused. "It seems that there is an active component of lurulu, which can be fragile."

Myron stared off into the night. "I doubt if I will ever chance upon such a state."

"How so?"

"My 'yearnings', if that is what they are, can never be reconciled; they pull in different directions. One involves a certain Tibbet Garwig, who lives at Duvray, on Alcydon. Second, my Aunt Hester has done me harm; she represents an itch I desperately want to scratch—call it a component of lurulu, if you like. Then there is the *Glicca;* I can not stay aboard the *Glicca* forever, and the prospect of any other life is dismal."

Maloof drained his glass. "For each of us, lurulu is in the nature of a far-off dream. But for now, it occurs to me that the night is still young, and that a short walk along Pomare Boulevard will bring us to the Pingis Tavern, where we might risk a Pooncho Number Two, or even a Number Three, depending upon the portents."

Myron was instantly on his feet. "The idea is constructive! As dauntless spacemen we may safely ignore portents, unless they take the form of Civil Agents—in which case we reconsider our plans."

The two descended the gangway, crossed the field, and set off up Pomare Boulevard toward the Pingis Tavern.

5

The sojourn of the *Glicca* at Coro-coro had reached its final days. Without enthusiasm, the crew began to prepare for departure.

One morning during a visit to the transshipment dock Myron provisionally accepted a parcel of cargo for a world somewhat to the side of the direct route to Blenkinsop, the next scheduled port of call.

Back aboard the *Glicca*, Myron reported the tentative transaction to Captain Maloof. "The parcel consists of thirty-two
carboys of chemical—kasic, to be specific. It was shipped from
Cax and off-loaded here for transshipment to Star Home."

"Star Home?"

"An obscure world on a dogleg off the direct run to Cax. I
am told that the Port Director will pay charges of three hundred and twenty-five sols, which seems reasonable. The course
is not impractical, and I accepted the parcel—subject to your
approval, of course."

Maloof looked into *Handbook to the Planets*. He found 'Star
Home' and read aloud.

" 'Star Home, second planet of the white dwarf Mireille, is
a small, dense world with a breathable atmosphere, a congenial
climate, and gravity close to Earth-normal. The sidereal day is
twenty hours and twenty-three minutes. There are two continents: The smaller, to the north, is a dreary waste of stone and
ice; the second is characterized by flat steppes overgrown with
chest-high grass, with a few ranges of ancient hills and a minor
upthrust of mountains in the far south.

" 'At first viewing, Star Home offers no great attraction either for the scholar or the casual traveler, though the sparse native population enlivens the scene. The "Ritters" are a patrician
caste of uncompromising nomads, guided only by the unwritten
doctrines of "Ritterway". They wander the seaside littoral,
pausing as the mood strikes them, mingling with other groups,
then separating into clan-like units. There are no settled communities of any description, and no formal social structure.

" 'The Ritters are versatile, and skilled at many small crafts,
but are most notably expert in the fabrication of exquisite rugs,
which they export off-world in return for needful articles beyond their ability to produce, such as tools, food synthesizers,
and household utensils. Generally placid folk, they live without
hostility and are indifferent to the presence of off-worlders.
Crime is unknown, as is reprehensible behaviour—except for the
antics of feckless young gallants, whose misdeeds are charitably
ignored as "a sowing of wild oats". The single spaceport is Port
Palactus, situated inconveniently in the center of the Great Mer-
maz Steppe. The facilities are meager: a pair of dilapidated warehouses and a structure serving as combination bank and port

office. There is neither a machine shop nor tourist accommodations.

"'Star Home flora is not abundant, but includes a dozen species of grass, among which is a lordly bamboo with black stalks and pale green leaves. Fauna, like the flora, is not various but includes the savagely ferocious "mereng", a predator which lives hidden in narrow tunnels under the grass. Merengs are supple, six-legged creatures with long fanged snouts, which may attain a length of twelve feet; they are dreaded by the Ritters but are occasionally hunted for meat and hides. Impressive and of mild disposition are the gigantic herbivores known as "wumps", ponderous creatures often forty or even fifty feet long and twenty feet high. Wumps walk on six heavy legs, ingesting grass by means of a sinuous snout, which brings grass to the maw. The Ritters domesticate wumps and build small residences called "trimbles" upon their broad backs. Some trimbles are quite picturesque, with peaked roofs; always at the rear is a workroom where rugs are produced.'"

Maloof frowned and looked up. "The article ends." He reread the section silently, fingers thrumming the table, then thrust the *Handbook* aside, in a mild show of vexation.

"The *Handbook* tells me less than I would like to know. Why is their spaceport located in the middle of a steppe? And there is little to suggest an explanation why the 'Ritters', as unconventional or peculiar as they are, might need thirty-two carboys of chemical."

Myron shook his head. "I cannot so much as guess."

Maloof waved the problem aside. "Still, it is none of our affair. More to the point, when we put down at Port Palactus, will anyone be there to receive the cargo? The Ritters might not trouble with such incidentals."

"The *Handbook* mentions a port office," said Myron dubiously. "That would seem to imply a Port Director."

"That is logic as seen from here," said Maloof. "Logic on Star Home might mean something else again. At out-of-the-way places like Port Palactus, the extraordinary is often the usual; the poor spaceman must look in all directions, and be ready for odd surprises."

Myron ventured a suggestion. "I can write a clause into the contract stipulating that if the cargo cannot be discharged within

three days after our arrival, owing to absence of proper spaceport
personnel, title to the cargo devolves upon the carrier—which is
to say, the *Glicca*."

Maloof indicated approval. "A good idea. Write the provision into the contract, and we'll take our chances."

During the afternoon, thirty-two carboys were loaded aboard
the *Glicca*, into the space previously occupied by the pilgrims.

6

The following morning, Moncrief and his troupe boarded the
Glicca and took up their old quarters.

Moods varied; Flook, Pook, and Snook were disconsolate at
the prospect of leaving Fluter, perhaps forever. Hunzel and
Siglaf took themselves to a corner of the saloon and gruffly discussed secret plans. Hoping to elevate the morale of his company with good cheer, Moncrief beamed on one and all and
went so far as to dance a jig.

Myron composed and sent off a letter to Miss Tibbet Garwig.
Schwatzendale and Wingo consumed final Pooncho Punches at
the Pingis Tavern but returned to the *Glicca* in good order during
the early evening.

On the following morning, two hours after sunrise, the *Glicca*
rose from the Coro-coro spaceport and set off on a course for
Star Home.

SEVEN

1

A rriving from space, the *Glicca* descended upon the night side of Star Home, to land at Port Palactus by the light of the waning moon.

In the pilot-house, Captain Maloof disengaged the ship's dynamic systems and went to look from the observation window. The steppe, colorless in the pale moonlight, spread away under a blanket of grass past the edge of vision. Otherwise there was little to see. The old warehouses huddled dark and quiet; a few yards beyond and to the side stood a small square structure. Nothing stirred; in particular, no one appeared to register the arrival of the *Glicca*. The ship's crew composed itself to wait for dawn before venturing out upon the landscape.

After a time, a glimmer of gray appeared in the east, then a slow flush of yellow. The white sun rose from behind a bank of clouds, and wan light seeped across the steppe.

The *Glicca*'s entry port slid open, and the gangway dropped to the ground. One by one, the ship's company descended to the surface of Star Home, where they stood in silence, taking in the immensity of the landscape. In the immediate vicinity of the spaceport the grass had been cut short and compressed to create a mat of turf; elsewhere it grew in a uniform carpet four feet tall. After a moment the group discovered in the far distance several enormous gray hulks, moving slowly across the steppe. They trundled through the grass on six thick legs; with twin proboscises they cut grass and conveyed the forage to ventral maws.

Myron took it upon himself to explain the creatures to the passengers. "The local folk know them as 'wumps', though of course this is not proper nomenclature. It is hard to gauge their bulk from this distance, but they are of prodigious size: some forty or fifty feet long and twenty feet tall. According to the *Handbook*, their temperament is so mild that the Ritters domesticate them and build huts on their backs to live at ease while traveling beside the sea and across the steppe."

Moncrief spared the wumps a single dismissive glance. An encounter with Siglaf and Hunzel had left him in a testy mood, and Myron's display of knowledge was an added irritant. He pretended to search the surroundings.

"Are you sure of your facts? Star Home appears to be deserted; at least, I see no Ritters, nor anyone else! Might they be hiding under the grass?"

"The *Handbook* is quite definite," said Myron. "The Ritters are nomads who have rejected all technical adjuncts. For relaxation, they create rugs of high quality and attend banquets where they sing, dance, and vie in the high jump. They lack social cohesiveness but are ruled by an implicit system which seems to satisfy everyone. Some of their customs are quaint: for instance, if you admire a woman's rug, you must marry her. In any event, Ritters are not to be found hiding under the grass."

"The *Handbook* is wrong!" cried Flook, pointing with both forefingers. "Just now I saw a face, staring at me from under the grass!"

Snook asked with interest: "Was he handsome?"

"Not really; he had a shifty expression."

"Tschah," muttered Moncrief. "Sheer flapdoodle."

"No," declared Pook. "I saw him myself."

Moncrief could not conceal his impatience. "It is well known that girls of your age are subject to delusions, which are often unsettling! Restraint and wise counsel are of prime importance; I advise sober reflection."

"Exactly so," declared Pook. "I saw him clearly. What could be more sober than that?"

Once again, Myron was able to provide authoritative information. "What you saw was probably a 'mereng'—which is, according to the *Handbook*, a sinuous creature that may reach twelve feet long. It glides under the grass on six squat legs and is said to be extremely dangerous. So do not wander out into the grass hoping for romance."

"Bah!" muttered Moncrief, and turned away to study the steppe.

Meanwhile Maloof, looking past the warehouses, noticed a rock-melt structure, evidently the port office and bank mentioned in the *Handbook*. He moved away from the group and crossed the turf to the lonely structure. To the side he found the door: a slab of dark wood hanging on a pair of iron hinges.

He stepped back and turned to survey the landscape. Steppe extended to the horizon, with nothing in sight but wind-blown grass. He turned back to the door and rapped once, twice, three times, eliciting no response. He tried the latch; to his surprise the door eased open. For a moment Maloof hesitated; then he leaned forward and looked through the crack.

There was little to see. Three high windows admitted more gloom than light; in the dimness, Maloof glimpsed a couch, a table, chairs, and a desk on which rested dog-eared documents, scattered papers, and a somewhat battered communicator.

In the shadows along the back wall, the outline of a door indicated a rear chamber. Maloof turned away, reluctant to trespass upon private premises. Then, prompted by a troubling thought, he stopped short. Where was the Port Director? Might he be lying behind that door, ill, or otherwise incapacitated? Maloof put aside his scruples and entered the office.

The silence was complete. On the wall to his left, a hanging caught his attention: a rug, or section of a rug, about four feet on a side, framed in dark wood. He looked closely; the rug was clearly a work of high virtuosity. The craftsmanship was meticulous, and the patterns were worked with intricate shapes and unconventional colors: stinging blues, lime green, sulfurous reds, black, pomegranate, the bitter off-white of potash dye.

Reluctantly he turned away from the hanging and approached the door. He halted, stared at the panel, then raised his hand and knocked. He listened, but the silence was heavy. He knocked again, more vigorously; the silence was as before. But what was that? The ghost of a sound, no more than a whisper.

Emboldened, Maloof knocked again. From within came the tragic moan of a man aroused from a deep and beneficent slumber.

Again Maloof knocked, and now he heard the mutter of a thick voice: "Who pounds at my door? It is not yet daylight; have you no pity? I deserve my rest."

Maloof called: "Where is the Port Director? Why is he not on duty?"

"All in good time," came the grumbled response. "Allow me to collect my wits."

Maloof set himself to wait.

Time passed; Maloof became restive. He stood once again in front of the door and raised his hand to knock—but at that instant the door swung aside, to reveal a stocky man wearing a voluminous orange nightgown, which draped his portly physique from neck to ankle. He stood blinking at Maloof with a surly expression.

"I am Port Director Oswig. How do you explain your boisterous conduct?"

"I am Captain Maloof, of the ship *Glicca*. We arrived several hours ago; when you failed to appear, I came to make sure that you were not ill. We carry a cargo of thirty-two carboys for Port Palactus. All is ready for discharge, as soon as the freight is paid."

Oswig cried out in outrage. "What sort of fandangle is this? All freight is prepaid, at Cax on Blenkinsop!"

"Not in this case. These goods were taken aboard at Corocoro as a cargo of opportunity. The bill of lading will make this clear."

Oswig held out his hand. "Show me the document, if you please."

Maloof tendered the paper, which Oswig scrutinized with care.

"Give special attention to the footnote," said Maloof politely. "You will notice that the freight charges must be paid within three days; if not, officers of the *Glicca* may confiscate the cargo and depart without formality."

"Bah!" muttered Oswig. "It is too early in the day for chaffering. Wait until I can deal with you on an official basis. Be seated and compose yourself." He stepped back; the door swung shut.

Instead of seating himself as Oswig had suggested, Maloof returned to study the wall hanging. The article exerted the same fascination as it had before; the craftsmanship seemed flawless, the colors were no less pungent, and the composition was even more clever and intricate than his first look had revealed.

The door slid aside; in the opening stood Oswig, now wearing his official regalia: a gray tunic, loose white breeches, and a white cap with a short black bill pulled down over dark ringlets. He advanced into the room and halted to inspect Maloof. He noticed Maloof's interest in the hanging, and his manner changed.

"That is an experimental panel created by my daughter Treblinka. She is twelve years old, but her work is of good quality."

"She would seem a prodigy," said Maloof.

"So it may be! But at this time I must see to business. There is reason for haste. Transport is my first concern; three wagons should suffice. I will call Dockerl at Farol Depot, and if he is brisk, the wagons will be here in three or four days. If the Lallankars are caught off guard, all will go well."

Oswig crossed the room to his desk and worked the controls of his communicator. At the tinkle of a chime he punched buttons, then sat back to wait.

Minutes passed. Oswig became impatient and drummed his fingers on the desk.

Finally, a gentle voice issued from the screen. "Wagon Master Dockerl here. Who calls, with such happy brio?"

Neither the wait nor Dockerl's flippant salute eased Oswig's disposition. Hunching forward, he issued a flood of instructions so energetically that Dockerl was unable to respond. Oswig stopped for breath and noticed that the screen had gone dead.

He leaned back in his chair, mouth drooping, then slowly swung around to face Maloof.

"Have you ever known the like? It is more than just a sorry joke." He came back across the room.

"When schmeer is scarce, the wagons cluster around the port like bugs on a corpse. When schmeer pots are full, with the rugmakers grinning from ear to ear, where are the wagons then?

At Miskitter Marsh, or Blackwater Camp or Sluiceway River-side, or off at the fringes of the steppe! At Palactus, we can only pray that they rumble their wumps and arrive within four days." Oswig gave his head an angry shake.

Maloof suggested, "Somehow you should enforce better service."

"We are Ritters; we enforce nothing! In the old days service went smartly. Wagons were assigned to the port. They took the cargo as soon as it was discharged; the Lallankars were helpless, and distribution was conducted properly. But the radio is a modern abomination! If the Lallankars pick up my signal, they trundle in from the steppe, preempt the carboys from under my nose, then ramble away, shouting slogans."

"Exasperating!" said Maloof.

Oswig nodded grimly.

After a pause Maloof ventured a cautious remark. "There is something here which I find mystifying. It would seem a true paradox."

Oswig showed little interest in Maloof's quandary. "You are an off-worlder; our way of life will baffle you."

"No doubt, but after making all allowances, the mystery remains. Perhaps you can throw some light on the matter."

"I am not a pundit," said Oswig brusquely. "Nor is there time for idle rumination."

"I will be brief. You might even be interested, since the matter touches upon yourself."

"Oh, very well," growled Oswig. "Let us hear this famous conundrum, and be done with it."

"Thank you. The situation is this: I have known you for only a short time, but already I can sense the broad outline of your character. In my opinion you are a strong, practical man, neither timid nor meek, and certainly not submissive."

Oswig gave a snort of dour amusement. "I will not try to refute you, but—more to the point—where is the mystery?"

Maloof held up his hand. "Oddly enough, at this moment I have come upon a reasonable explanation, and the mystery has dissolved."

Oswig eyed Maloof with suspicion. "That is good news, or so it seems, and now we can get on with our affairs. But what was the nature of this so-called 'mystery'?"

"It starts with the fact that I am a rational being; I could not understand why a man of your character should not defend his carboys to better effect. Then a new idea occurred to me, and the mystery dissolved. I realized that the Lallankars must be a reckless, ferocious race, whom Director Oswig—brave though he might be—was forced to allow to depredate and despoil as they chose, while he sought safety in a secret place. Am I right?"

"You are wrong!" thundered Oswig. "In every degree, respect and particular! The Lallankars are vermin, and I am a Ritter, of Star Home! I am self-guided, self-determined, and autonomous! On Star Home there are neither rules nor statutes. To even attempt to regulate the Lallankars would be to deny the Ritter franchise." Oswig made a sweeping gesture, to indicate that the topic had been exhausted. "Now then, let us look to the cargo. As I recall, there were thirty-two carboys of kasic, ready for discharge."

"Correct! By the way, what is kasic? I ask from sheer curiosity."

Oswig's response was tart. "Ask any way you like. The facts are immutable."

"Hm," said Maloof. "On a strange world, where paradoxes are rife, this is good news."

"Bah," muttered Oswig. "If I explained every detail, you would know no more than you do now."

Turning on his heel, Oswig marched through the doorway out into the pale light of morning, with Maloof following.

Oswig stopped short, as if at a sudden recollection. "Now it occurs to me! The warehousemen are not on duty—they have gone off to games at the Ballingay Traces. But there should be no real inconvenience; I expect that your crew will discharge the cargo for us, as a courtesy."

"Certainly," said Maloof. "We have done such work before, and we can do it again. Our fee will be the standard fifty sols."

Oswig cried out in shock. "Do my ears hear correctly? Did you truly mention the sum 'fifty sols'? Have you no morality whatever? How can a gentleman swindle with such aplomb?"

Maloof held up his hand. "I will answer your questions in the order they were asked. Yes, your ears are functioning properly. Yes; the price quoted was fifty sols. Yes, I use the morality of the working spaceman, which is compact but versatile. And I can explain the basis of our rates: often an official begs for a free service, as a courtesy, then puts the savings into his own pocket. Our schedule of fees is intended to curb this nuisance."

"Sheer bullypup!" stormed Oswig. "Save your excuses for ears more innocent than mine!" Swinging about, he re-entered the office and went to his desk. Opening a drawer, he snatched out a handful of pink and blue currency, oblivious to the notes which fluttered to the floor. He waved the notes in Maloof's face. "As you can see, your fee is secure!"

Maloof said: "I am interested less in security than in the money itself."

Oswig grimly paid over three hundred and seventy-five sols.

"Now then, your demands have been met. You may put your crew to work."

"Just as you say."

2

Maloof and Oswig stood to the side, watching as the work proceeded. In the cargo bay, Wingo operated the overhead hoist, shifting the carboys and lowering them to the turf, where Myron and Schwatzendale waited with power-dollies. Pursuant to Oswig's instructions they trucked the carboys into the far warehouse, which Oswig considered most secure from depredation. Moncrief strolled across the turf to join Maloof and Oswig.

Moncrief's romantic temperament disposed him to more or less innocent flights of fancy, which served to amuse him and relieve the tedium. On this occasion, he introduced himself to Oswig with flair: "I am Master Marcel Moncrief, roving polymath on the staff of the *Galactic Sentinel*, on open assignment."

Oswig inspected him without cordiality, while Maloof listened with raised eyebrows.

Moncrief enlarged upon his fabrication. "I have no explicit program for this planet, aside from my usual survey of a world and its culture. However, my references mention certain remote villages where ancient customs are preserved; if time permits, I would like to visit one or two of these villages to study their folk art, and perhaps record a few staves of their ceremonial chants."

Oswig gave a contemptuous snort. "You have been reading too many books. The Ritters are nomads. Villages are non-
existent, and our most poignant music is the cries of woe heard
when schmeer pots run dry."

"What is 'schmeer'?"

Oswig replied gracelessly: "Schmeer is the adhesive which
binds our rugs. It is indispensable."

"Interesting. The carboys, then, contain schmeer?"

"Naturally not—the carboys contain kasic, a catalyst which
is used to make schmeer."

Moncrief gave his head a smiling shake. "You are an artist
with words, so much is clear, but you paint with too broad a
brush. The pictorial scheme is striking, but the details are lost
in a blur."

Oswig screwed up his eyebrows. "I confess to bafflement.
Please clarify your remarks."

Moncrief considered. "Essentially, what I am asking is: what
is 'kasic'?"

Oswig glowered, then decided to humor this unlikely savant.

"Kasic is a component of schmeer. When poured from the
carboy, it is a semi-viscous, dark brown liquid, with a bad smell.
For each forty gallons of schmeer, two gills of kasic are required."

"And who does the formulation? A special caste of adepts, I
assume?"

"Not so! The Ritters are a single race. There are no castes,
except, perhaps, for the Lallankars."

"Then who makes the schmeer?"

"Everyone! My daughter Treblinka is an expert."

"And what is her method?"

"The recipe is standard. Into a forty-gallon vat she pours
twenty gallons of green grass gum, then adds ten gallons of barnacle slurry, ten pounds of mereng bladder-wax for unctuous-
ness, three gallons of boiled red kelp, a jug of emalque extract,
a gallon of fire oil for bite, and two gills of kasic. The vat is
brought to a boil, simmered for two hours, strained, and allowed
to rest. After a week the schmeer is ready."

"Most interesting!" Moncrief looked toward the *Glicca*, where
the work of unloading was still under way. "With so much kasic,
you will be inundated in schmeer! How can it all be put to use?"

"Curb your wonder!" Oswig told him. "Thirty-two carboys of kasic is barely adequate. The rugmaker's worst fear is that his pot will go dry."

Moncrief asked plaintively: "But where is the need for so many rugs? It seems that the rugmakers are driven by obsession. Surely these rampant energies could be put to better use."

"Indeed? What do you have in mind?"

Moncrief considered, tapping his chin with his forefinger. "First, a civilized town or two, with tourist hotels, cafes, and arcades where the best rugs could be put on display. This would seem a progressive program."

Oswig studied Moncrief for a long moment.

"Doubtless, you are a deep-dyed scholar, and a past master of poodle-de-doodle. Also, you have read several books. Still, your knowledge of Star Home is a muddle, and your theories are bunk."

Moncrief blinked but maintained his sangfroid. "I will give your comments careful study. They may well illuminate the unusual quirks of local custom."

"While you study, remember this," said Oswig. "We Ritters are nomads, wandering the steppe as the mood takes us, by the white light of day, through the pale moonlight by night. The vistas are never the same; the grass undulates in long swells, where it is moved by the wind. Sometimes rain sweeps down upon the trimbles—but the wumps amble on, taking no notice. Inside the trimbles, the rugs are worked on the racks. It is a placid life, so long as kasic is available on a timely basis. If Lallankars intercept the shipment, then rug-makers with short pots of schmeer become anxious."

Moncrief put a delicate question: "What, then, is a 'Lallankar'?"

Oswig spat on the ground. "The topic is tiresome; still, it cannot be ignored. Sometimes a youth with doting parents becomes an adolescent convinced of his own sublime importance. He daydreams, shirks his work, and joins the girls at play; he makes no effort to learn the way of the Ritters. No one interferes; they are Ritters, and each must pursue his own destiny! He has no friends but consorts with others of his own sort. They think of themselves as gallant bravos, entitled to the sweetest fruits on the tree of life! Their favorite ploy is to preempt a shipment of kasic, which becomes their property through the exigencies of the Ritter creed. Each Lallankar claims for himself a carboy of kasic; never in his life will he need more.

"The Lallankars make for an important camp, such as Blackwater Camp, and barter with the kasic. What is left is given over to a haphazard distribution—which is better than no distribution at all. The Lallankar now looks to his own affairs. He decorates his trimble with red satin cushions and sluices down his wump with floral water. He stocks his pantry with delicacies, flasks of brambleberry wine, and rare confections from the synthesizer. He ties a blue sash around his waist and sets off to find his favorite among the pretty girls, whom he invites up to his trimble. He seats her upon a cushion, then pours soft green wine into dainty cups of carved bamboo. Presently he serves a banquet of unusual viands, and the afternoon passes. At sunset, he displays a jug of kasic and asks if he might offer such a gift to signalize his fervent regard. The girl responds with joy and gratitude. Meanwhile the wump ambles across the steppe through the gathering dusk.

"And so it goes. Elsewhere the rugmakers scrape the bottoms of their schmeer-pots. Across the steppe, at every sweetwater pond, along every strand, on every hillock where the wumps encircle a camp, the rug-makers sing the same song, and it is a sad song indeed."

After a moment, Moncrief asked: "Could not the system be altered, so as to provide schmeer for these unfortunates whose pots have gone dry?"

Oswig was unmoved. "Thirty-two carboys of kasic yield a precise volume of schmeer. This is the basis for an orderly distribution of kasic."

"Aha!" cried Moncrief, his eyes bright with enthusiasm. "You have cited a problem to which I have the answer!"

Oswig had lost interest in the topic and turned to address Maloof, but Moncrief was not to be denied. "My concept is simple but elegant! I commend it to your attention."

Oswig heaved a patient sigh. "Very well! Explain this noble concept, if you will."

"With pleasure. You merely ship twice as many rugs to Cax; they will send back twice as much kasic. This cargo must be discharged at a site secure from the Lallankars, and that is the crux of the scheme. The kasic now is distributed with open-handed grandeur, and the song of the rugmakers will be heard no more."

Moncrief stepped back, in smiling anticipation of Oswig's plaudits.

"Startling!" Oswig admitted. "Particularly in view of its implicit purport."

"Oh?" said Moncrief, nonplussed, his smile fading. "How can this be?"

Oswig said: "Your scheme imputes to the Ritters a bewildered foolishness, from which they are rescued by the advice of a kindly off-world savant."

"Ahem," said Moncrief. "I fear that your meaning eludes me."

Oswig paid no heed. "The advice is spurious for several reasons. First, a flood of mediocre rugs would choke the repository. Second, doubling the amount of schmeer doubles the quantity of the other materials, which are tedious to collect. Third, even at this time, there are many who wish to limit the import of kasic to ten carboys. Fourth—but perhaps you have heard enough. In essence, your scheme cannot be recommended."

Moncrief performed a stiff bow. "No further expatiation is necessary. And now, please excuse me; I have urgent business elsewhere." He swung about and marched off toward the *Glicca*, where the discharge of cargo had now been effected.

Oswig turned to Maloof. "What, may I ask, is your next destination?"

"We carry goods for Cax, which will be our next port of call."

"In that case, I can offer you a parcel of freight for Monomarche, at Cax, if you are interested."

"I am interested, certainly."

"The parcel consists of fourteen rugs, rolled into bundles about six feet long. They are now in the repository at Torqual Downs. I can order them out by wagon, which means a delay of two weeks, but there is a better way.

"Dockerl will arrive within three or four days, along with my assistant Zitzelman. As soon as Dockerl picks up the carboys of kasic, I suggest that you shift the *Glicca* to Torqual Downs, where the rugs can be loaded efficiently. The freight charges will be prepaid at the standard rate of one hundred and seventy-five sols."

Maloof considered. "As a matter of curiosity, what value is placed upon a single rug?"

Oswig glanced at Maloof with a flicker of suspicion; still, he responded without hesitation.

"There are several categories. The export grades command a price of three hundred sols. Occasionally, when we need a special item of machinery, such as a new food synthesizer or the like, we include in the shipment an extra rug, and the transaction is accomplished."

"And you sell only to Monomarche?"

"Correct. It is a long-standing arrangement."

3

Back aboard the *Glicca*, Captain Maloof told the ship's company of the altered schedule. "We will be delayed at Port Palactus for several days, until Director Oswig has cleared away his carboys. Then we move to Torqual Downs to take on freight for Cax. You may think of the period as a three-day vacation!"

Moncrief slapped the table and rose to his feet. "The layover comes at an opportune time. But for the Mouse-riders, it will not be a vacation. I have worked up several new routines, which I hope will play well at Cax. They differ from our usual entertainment and must be presented carefully, since the audiences at Cax are somewhat special."

Moncrief displayed a sheaf of papers. "These are my notes. I propose that we run through them now, and perhaps we will hold a scratch rehearsal later in the day. This way, if you please."

Moncrief set off across the saloon, with Flook, Pook, and Snook dancing and skittering at his heels. The Klutes sat watching silently with sardonic expressions; for a moment they muttered together, then lurched to their feet and sauntered across the saloon after the others. The girls, winsome and demure as always, settled upon a couch; the Klutes leaned contemptuously against the wall.

Moncrief placed his papers upon the table. "You might like

to know that at Cax we will be performing at the Trevanian, which is an exceptionally large theater.

"The Trevanian is popular with ordinary Blenks and the upper classes as well. They come to relax and have a good time, and the audiences are boisterous; if they like the performance, the artists are rewarded, but if the audience is bored or displeased, the performers quickly learn of the fact, and even then must be gracious! The Trevanian will be an interesting experience for all of us. So: to work.

"These sequences are unlike our usual material, in view of the responsive audience. The first sequence is a tropical extravaganza. The girls wear costumes of green feathers and bird masks; they perch in the foliage of a lush jungle and produce fluting melodies based upon bird-calls. Suddenly, they mime terror and become silent. From off-stage comes a low, rumbling mutter—a sound felt rather than heard. The bird-girls hide in the foliage as best they can. The rumble becomes heavy, and slave-takers appear: massive creatures, wearing the iron armor of Bugasky warriors. They discover the bird-girls and set about their craft. The bird-girls are clever and use all manner of tricks to evade capture, and in the end the slave-takers are caught in their own snares and are hoisted high to hang by their heels. The green-feathered bird-girls cavort and dance gleefully. At last the slave-takers escape and chase the bird-girls into the jungle. From far away comes a horrid sound. Lavender murk slowly falls over the scene, and that is the first sequence." Moncrief looked from face to face, hoping for enthusiasm.

Hunzel muttered: "It sounds complicated, and I don't like hanging by my heels."

"It will please the audiences," said Moncrief cheerfully. "For the second sequence, I plan to use the old Zagazig routine, modified a bit, possibly. I wonder if we could lure enough daredevils from the audience. Hm. Perhaps not; the Blenks are somewhat self-conscious.

"In any case, for the third sequence I am inclined to try a truly innovative scheme, which is simple but which still should amuse the Blenks, who are always ready for a frolic." He chuckled. "They will remember the Mouse-riders to the end of their days!" He picked up his papers. "But now, and most urgently: the jungle sequence!"

Moncrief tendered papers to Flook, Pook, and Snook, but when he turned to the Klutes, they thrust the papers aside and stood with arms folded. "You may perform a private act with your papers," Hunzel told him.

Siglaf was less offensive but no less definite. "The sequences are irrelevant. We are here to collect our money, and for no other reason."

Hunzel added: "We want no evasions—chuckles and winks will no longer suffice! The money must be paid in full."

Moncrief sighed. "At the moment Mouse-rider finances are not robust, nor, for a fact, can I guess the extent of your demands. Can you draw up a detailed invoice?"

"That is unnecessary," said Hunzel. "We can calculate the total in this fashion: for Siglaf and myself, six sols per day each. For the girls: four sols per day. In all, the amount is twenty-four sols per day, or in fair estimate: one hundred twenty sols per week. We have served you for three years, which indicates a total of about eighteen thousand sols."

Moncrief's eyebrows rose high in shock. He started to speak, but Hunzel continued. "From this figure, we deduct a reasonable sum for layover times, moneys advanced to us, and miscellaneous items and arrive at a figure of fifteen thousand sols. That is our just demand."

Moncrief heaved a deep sigh. "This is astounding! You have plucked an inordinate figure out of the air and pretend that it is a logical demand. I dispute the accuracy of this figure, from one end to the other. If you want me to take you seriously, you must present a carefully detailed account. That will be the basis for negotiations."

"We want no negotiation," stormed Siglaf. "We want money! Do you intend to pay?"

"Your demands are preposterous! Prepare a careful invoice, and I will give it my attention, at the very least. As I have indicated, the Mouse-rider reserves are currently scant."

"That is not what we wanted to hear! We are listening for the crackle of financial certificates and the chink of sols!"

Moncrief tried to soothe the ruffled feelings. "Let us all be reasonable! We cannot allow a little tiff to spoil the game! I hope for great success at Cax, and you must be ready to share the acclaim!"

Siglaf produced a harsh grunt of what might have been laughter. "There will be no 'acclaim' if there are no Mouse-riders! Unless we are paid, we leave the ship at Cax."

Moncrief chided her: "That is sorry talk—if you leave the ship without funds, you will end up begging in the streets."

"Do not worry on our behalf!" Hunzel told him, leering. "We and the girls will quickly set up a profitable enterprise. We shall not lack funds."

Moncrief's jaw dropped as the implications of the program became clear to him. He spoke in a hushed voice: "You cannot be serious! The idea is unthinkable!"

"Not really," said Siglaf. "If you do not pay us our money, then we must rely upon what assets are under our control. You must accept the inevitable."

Moncrief had found his voice. "I accept nothing! The girls shall not leave the *Glicca*."

Siglaf produced her harsh laugh. "You are a foolish old man. You refuse to pay us our money, then you squeal at the consequences."

"The girls will go ashore with us at Cax," said Hunzel. "They have no choice—they are bound to us until their indentures are dissolved. The law will support our case."

Moncrief put on his most winning smile. "Truly, this talk is neither helpful nor progressive." He glanced across the saloon. "There is Captain Maloof—perhaps he can help us resolve our problem."

"Let him be," growled Siglaf. "This is none of his affair."

"Everything aboard the *Glicca* is his affair," Moncrief told her. He signaled to Maloof, who sauntered across the saloon.

Maloof looked from face to face. "No one seems happy. Are there difficulties?"

"Yes," said Moncrief. "We have reached an impasse. Your advice might be helpful."

"My opinions may please none of you. However, I will take the risk, if you will do the same."

Moncrief described the dispute, using as few words as possible and trying for objectivity. Siglaf and Hunzel made several more or less acerbic comments; then the three girls stated their points of view.

Maloof looked down at the table. "What papers are these?"

"Just my notes on Mouse-rider sequences," said Moncrief.

Maloof looked around. "Can any of you show documents to verify his or her demands?"

"We need no documents," growled Hunzel. "We base our claims on mathematical truths."

Maloof looked at Moncrief. "And what of you?"

"I can show only miscellaneous notes, a few receipts, per-haps a production ledger or two, also indexes and a few outlines for future Mouse-rider productions. They may cast a glimmer of light upon this miserable affair, or so I hope."

Siglaf snapped: "We want more than a glimmer of light. We want our money!"

Maloof rose to his feet. "My advice is this: each party should assemble all available documents, memoranda, contracts, notes, and anything else relevant, then prepare a careful schedule of claims, as detailed as possible. Then we can return to the nego-tiations whenever it becomes convenient."

Siglaf and Hunzel grimaced in dissatisfaction and stalked off to their quarters.

Moncrief said glumly: "I am a trained impresario, gifted with both creativity and wit. I have organized Mouse-rider pageants, and much else, but I am not a man for trifling detail."

"You must search your records with care," said Maloof. "One number is worth a dozen suppositions."

The deliberations Maloof had envisaged were forestalled by an unexpected event. During the night, unknown entities came in from the steppe, as furtive as ghosts. They halted behind the far warehouse and worked with silent efficiency. When they de-parted, the thirty-two carboys of kasic were in their possession.

4

Wingo, arising early, had gone for a morning stroll with his camera, hoping to surprise a mereng at one of its interesting ac-tivities. As he passed behind the far warehouse, he noticed evi-dence of the depredation, as well as confused tracks in the grass and a pair of ruts leading off into the northeast.

Wingo reported his findings to Maloof, who sent Myron to notify Director Oswig.

Myron found Oswig making a breakfast of porridge and tea. Neither tact nor delicacy was practical; he said: "Bad news, sir! The kasic has been stolen."

Oswig stared at him impassively, jaws moving as he ingested the last of his porridge. Then he turned to his radio.

Myron, standing by, heard Dockerl's cheerful call issuing from the mesh: "Dockerl here!"

Oswig's voice cracked with emotion. "You have not yet made instant departure for Port Palactus, as I instructed."

Dockerl made haste to explain. "We prepared to depart while dealing with a dozen emergencies! They are now defeated, and our departure is imminent!"

"Do not trouble yourself unduly," Oswig told him drily. "The Lallankars have preceded you. The kasic is gone. Allow me, if you will, to criticize your torpid activity—I ask only that you compare it with the Ritter's code of duty!"

When Dockerl finally was able to interpose a remark, he cried out: "Instead of taxing me for something, which is nothing, you should compliment my sagacity for avoiding a fruitless mad dash across the steppe! I avoided an exercise in futility and also saved you a howling embarrassment—have you no gratitude?"

Myron returned to the *Glicca*, to find Captain Maloof conferring with Wingo and Schwatzendale. He joined the group and listened with interest to the discussion.

"There should be no great risk, and the advantages are obvious," said Maloof. "Are there contrary opinions?"

"None at all," said Schwatzendale. "The scheme is sound."

"That is my personal feeling," said Maloof.

"Make your arrangements, and be on your way."

Schwatzendale, Wingo, and Myron lowered the ship's flitter to the turf. They boarded the craft and took it aloft; below, the steppe expanded far and wide, beyond the horizons, uniform but for a few slow waves where the wind touched the grass.

The twin tracks of the Lallankar wagons led away into the northeast. Flying at an altitude of a thousand feet the flitter followed the wagon trail, and after half an hour the quarry came into view, a column of five wumps, each carrying on its broad back a small cottage with a front and back deck. The high-pitched roofs were artfully concave, with quaint upturned eaves.

The decks were vacant, the Lallankars apparently resting within after the night's work and subsequent carousing.

A long rope trailed from the last wump in the column, pulling a wagon loaded with carboys.

Aboard the flitter, Schwatzendale, Wingo, and Myron took counsel and agreed upon a strategy which seemed simple and direct.

Schwatzendale brought the flitter down until it skimmed the grass, then approached the column from the rear until the flitter almost nosed the last wagon. Myron jumped into one of the ruts where the grass had been smashed flat and ran to the front of the wagon; with a sharp knife he cut the rope, and it fell slack and trailed away through the grass after the receding wump.

Myron returned around the wagon to the flitter, before a mereng might emerge from the grass and seize his leg.

The column of wumps continued into the northeast, the Lallankars oblivious to the loss of their booty.

Schwatzendale made contact with the *Glicca* and reported events to Captain Maloof. "The Lallankars seem to all be asleep! Their wumps have made off into the distance, and all is serene. They will be surprised when they rouse themselves."

Fifteen minutes later the *Glicca* drifted down from the sky, to settle close beside the wagon.

The cargo doors were thrown open, and the carboys were transferred into the hold. The *Glicca* rose into the air and returned toward Port Palactus, to land in the grass a mile south of the spaceport.

"We are here for a purpose," Maloof told his crew. "Oswig is a complicated man, and he is also a Ritter. All in all, I would rather deal with him out here than in his own office."

Schwatzendale was skeptical. "Your theory is sound," he admitted, "but will Oswig come to the ship?"

"That remains to be seen. In any case, you may now approach him at his office and invite his presence aboard the *Glicca*."

Oswig was recalcitrant, as had been expected, but Schwatzendale finally prevailed upon him to board the flitter and fly out to the *Glicca*.

Maloof met Oswig at the port and ushered him aboard. The

two sat at the conference table in the corner of the saloon. Wingo brought tea and cakes, which Oswig ignored.

"Why have you brought me out here, in the long grass?" Oswig demanded. "I prefer to deal with you in my official premises."

"Just so," said Maloof, "but I thought that we might be more comfortable out here."

"Whatever the case, it is immaterial. Be good enough to reveal the purpose of this meeting."

"First, I wish to commiserate with you upon the loss of your carboys."

Oswig shrugged. "Do not trouble yourself. As a Ritter, I take all with the same equanimity. The vector of my life is Ritterway."

"You are indifferent to the theft?"

Oswig scowled. "Your terms are curiously askew; naturally I prefer that the kasic should be distributed by the designated authority—which is to say, myself. But as usual, the Lallankars have flouted propriety. They are rumbling their wumps across the steppe, to Maiden Water or some other notorious resort, and will convert the kasic into a grand poomsibah of sybaritical follies."

Maloof spoke. "Happily, I can now reveal that the Lallankars will enjoy excesses only of grief and anguish, for this reason: my crew followed the Lallankars and cut the carboys loose. They are now aboard the *Glicca*."

For a time Oswig sat in silence, mulling over this unsettling new situation. He spoke, straining to keep his voice civil. "What do you propose to do? I hope the kasic will revert into its proper custody."

"That is a possibility," said Maloof. "At the moment, we ourselves are the proper custodians, since we rescued the kasic from the irresponsible Lallankars. Still, under certain conditions, the kasic might well be transferred back to you."

Oswig asked in a frosty voice: "What are these conditions?"

"I shall be blunt," said Maloof. "You have told us that at Torqual Downs hundreds or even thousands of rugs are stored in the repository."

"I have said something to this effect," Oswig agreed tonelessly.

"Eventually these rugs will moulder and rot away—a great pity to waste these treasures, and their vibrant beauty, when they might be put to constructive use."

"Tragically, this is true."

Maloof nodded. "Fifty or sixty of these rugs could be put to very constructive use, and they will never be missed."

Oswig said cautiously: "Theoretical possibilities exist, provided that certain standards of—decorum—are recognized."

"That goes without saying!" declared Maloof. "We move to Torqual Downs in any event, to load the rugs for Monomarche. I suggest that the loading proceed quietly; the process can be accomplished expeditiously, with no one the wiser, if we do the loading ourselves."

"And the kasic?"

"The carboys will be relinquished into your care wherever you specify."

"That should be satisfactory," said Oswig.

Eight

1

An hour before sunset, the *Glicca* departed Star Home with sixty-two rugs bundled into the aft cargo bay. A parcel of fourteen rugs would be delivered to Monomarche at Cax; forty-eight rugs Director Oswig had transferred to Captain Maloof, in exchange for thirty-two carboys of kasic. Two of these rugs had been preempted by Myron Tany for his private purposes; the remaining forty-six would be marketed to best advantage by Captain Maloof, wherever conditions made such a transfer practical.

On the morning of the second day out, Captain Maloof and the Mouse-riders resumed the business which had been interrupted several days previously at Port Palactus.

The group gathered at the same table as before. Captain Maloof was first to arrive, followed by Moncrief and the three girls, and finally by the sullen Klutes. Maloof seated himself at the head of the table; the Klutes sat at the opposite end, Moncrief to the right, and the girls to the left.

Maloof surveyed the group but found no more bonhomie now than at the previous session. The Klutes muttered together, glaring at Moncrief from time to time. Moncrief sat with an expression of mild forbearance, hands clasped modestly on the table.

Maloof spoke, trying to project positivity. "Today we take up where we left off, and I hope that we can reach an accommodation which everyone will find tolerable, at the very least. I will act as an impartial arbiter. I am not a legal expert, but during my stint with the IPCC, I gained a working knowledge of Gaean law, which I have not forgotten. At our last meeting, I asked that you look through your papers and bring to the table whatever pertinent material you came upon. I hope that this has been done."

Siglaf said gruffly: "We found no papers of the sort you have in mind, but no such documents are needed, since we will prove our claim by the use of ordinary mathematics."

Maloof turned to Moncrief. "And what of you, Sir Mouserider? Have you anything you care to show us?"

Moncrief smiled, almost apologetically. "I have looked through my files and found a number of invoices, receipts, statements, and general memoranda, mostly items of little consequence. However, in the clutter I came upon a few documents which may be of interest." He reached into his pocket and brought out a brown folder, which he placed upon the table.

Maloof turned back to the Klutes. "What, exactly, is the substance of your claim?"

"It could not be more basic," stated Hunzel. "Moncrief owes us money. He can doodle and dodge no longer. Now he must pay."

Siglaf tilted her head and showed a grin which was almost a leer. "He will plead poverty, with tears in his eyes! But pay no heed—he carries a bundle of wealth among his effects."

Moncrief laughed sadly. "If only it were true. Here would be lurulu of the most exalted degree! I would never go mouseriding again."

"Bah," muttered Hunzel. "Your mockery is in poor taste, and no one is amused. Instead of wasting our time with your foolishness, pay us our money."

"I was not aware that I owed you money."

The Klutes stared at him incredulously; then both uttered short sardonic laughs. "That is another of your jokes," said

Hunzel. "No matter; we can prove our case. You have not a leg to stand on."

"If you please," said Maloof, "you may present the details of your case."

2

"Moncrief first saw us at Frippen, near the Bleary Hills on Numoy," Hunzel began. "We had come down from the hills to make our report to the Enders Valley Foundling Farm, where we had taken custody of the girls two years before.

"For some reason, Moncrief became interested in us. He spoke to us; then he spoke even longer with the girls. He said that he was head of the famous Mouse-rider troupe, and at the moment there were vacancies that he was trying to fill. He asked if we would like to join the troupe; he told us fine tales of exciting adventures and star travel, of wonderful places we would visit, and the hundred kinds of strange people we would meet—and all the time we would be earning money.

"He saw that we were interested, and made offers of how we would work. He spoke of this and that, and the various advantages of the plans until we were quite confused. Then he wrote out the choices. We chose the plan that seemed most advantageous, and so we became Mouse-riders.

"For a time we toured the provinces of Numoy. Then a spaceship took us to Lally Komar Town on the world Spangard. After that we moved from here to there, and as Moncrief had promised, everywhere was different—some good, some not so good.

"But whenever we wanted money, Moncrief went into a nervous spasm—he would twitter, and chuckle, and dance from foot to foot, then say that he must consult his books. Sometimes, his mouth pinched up and his eyes went dim while he reached into his pocket, brought forth a few sols, and passed them into our hands, one by one. So it went until Siglaf finally calculated how much he owed us.

"He had contracted to pay Siglaf and me six sols each per day, and the girls four sols each per day, all money payable to us— since the girls are indentured and working under our supervision.

They have never attempted to amortize the indentures, which are four hundred sols each."

Siglaf hunched forward. "Moncrief is subtly sly. At Frippen he tried to confuse us, talking first out of one side of his mouth, then the other! But we were too wise for him, and now he is distraught—he has tried every trick to defraud us, but we are decided. If he fails to pay us, we leave the Mouse-riders at Cax."

Maloof held up his hand. "You are going too far, too fast. How much, by your calculations, does Moncrief owe you?"

"The figure is easily determined," said Hunzel. "We reckon five days a week and fifty weeks a year. Siglaf and I earn six sols per day, or thirty sols per week, to the sum of fifteen hundred sols per year. After three years, each of us has earned forty-five hundred sols, to a total of nine thousand sols. The girls earn one thousand sols per year, and for the three of them for three years, a total of nine thousand sols, to a grand total of eighteen thousand sols."

"Hm," said Maloof. "That is a substantial sum."

"So it is," said Siglaf. "From time to time Moncrief doled out a few sols: five sols now, ten sols later, a few more dinkets when he felt munificent. Over the years, during his fits of guilt, he has given as much as two hundred sols! On the other hand, we are large-handed; as a token of our personal generosity, we will demand only fifteen thousand sols. But this he must pay, or at Cax we leave the troupe, and Moncrief can dance the kazatzka at the Trevanian while playing the flute."

Moncrief shook his head in wonder. "Never have I suspected the Klutes of such extravagant imaginations. Their statements are, of course, factitious."

Maloof sighed. "What, then, is your version of events?"

"I will explain with pleasure," Moncrief stated. "I first encountered the Klutes and the three girls at Frippen on Numoy. They made a dramatic impact upon me. I was in the process of reorganizing the Mouse-riders, and I was on the lookout for fresh personnel; I could see that the Klutes, with their hulking bulks and ferocious faces—in striking contrast to the three girls, with their charm, innocence, and mischievous precocity— could be valuable adjuncts to the Mouse-riders. I offered them employment with the troupe, and all five accepted without hesitation.

"The Klutes wanted to know how much they would earn. I explained that they could join the troupe and receive a share of the profits after expenses, or they might choose a second option and work by the hour, during performances, rehearsals, and whenever they might be busy with troupe business, in which case they must pay their own expenses.

"For the previous three months the troupe had been touring the provinces of Fiametta, playing two performances a day. The Klutes could see that under these conditions their earnings would be very consequential, and they decided to work by the terms of the second option.

"To make sure that they understood their choice, I prepared a paper detailing the terms of Option One and Option Two as clearly as possible. I insisted that they indicate their choice of option and sign their names, which was done. They explained that the girls were under indenture and therefore need not sign, which I accepted."

"And you have retained this document?"

"Just so! Over the years I have learned the value of meticulous records."

Moncrief opened his brown folder and removed a sheet of paper, which he handed to Maloof. The Klutes watched with narrow-eyed suspicion.

Maloof scanned the document. The second paragraph was endorsed by a pair of signatures, in handwriting so eccentric as to be almost illegible. He looked down the table to the Klutes. "I presume that you recall signing this paper?"

The Klutes shrugged and looked at each other. Siglaf said: "That happened three years ago. The paper is faded and old, and the writing is obsolete. Put the paper aside, and let us deal with affairs as they are now."

Maloof shook his head. "This may be the custom in the Bleary Hills, but elsewhere in the Gaean Reach things go differently."

"No matter," said Siglaf. "Our figures cannot be faulted."

"They are fine figures indeed," said Maloof. "However, they lack all connection with the business at hand."

The Klutes stared at him mulishly.

Maloof looked to Moncrief. "Do you have more records?"

Moncrief opened his folder again and drew out two notebooks.

"In the black notebook, I record details of all performances and associated rehearsals. In the green notebook I keep a record of all expenses incurred by the troupe.

"I copy these into my information machine whenever it is convenient, which gives me access to all manner of purchases and payments—for a fact, the machine provides more information than I need. I can learn the time worked by both the Klutes and the girls, and the wages they have earned.

"In the green book are recorded all expenses pursuant to Mouse-rider operations. The figures include costs of food, shelter, and transportation incurred by the Klutes and the girls. I will point out that, despite their contract, the Klutes have paid not one dinket of these expenses, which were not inconsiderable.

"Why have I allowed this delinquency to continue? Because I knew the total of their earnings, and I saw that these two amounts were at all times reasonably close. And whenever their earnings exceeded the expenses by any substantial sum, I paid over sufficient money to restore the balance. I have receipts to prove that during the three years I have paid over about nine hundred sols. There may be some small differential now; I have not checked recently."

Maloof turned to the Klutes. "You have heard Moncrief's explanation. Do you care to examine his books?"

Siglaf muttered: "To what purpose? We cannot decipher his worm-tracks. We are confident only of our own figures, which represent three years of toil."

Hunzel said: "Moncrief must make a definite commitment, or we leave the ship at Cax. That is our only recourse."

Moncrief held his arms wide, in a plea for moderation. "How can I pay money which I do not have? You ask the impossible!"

Siglaf uttered a coarse grunt. "We may have come down from the Bleary Hills, but we are not tumblewits. We know that you have a great bundle of sols hidden away among your things. We want our share."

Hunzel said, "The issues are clear—either you pay us, or the five of us will leave the ship at Cax."

Moncrief clicked his tongue in desperation. "You cannot take the girls! They belong with the troupe."

"Nevertheless, they go with us."

"This is merciless bluster! Cax is a dreary place; you would wander back and forth, cold and hungry. You can't subject the girls to such misery!"

"Give us credit for forethought!" said Siglaf. "We will set up an enterprise, and put the girls to work. With their endowments they will bring in a great deal of money, and we will keep our prices high. It will be a fine novelty for them."

Moncrief found his voice. "The idea is abominable! We will not allow the girls to leave the ship!"

Hunzel uttered a jeering laugh. "It is something you cannot avoid! We hold the indentures, and the girls are under our control. That is the law; defy it at your peril."

The girls looked back and forth between Moncrief and the Klutes. Flook asked: "What are you talking about? It seems to concern us; you must tell us what is going on!"

Moncrief spoke in a measured voice. "The Klutes intend to take you off the *Glicca* at Cax. They will bring men to look at you and will take money from whatever man wants to use you in his bed for the night, whether you like him or not. That will be your occupation."

The girls looked incredulously at the Klutes. "This cannot be true—would you do that to us?"

"It is a quick way to make money," said Siglaf. "On Cax we will need money, and you will quickly become accustomed to the work. It is better than being hungry and shivering in the rain."

"I do not want to be either hungry or shivering," said Flook. "But I don't think that I will care for that sort of work."

Pook said, "I prefer to stay aboard the *Glicca* and work with the Mouse-riders."

Snook said, "If Siglaf and Hunzel wish to take up that line of business they may do so, but we prefer to stay aboard the *Glicca*."

"Your preferences are not important!" snapped Siglaf. "You are indentured, and you must do as we say. That is the law, and you have no choice."

The girls sat silent and crestfallen.

Maloof rose to his feet. "I have heard statements from both parties, and in my opinion, Moncrief's records are convincing. My advice is that the Klutes carry on as before, but keep more careful records. If they would like to leave the ship at Cax, they may do so, but as for taking the girls with them, no tribunal in all the Reach would stretch the power of indenture to include such sordid purposes."

Maloof reflected a moment, then addressed the Klutes. "I would like to look over the certificates of indenture, if I may."

"You may not," snapped Hunzel. "They are private papers."

"Not necessarily," said Maloof. "The girls obviously have a right to examine them whenever they like."

Hunzel spoke to the girls. "You do not want to look at these papers now, or so I assume. Am I right?"

Flook said, "I am curious; I would like to look at the papers."

Pook said, "I am curious too. I want to see them."

Snook said: "And I as well."

Siglaf's eyes glinted. "Very well—you shall see them, when it is more private."

Flook asked: "Why not now? There is no one here but Moncrief and Captain Maloof—that is private enough."

The Klutes sat straight in their chairs, rigid as stone figures. After a moment Hunzel muttered, "It is not a convenient time to disturb our belongings for foolishness."

Maloof said: "One time is as good as another. Bring out the papers yourselves, now, or I must use my authority as master of the *Glicca* and locate them myself."

The Klutes looked at each other, then Siglaf heaved herself erect and strode off to the cabin she shared with Hunzel. After a moment she returned with a buff envelope, which she tossed upon the table in front of Maloof.

Maloof looked at the three girls. "Shall I open the envelope now?"

The girls nodded, sensing the possibility of imminent change in their lives.

Maloof opened the envelope and withdrew three sheets of heavy buff paper. He laid them on the table and began to read. After a time he smiled, then he chuckled.

Moncrief came to look over his shoulder. He spoke in a strange, emphatic language: "Ton-ton eskoy!"

"Exactly," said Maloof.

Pook asked anxiously: "What does that mean?"

Maloof spoke softly, as if he were reciting a fragment of

lyric poetry. "The grotesque sometimes reaches such exalted levels that it becomes almost sublime." He glanced toward the Klutes; they gave back impersonal stares.

Maloof spoke to the girls. "The papers appear to be official forms, issued by the Enders Valley Foundling Farm, for Maundry Vale Province, at Frippen on the world Numoy. That is the heading at the top of the page." He turned to the papers and read: " 'This paper grants custody of Prasilian Sklavo, age fourteen'—"

"That is me," said Flook.

"—'into the guardianship of Siglaf and Hunzel Podeska, of Cawterfel Farm of Tado Township in the Hills of Maundry Vale Province, subject to the following provisions: the guardians undertake to provide comfortable and secure lodgings for the ward, and to serve nutritious food of good quality to the ward's taste. The guardians must arrange for standard education for the ward, also medical and dental services when necessary, and try to provide a cheerful home atmosphere, along with normal recreational facilities. The ward is to be allowed leisure for appropriate social activity, but at the same time must be protected from unwholesome companions. The ward will not be required to perform labor other than minor household chores of an ordinary nature. The ward may not be asked to perform difficult, arduous, or dangerous work. The premises of the ward's residence will be regularly inspected by Institute personnel to ensure compliance with Institute regulations.'

" 'The grant of custody is valid only within the province of Maundry Vale. The ward may not be removed from the province, or otherwise away from the authority of the Institute; if such transgression occurs, the grant of custody is revoked.'

" 'If the guardians are put to extraordinary expense of legal and justifiable nature, the guardians may place an obligation or indenture not to exceed four hundred sols against the ward. This documentation will serve as authorization for such indenture so long as the debt is incurred, and discharged, inside Maundry Vale Province, and the Institute is notified.'

" 'If the ward is removed from the province, any indenture is dissolved. Signatures of both parties will be appended below.' "

Maloof looked at the other two sheets. "The documents are all the same, except that one names Lulanie Sklavo, and the other Thalasso Sklavo, who I presume are Pook and Snook."

"That is quite right," said Pook excitedly. "Are we free of indenture, and need not obey the Klutes?"

"Precisely so."

Flook asked anxiously: "Are we to leave the ship at Cax?"

"No," said Maloof. "You owe nothing to the Klutes. They have no control over you. If you wish to become Mouse-riders and work with Moncrief, you are free to do so—and I think that he will agree to the arrangement."

"That would suit us very well," said Snook. "And the Klutes—what of them? Will they leave the ship at Cax and set up their enterprise?"

Hunzel and Siglaf sat stiffly. After a moment, Siglaf said off-handedly: "Perhaps we will stay with the Mouse-riders. We have nothing better to do."

Moncrief looked at the Klutes thoughtfully. "I will take the idea under advisement. I can't deny that you play a valuable role in many of the routines. Still, you could be replaced. We shall see."

After a pause, Maloof spoke. "The dispute which was initiated on Star Home has been resolved. I hope that all concerned will assure themselves that resolution was scrupulously just."

Siglaf and Hunzel, making no comment, rose to their feet and went to their quarters.

NINE

1

Excerpt from *Handbook to the Planets*: Blenkinsop, Moulder 17

The orange star Moulder controls twenty-two far-flung planets, including a single habitable world to which the locator Abel Blenkinsop attached his own name. Now, three thousand years later, the world is home to a dour, dark-visaged race: the Blenks, who live in five great cities and work at the vast industrial yards which provide goods for half of the worlds in the local sector.

Neither the climate nor the geography of Blenkinsop can be considered congenial. More often than not, the sky is layered under a thin overcast through which the giant star Moulder shows as a dim orange disk. One season is much like another, though during the nominally winter months rain squalls and bitter winds more frequently range along the narrow city streets, driving pedestrians into their bungalows or underground into the subway system.

The polar continents to north and south are bitter
wastes of glaciers between mountains of black gabbro.
Of the six remaining continents, four are sodden marshes
threaded by slow waterways. Two other continents have
gentle terrain with rolling hills in the south, and here the
Blenks have established their cities, for reasons lost to
memory, each to the north of the hills, with the industrial
yards still farther to the north.

Across the years, the population has created within itself three classes of citizenry, which have congealed into
distinctive castes. The most prestigious are the relatively
few Shimerati, who live along the ridges of the southern
highlands in palaces behind exotic gardens. The next
lower caste is the Hummers, comprising high-level finan-
ciers and mercantilists, legal, medical, and technical pro-
fessionals, and general intelligentsia. Their mansions,
situated along the slopes of the highlands, are notably
more pretentious than the simple and elegant Shimerati
palaces. The third caste encompasses the working classes
of Blenkinsop, who live in solid little bungalows ranged
side by side along the interminable streets of the cities.

There is little traffic along the narrow streets of the
cities: drays and delivery vans, pushcarts operated by
sturdy old women, and a few high-wheeled motorized
rickshaws, which serve the Blenks as taxis. For general
transportation, most Blenks ride the subway systems,
which underlie the streets.

Despite occasional variation, the working Blenk is easily defined. He is of middle stature and stocky physique,
usually a few pounds overweight—a fact to which he is
indifferent, since he has little vanity. His clothes are chosen for durability rather than style, and if he chances to
look into a mirror he accepts his image without reaction;
this is himself in his singular individuality. His personal
manner is abrupt and brusque, lacking both tact and
grace, but to his credit he is loyal, generous, gentle with
wife and children, and totally brave. At work he is com-
petitive, since his basic goals are advancement in status
and rank.

A typical Blenk visits the vast theater known as the

'Trevanian' often, sometimes with his family and sometimes alone. In the warm blur of the murmurous darkness, the stresses of his daily life ease away; he is at peace
with himself and his surroundings. At the end of the
evening he reluctantly rises from his seat and slowly
leaves the hall, still lost in a semi-euphoric mood, to ride
the subway home, where the children are asleep and his
wife has a bowl of hot soup waiting for him.

The Trevanian is also patronized by the upper castes.
The Shimerati occupy the high balcony, where they can
be glimpsed by the players onstage should they trouble to
look—though they would discover only a few pale oval
blurs, devoid of animation. The Hummers on the balcony
below are more conspicuous; they wear their most splendid costumes and conduct themselves in accordance with
a ritualized etiquette. The ladies indulge themselves in
monumental coiffures sparkling with small luminosities
and streaming with colored ribbons. Their behavior is ex-
aggerated for the occasion; they gesture with fluttering
fingers, they simper, pout, and gaze toward the ceiling in
mock-agony when their desires are inexcusably ignored.
They beckon and chirrup to acquaintances and toss
nosegays to their favorites, meanwhile enjoying the re-
freshments served by liveried attendants.

The same partiality for extravagance and exaggeration
is apparent in Hummer architecture, dictating the unusual, bizarre, rococo, and fantastic. From hillside foun-
dations, Hummer mansions loft three stories high, each
with its complement of cupolas, bays, balconies, private
decks, and pendant glass globes, furnished for the convenience of those who choose to take tea, and enjoy petits
fours or frozen creams while swinging gently in the dim
orange sunlight.

Far different are the palaces of the Shimerati, which
are low, irregular, and deceptively simple, built to the
terms of an understated elegance using porphyry, moon-
stone, jet, and an occasional column of malachite.

2

From the pilot-house of the *Glicca*, the star Moulder first appeared as an orange spark on a background of far dim constellations. As the *Glicca* approached, the spark became an enormous orange disk, with a retinue of twenty-two planets.

Captain Maloof directed the *Glicca* toward the seventeenth of these worlds, which long ago the locator Abel Minger Blenkinsop had registered, using his own name.

The world expanded below. Maloof made contact with the space-control office at Cax and received landing instructions. The *Glicca* dropped through overcast and down toward the early morning face of Cax. Maloof located the landing field and guided the *Glicca* to its allocated plat.

As soon as the exit port was slid open and the gangway lowered, three uniformed officials left the port offices and trotted across the field to the ship. They conferred a moment, then climbed the gangway and entered the saloon. For half an hour they subjected the ship's company and the ship itself to standard entry formalities.

As soon as they issued clearances and departed, Myron crossed the field to the long, low terminal building, where he expected to find the office of the Port Director. He climbed a ramp to the cargo dock.

A few yards to the left, a corridor opened into the building. A sign with a pointing arrow read:

TO THE PORT DIRECTOR

Myron turned into the corridor and almost at once came upon a tall door, where another sign read:

RICO YAIL
DIRECTOR OF THE PORT
COME AT WILL

The door slid open to Myron's touch; he entered a large room sparsely furnished with a desk, a few chairs, and a tall cabinet. The walls displayed a single decoration: a poster printed in tones of black, gray, and mulberry, depicting twenty-five types of spaceship currently in operation.

At the back of the desk, a large man of indeterminate age, languidly handsome, sat at his ease. The desk bore neither documents, ledgers, nor files; the director, if this were he, seemed unoccupied and rather more casual than Myron had expected. He spoke courteously: "I am Rico Yail; please be seated and explain how I can help you."

Myron sat down and laid his sheaf of documents upon the desk. "I am Myron Tany, supercargo of the *Glicca*, which has just arrived. We carry a mixed cargo, including ten bales of skins from the world Madlock, some miscellaneous parcels from Fluter and elsewhere, and from Star Home a consignment of fourteen rugs for Monomarche, which I take to be a local merchandiser."

"In the broadest sense, you are correct," said Yail. "In each city of Blenkinsop, there are one or more great magazines similar to Monomarche, though on a lesser scale. These magazines purvey goods of every sort, both local and off-world. They deal with the ordinary Blenks and the upper castes as well. Monomarche is the most prestigious of the group and commands considerable influence. They will send a man for the rugs, so you may put them from your mind; also, I will send a crew to discharge the rest of the freight for Cax. Your responsibilities will be at an end."

Myron was puzzled. He indicated the documents he had placed on the desk. "Here are the applicable manifests, invoices, certificates, and a few forms which should be filled out immediately."

He started to pass them across the desk, but Yail raised his hand to forestall him. "A clerk is usually on hand to deal with such matters, but today he is away—so you may drop the papers into yonder trash basket, where they will do us no harm."

Myron's jaw dropped. "Are you serious?"

"Of course! A clerk will be here tomorrow; he can sort through the trash, if he likes—that is his prerogative. But we have more important things to do."

Without further demur, Myron obeyed the instructions.

"Good," said Yail, leaning back in his chair. "Now then: what are your next ports of call?"

"The schedule, so far as I know, is not yet definite," said Myron. "We have no outstanding commitments; we are at liberty to accept such cargoes as you might wish to move."

"Excellent. We can offer cargoes to a variety of ports, mostly, I must say, off the standard shipping routes—not necessarily a disadvantage, since non-conventional itineraries are often profitable! To compensate for exceptionally distant ports, a twenty percent adjustment in freight rates may be possible."

"That might well be an inducement," said Myron. "If you will give me a list of these cargoes and their destinations, and the projected freight charges, I will take it to Captain Maloof, and tonight we will work out some routings."

Yail turned to his information machine. He touched buttons; the screen glowed pink, with lines of bright blue-green text. Yail scanned the display, made a few changes, and pressed a button, and a sheet of paper issued from a slot. He gave the paper to Myron, who tucked it into his pocket.

"We will work on this tonight," Myron said. "If we have any success, I will let you know as soon as possible."

Myron prepared himself to leave, but hesitated. Yail looked inquiringly across the desk.

Myron spoke, half-apologetically: "If you have a minute or two to spare, I would be grateful for your advice."

"As of now, nothing presses," said Yail. "State your problem, then I can tell you whether my advice might be useful."

Myron arranged his thoughts. "The situation is this. On Star Home we shifted the *Glicca* from Port Palactus to the rug repository at Torqual Downs, where we would take aboard the rugs for Monomarche. At the repository we noticed hundreds of rugs in storage, the best of the best. A few days before, thieves had stolen thirty-two carboys of kasic from Port Palactus; we chased down the thieves and took back the carboys. The port director was anxious to recover the carboys, and so we traded forty-six rugs from the Torqual repository in exchange for the kasic. These rugs are now in our aft cargo bay, and we want to dispose of them to best advantage. But we do not know how to proceed."

Yail nodded thoughtfully. "You have correctly perceived the difficulties; as soon as you made a move, you would be wrapped up in a cocoon of red tape. But do not let me alarm you—proper tactics can circumvent these obstacles. After all, authorities cannot tax or regulate what is unknown to them; this is a universal law!

"Monomarche has achieved a virtual monopoly on the Star Home rugs, which it sells to the Shimerati—no doubt at a handsome profit. The other magazines would be happy to break this monopoly, I'm sure; perhaps they could be discreetly approached." He hitched himself forward. "What sort of price are you contemplating? For instance, would you accept three hundred sols per rug?"

"Hm," Myron mused. "Three hundred multiplied by forty-six equals thirteen thousand eight hundred, which is an impressive sum. But I must consult my colleagues before making a commitment."

Yail turned to look out the window, frowning in deep cogitation. At last he turned back to Myron. "The figure I mentioned is, of course, tentative. If you attempted to handle the business yourself, I imagine that the best offer you would hear might be a grudging two hundred sols. With my guidance, the price would be somewhat higher; however, I would expect a reasonable fee. I suggest that this might be twenty percent of any excess over three hundred sols per rug. For instance, if I sold a rug at four hundred sols, my fee would be twenty percent of one hundred sols, or twenty sols. You would be selling the rug for three hundred eighty sols. Would you accept such an arrangement?"

"It sounds better than two hundred sols per rug," said Myron. "Still, I can agree to nothing definite at this moment."

3

Myron returned to the *Glicca*, where he found Captain Maloof in the galley, along with Wingo and Schwatzendale.

Myron described his meeting with Yail. "He is a surprise—not the Blenk we have been led to expect. He is relaxed and easy; if he suffers nervous tensions, I saw no symptoms."

Maloof asked: "Does he have cargo for us?"

Myron produced the list which he had received from Yail. "There seem to be a number of parcels to ports somewhat off the usual shipping routes—I told him that we would look over the list, and try to work out a practical itinerary."

Maloof studied the list, with eyebrows raised. "I have never heard of most of these ports. I suspect these so-called 'parcels of cargo' are a collection of odd lots, which no other carrier will accept; they have been languishing in corners of Yail's warehouses like a band of lost waifs, waiting and hoping for a miracle." Maloof put the list down on the table. "Still, they seem to make up a proper cargo, which might turn us a profit, especially if we collect a twenty percent surcharge on the most inconvenient legs."

"And we might pick up a lot or two of cargo along the way," Myron theorized.

"That is always a possibility." Maloof picked up the list and scanned it again. "Hmf. These places are truly obscure, but I suppose they must exist, since Yail is sending them freight! Tonight we will use the Index to locate them on our charts, and sort out a route."

"For a fact, it will be something of a challenge," Myron mused.

"Yes, but perhaps by exercising our joint ingenuity, and throwing in a few zigzags, we may still produce a workable itinerary." He paused. "Even so, it is not good policy to travel a hundred light-years to deliver a sack of birdseed."

After a moment, Myron said: "I also mentioned our rugs to Yail, and asked how we could sell them to the best advantage. He warned me against trying to sell them ourselves, for fear of bureaucratic complications. He asked what price we had put on the rugs; I told him that our thinking had not gone so far, but he asked if we would be satisfied with three hundred sols per rug, or thirteen thousand eight hundred sols for the lot. I said that I would confer with my shipmates and get back to him as soon as possible.

"He went on to say that if we so chose, he would act as our agent, and that his commission would be twenty percent of the difference between three hundred and the final selling price; for instance, if he sold a rug for four hundred sols, he would earn twenty sols, while we would get three hundred eighty sols."

Schwatzendale wrote figures on a sheet of paper. "If we sold forty-six rugs, we would take seventeen thousand four hundred eighty sols, and Yail nine hundred twenty."

"Fair enough," said Maloof, "provided we are paid in cash at the time the rugs are delivered."

Myron returned to Yail's office. As before, he sat relaxed behind the desk.

Yail signaled Myron to a chair. "Do you have instructions for me?"

"I do. Your proposal is accepted, as long as payment is made in cash at the time that the rugs are delivered."

"The terms are accepted," said Yail.

"Now, to work. There are eleven magazines large enough to consider a transaction of this magnitude, including Monomarche. The trade is profitable, since the Shimerati control so much wealth that they ignore price and pay whatever is asked. But Monomarche has no need to be avaricious, and so far as I can gather the rugs are priced at about five hundred sols apiece.

"I will test the market. Come back later—I may have news for you."

4

During the early afternoon, the rain of the morning abated to a fine drizzle, then came to a halt altogether, and the orange disk of Moulder appeared behind the overcast.

An hour or two previously, the Klutes had wandered away from the *Glicca*, planning to explore the city on their own account. The circumstances were dismal; a light rain was falling, and the streets exhaled a sour odor. They marched along the narrow streets, rain-hoods pulled over their heads. At intervals, small, narrow-fronted shops overlooked the street, dark within, sometimes with the pale face of the proprietor half-seen peering through the grimy front panes. Otherwise, the Klutes saw little to interest them.

After a time, they returned to the space-port, grim and dissatisfied, striding through the rain and stamping through puddles to finally reach the *Glicca*.

They changed into dry clothes and went to the galley, where Wingo served them hot tea and scones.

"How did you find the city?" asked Wingo cheerfully.

"The streets were like dark passages, and smelled of dead dogs. The rain was incessant and coursed down our necks in a freshet. We tried to find a tea shop where we could refresh ourselves, but there was none to be found."

Siglaf added: "I believe that, despite its giddy foolishness, I prefer Fluter."

After a pause, Wingo asked delicately: "So then; are you staying with the Mouse-riders?"

Hunzel thought for a moment, then gave an ambiguous grunt. "We face some hard choices. We are in a state of flux."

Siglaf amplified the remark. "In effect, we are open to any propitious offers."

5

Meanwhile, Moncrief had embarked upon adventures of his own. After dressing with care, he had set off to find the Trevanian, where he hoped to secure favorable bookings for the Mouse-riders.

In front of the port offices he commanded the services of a motorized rickshaw, operated by a weedy, hollow-cheeked youth with long varnished mustachios. Before consenting to activate his vehicle, the operator looked Moncrief up and down, then asked: "What is your destination?"

Moncrief said grandly: "You may take me to the Trevanian, at best speed."

The operator nodded curtly, to indicate that he found the destination acceptable. "Climb aboard. The fare is ten dinkets; I will not move a man of your bulk for less."

Moncrief did not care for the operator's manner, which, so he thought, verged on the disrespectful—the more so when he found fault with Moncrief's method for climbing aboard the vehicle. "Briskly, now, Grandfather—the day is for jumping and running; sleep somewhere else if you are tired."

Moncrief, using all dignity, scrambled onto the narrow seat of the vehicle. The operator engaged gears, and the taxi set off across the field, careening dangerously through puddles while Moncrief held on for dear life.

The taxi trundled off the field to the street and presently arrived at the Trevanian. Moncrief alighted stiffly and for a moment gazed in awe at the great Blenk entertainment hall.

The operator tapped his hooter impatiently. "Come now, old toddler! Pay the ten dinkets at once, or I will charge a waiting supplement."

Moncrief hurriedly paid over the fare, which the operator accepted without comment. Cutting a final curvet through a puddle, the rickshaw departed.

Moncrief crossed to the Trevanian. A massive door of iron and glass slid aside at his approach; he passed through the opening into a short hall, which took him into a large octagonal foyer, notable for the corridors which led away from each of the wall-segments.

He stopped short; a multiplicity of choices confronted him. Which corridor led to the office of the Director of Production? On the opposite wall he noticed a long white panel printed with lines of informational text: a directory? He crossed the room and studied the panel.

The printed text was not immediately clear. Aha! A reference to Overman Murius Zank, Director of Production. Moncrief read the associated text and came upon the phrase: 'To reach the office, use the orange indicator.' Moncrief frowned; the words were cryptic indeed. What was an 'orange indicator'? Moncrief stood back and searched the chamber for indicators, of any color whatever, and was enlightened at once.

Each corridor exhibited a distinctive colored stripe along its centerline. Moncrief looked here and there and found a corridor marked by an orange stripe. The corridor and the stripe receded into the distance; without hesitation Moncrief set off into the bowels of the Trevanian.

At intervals, numbered doors appeared to right and left. Moncrief presently arrived at a pair of doors with a plaque reading:

OVERMAN MURIUS ZANK
DIRECTOR OF PRODUCTION

Moncrief touched the latch, and the doors swung aside. He entered a large, high-ceilinged room; a counter separated him from a business office, where a dozen clerks worked in attitudes

of remarkable diligence. Moncrief advanced to the counter,
where he assumed a posture of importance and waited for a
clerk to approach and inquire his needs.

While he waited, Moncrief took occasion to assess the
room. At the far end of the section where he stood, a carved
wooden balustrade created what seemed to be a special waiting
area, which was at the moment vacant. A door from the waiting
area led into an inner office. Over the door a panel read:

OVERMAN MURIUS ZANK
DIRECTOR OF PRODUCTION
ENTER AT THE GREEN LIGHT

A red light now glowed above the door.

Moncrief turned his attention back to the office. He became impatient and thumped on the counter with his knuckles.
The signal went unheeded.

The desk nearest the counter was occupied by a fresh-faced
young man, a trifle plump, dressed in natty garments. A sign
on his desk read: BAYARD DESOSSO. Like his colleagues, Bayard
worked so diligently as to be oblivious to all else. Moncrief stared
at him, trying to compel his attention by sheer force of will. He
met no success; if anything, Bayard exerted himself even more
energetically.

At this moment, a sudden tumult issued from the inner office; enraged voices, pounding and stamping, outcries and cat-
calls. Startled, Bayard looked up, and his gaze met Moncrief's
insistent stare.

Moncrief instantly pointed his finger. "You there, Bayard!
Come here at once!"

A sad expression crossed Bayard's face, altering at once to
resolute courtesy.

"Certainly, sir! By all means!" Bayard strode to the counter.
"How can I help you, sir?"

"I am Master Moncrief, director of the famous Mouse-rider
troupe. I am here to see Director Zank; he will wish to fit the
Mouse-riders into his schedule. Time is of the essence."

Bayard looked over his shoulder; the red light still glowed.
Bayard said regretfully: "The Director may not be disturbed at
this time."

Moncrief cocked his head to listen. "He is either rehearsing a very frolicsome act, or he is being soundly thrashed."

"Such a liberty would be unthinkable!" cried Bayard, but he turned an apprehensive look toward the inner office.

"I suggest," said Moncrief firmly, "that you at least announce that Master Moncrief of the famous Mouse-riders is on hand. It is important that he see me at once."

Bayard shook his head. "You propose an enormity." He paused, to hear the sound of stamping feet. "He is even now trying to quell the Futin Putos, and as you will note, they are emphatic."

Moncrief inquired: "Who are 'the Futin Putos'?"

"They are a troupe of acrobats from the Dark Forest," replied Bayard. "Overman Zank is disgusted with their brutish antics; still, they are popular with a certain segment of the audience, and he feels obliged to use them from time to time."

The sounds from Zank's office had subsided to a murmur of voices, which suddenly waxed in anger, then went quiet.

Moncrief drummed his fingers upon the counter. Suddenly, the rear door from Zank's office flew open, and out to the waiting area came a tumble of ten hairy men, jostling, shoving, struggling for places on the upholstered benches.

After squirming, elbowing, grumbling, and growling, the Futin Putos began to stare across the balustrade at the office clerks, with the curiosity of visitors to a zoo.

Moncrief looked with disfavor at what he considered the most uncouth group of individuals of his experience. They were of ordinary stature, but so burly as to seem squat; lank black hair hung down to join heavy black beards, cut off square under the chin. They wore leather vests and short leather pantaloons, dank with soil and grease.

"Not a savory group," said Moncrief with a sniff, and turned away.

"Don't show them overt disapproval!" Bayard warned quickly. "If they perceive an insult, they will take a vicious revenge. On the stage, they perform spectacular feats, but if someone makes a mistake, they knock him sprawling, then kick him until he crawls away in humiliation."

"In front of the audience?" asked Moncrief in disbelief.

"Definitely. Their audience eggs them on."

Moncrief studied Bayard without approval. "When I entered the office and came to the counter, you ignored me as if I were made of air. How do you explain this conduct?"

Bayard put on a stubborn face. "We must act according to our new regulations."

"Do I hear you aright?" asked Moncrief. "Is it your policy to ignore patrons? This would seem eccentric—to say the least!"

"That is not our affair. In the main, our regulations are not unreasonable."

Moncrief glanced across the room, but the green light was not yet visible. He turned back to Bayard. "Tell me of your new regulations."

Bayard responded mechanically. "Article One defines the need for punctuality and correlates a scale of penalties with degrees of tardiness. Article Two bans conversation, song, banter, gossip, and the like. Article Three establishes work quotas for all office personnel—these quotas are considered stringent! Article Four curtails an old custom; in the past, when a client arrived at the counter, four or five clerks might greet him, to inquire after the health of his family and to chat and learn the details of his business. After that the client might be sent to a new department, or advised as how best to conduct himself before Overman Zank. The new rule has changed this procedure. When a client appears, the first clerk to notice him must hurry to the counter and help the client alone, with crisp efficiency. Unfortunately, the clerk who helps clients will never make up his work quota! But we have found a solution to the dilemma. Nowhere is it specified that clerks are required to keep a vigilant watch on the counter; hence, if the clerk focuses upon his work, he cannot be faulted for neglect."

"Ingenious!" declared Moncrief.

Moncrief was distracted from further comment by the light over Zank's door, which had turned green.

"The green light has appeared," called Bayard. "Come, if you wish to see Zank!"

Adopting a stately posture, Moncrief pushed through the gate in the counter and followed Bayard toward another entrance to Zank's office, at the back of the room.

The Futin Putos suddenly became quiet, then crowded the balustrade, where they hooted and jeered.

"Hoy there, old tumper! Why do you trot so briskly?"

"Tell old Zank that our memories are long!"

"If you forget, we will pull your nose, or whatever it is that dangles between your legs."

Moncrief ignored the raillery and followed Bayard across the room.

Bayard stopped at the door. "I will go in first and announce you. After the Futin Putos, Director Zank's sangfroid may be frayed."

The Futin Putos continued to call advice; Moncrief waited with as much aplomb as he could muster.

A moment later, the door opened and Bayard stood in the opening. He spoke, somewhat self-importantly. "I have mentioned the Mouse-rider troupe to Overman Zank, and I gather that he is favorably impressed. You may now enter. Be polite, but not ebullient. Come, if you will."

Moncrief followed Bayard into a large chamber, sparsely furnished, and unoccupied except for a thin old man who sat motionless behind a massive semi-circular desk.

Bayard assumed a formal posture and performed introductions. To Moncrief he said: "You are in the presence of Overman Murius Zank, Director of Production." To Zank he said: "This gentleman is Professor Moncrief, master of the Mouse-rider troupe. He hopes to present one or more programs at the Trevanian, if circumstances permit."

Zank stared at Moncrief briefly, then dismissed Bayard with a flicker of his fingers. Bayard bowed with punctilio and left the chamber.

The men surveyed each other. Moncrief saw a small, gaunt man with a bald, bony head. Zank's eyes were round; his nose was a small rapacious hook; his mouth was thin and without color. If he ever felt emotion, his features gave no indication.

After a moment, Zank spoke. "If you wish to sit, you may do so."

Moncrief gingerly lowered himself onto a straight-backed chair of rather fragile appearance, which creaked under his weight.

"In regard to our programs, you come at an inconvenient time," said Zank. "The schedule for the week is booked solid, except for a few slots in the after-midnight 'graveyard'. There is a single slot the day after tomorrow, which the Futin Putos claim as their own, in a most raucous manner. But I do not agree with them, and this has been the source of some contention. My preference would be to send them hopping back to the Dark Forest. I hesitate only because they are popular with a segment of the audience which I cannot ignore."

"Hm," said Moncrief. "They seem a most intemperate group."

The ghost of a grim smile twitched Zank's thin mouth. "They hope to intimidate me, but it is a vain hope."

The Futin Putos had failed to fully close the door to the waiting area. Through the crack, a number of glittering eyes peered.

Moncrief and Zank continued their discussion, unaware of the inspection. Moncrief said, somewhat sententiously: "As a stranger at Cax, perhaps I should restrain my opinions; however, they seem to me a gang of sadistic thugs, lacking all charm."

"It is a fair appraisal," said Zank. "Now tell me something of the Mouse-riders."

"With pleasure! I need not explain that our programs contrast notably with the grotesque capers of the Futin Putos. The Mouse-riders are inspired by a different vision; our sequences combine gallant adventure, romance, and mystery. We are known for our creative imagery, so that every sequence is a mix of music, beauty, and the glamour of far places. I have in mind three sequences, joined by one means or another into a unity. If I may say so, the slot on the day after tomorrow would suit us well, since our stay at Cax will be brief."

"That is reasonable," said Zank, after a moment of consideration. "Especially since it accords with my own inclinations. The Futin Putos shall play the graveyard. If they protest, they may chase each other back to the Dark Forest."

The door slammed open, and the Futin Putos burst in a tumbling rush into Zank's office.

Zank muttered to Moncrief: "Stand behind me, and say nothing."

Moncrief obeyed with alacrity.

Zank spoke harshly: "What are you up to? Leave at once—you trespass my office."

The chief shuffled a step forward. "But you are to blame! You have called us 'stinking brutes' and mocked our artistry;

you have schemed with that fat Mouse-rider and have given him our good slot; you have shifted us far and late past the midnight slot, to when the hall is empty! That is betrayal, and someone shall pay the price!"

Zank raised his hand and pointed his finger as if it were a weapon, bringing the Futin Putos to an uncertain halt.

"You are hysterical," he said in a low voice. "Take care, or it will be the worse for you."

Momentarily daunted, the Futin Putos stood crouching and glowering, ten feet from the desk.

Zank spoke again, his voice ringing with metallic overtones. "I am Director, and I arrange production as I see fit! Be happy with what I allow you, or take yourselves back to the Dark Forest! Go now!"

"Not just yet," said the chief. The Futin Putos began to inch forward, making guttural sounds, moaning, wheezing, and hissing.

Moncrief shrank back against the wall. The Futin Putos had closed their minds to reason! How sad, how strange, to die here in the Trevanian.

But Zank seemed unconcerned. "Are you going?" he asked.

"When we have taken our vengeance," replied the chief. "First we will give the Mouse-rider his due, and then we shall deal with you!"

Zank touched a button on his desk. The door into the office slid aside; Bayard stood in the opening.

"Yes, sir?"

"Clear away these intruders," Zank told him. "They are unwelcome."

Bayard faced the Futin Putos. "Clear the office! You heard the Director—you are unwelcome! Lively now; form a single file, if you please!"

The Futin Putos seized Bayard and tossed him back and forth like a large, sprawling bean-bag, ignoring his protests and threats. Finally, tiring of the game, they tossed him out through the door and turned back to Overman Zank. One step after another, they edged again toward the desk.

Without haste, Zank reached forward and touched another button. A heavy semi-circular glass panel lifted from a housing in the floor to create a barrier five feet tall around the desk.

Nonplussed, the Futin Putos paused again. Then the chief vented a contemptuous laugh. "What do you expect from that trifle? I can vault it using a single bound!"

The group howled with mockery.

Leaning back in his chair, Zank said lightly: "Do as you like. I recommend, however, that you leave the office at once, and in good order."

"Only after justice has been done," declared the chief.

"Justice is poised, and ready," said Zank.

The chief hunched his shoulders, crouched, then sprang to the top of the glass wall.

A dazzle of blue sparks ran up his arms and legs and caused all the hairs of his head and beard to expand and stiffen into the semblance of a great puff-ball, each hair crackling with sparks. He uttered a choking cry, then tumbled over into a backward somersault. Touching the floor, his feet spattered blue sparks, which gradually diminished as the chief danced and stepped high, his fellows looking on with slack-jawed wonder.

At this time, six Monitors in black and yellow uniforms filed quietly into the office. Without words they addressed themselves to the Futin Putos. After a brief scuffle, and a few taps with persuasion rods, the acrobats were shackled neck to neck along a chain and, at a signal, were marched unceremoniously from the office.

Moncrief sheepishly stepped from behind the desk. Resuming his place in the chair, he tried to act as if nothing in particular had occurred. After a moment he asked: "What will happen to them now?"

"Nothing very much," said Zank. "They ignore beatings, causing the Monitors to exert themselves to no avail. And incarceration only aggravates the Monitors, as the Futin Putos do nothing but sleep, waking only long enough to befoul their cells. If we send them north to Windy Isle, after a few months their audience raises a fearful protest. But if I write them into the midnight slot for three or four months, they will see the error of their ways, perhaps."

"Hm," mused Moncrief. "Are their threats to be taken seriously?"

Zank considered. "The best that I can tell you is that they are unpredictable. They are malevolent and vengeful without doubt, but whether the act depends upon opportunity, or whether they might be distracted by another exploit, it is hard to say. My advice to you is not to wander by night alone along dark streets." Zank straightened up in his tall chair. "But at this time you should consult Overman Skame to arrange for your stage sets." He touched one of the buttons on his desk.

Bayard limped into the room. "Yes, sir?"

Zank looked him over with raised eyebrows. "Bayard, you will please conduct Master Moncrief to the office of the stage manager."

"Yes, sir; at once!" spoke Bayard.

Zank inspected him coldly. "Then, before you resume your usual duties, step into the dressing room and freshen yourself. At the moment you cut a sorry figure. I insist that my staff take pride in a smart appearance."

"As you say, sir!" replied Bayard. He bowed stiffly, then turned to Moncrief.

"If you are ready, sir, I will take you to Overman Skame."

Moncrief expressed his gratitude to Overman Zank, then followed Bayard from the office.

6

By a cross-passage Bayard led Moncrief to a corridor with a blue stripe, which took them to a massive iron door decorated with a hundred silver rosettes. The plaque read:

OVERMAN LUCAN SKAME
DIRECTOR OF STAGE MANAGEMENT

Bayard spoke a few words of reassurance. "Overman Skame has an easy disposition and will always listen to your ideas. You may find him a bit startling at first, but pay no heed." He touched a pad, and the door slid aside. "I wish you luck."

Bayard bowed, then turned back along the corridor.

Moncrief stepped forward but was halted by the impact of what confronted him. Chaotic clutter appeared to occupy the entire volume of the office, except at the far end, where he saw

Overman Skame sitting at an extraordinary desk, opposite a pair of clerks hunched over workstations.

Moncrief was unattended. He blinked and looked from right to left, up to the high ceiling, and down to the floor. The room was full of tables laden with contrivances of unknown purpose, as well as more familiar devices.

Moncrief moved slowly forward, appraising the concatenation of shape, color, and complication that lay around him. Cases displayed hundreds of animals, the denizens of as many worlds; dolls wearing characteristic costumes stood in groups or worked at typical tasks. Everywhere, in no perceptible order, stood modeled structures from many times and places. There were replicas of private dwellings; pavilions and palaces, odd little bungalows, and mountain lodges; there were towers, and tumbles of cones and spheres. From the ceiling on bronze chains hung lamps and lanterns of a hundred styles, some old, some archaic, others primitive, all aglow with appropriate sources of illumination. Interspersed were hundreds of mechanical and electrical devices of unknown purpose. Along the walls, completely encircling the room, shelves supported tracks along which moved vehicles of many descriptions, some emitting small hoots and whistles.

Moncrief gave up trying to assimilate the variety contained in the office. He came to Skame's desk, an object of eccentric design, at its basis a long table almost four feet wide, bent into a semi-circle with the director seated centrally, clasped by wings to right and left.

Skame's attention was fixed upon the pages of a large folio, depicting fashionable young women, not necessarily Blenk, bodies and limbs twisted into odd postures, wearing garments of extreme style. So intent was his interest that he seemed oblivious to Moncrief, who had come to a halt in front of the desk.

Moncrief studied Overman Skame. Here, he thought, was a man of undoubtedly distinctive character. Like Zank, and perhaps Bayard, he appeared to differ from the typical Blenk stock, as if there might be an admixture of another blood-line. Shimerati? Moncrief wondered. Skame was tall and gaunt, with narrow shoulders and thin arms. His face was long, pale, and narrow, with a thin nose, pale green eyes under near-invisible eyebrows, and a wide crooked mouth. He wore a loose robe striped dark blue and green, with a globular opal, two inches in diameter, dangling from his neck on a fine iron chain; on his head was a flat-crowned hat of heavy tan stuff with an extremely wide brim, worn rakishly aslant.

Overman Skame at last became aware of Moncrief. Closing the folio, he swung around in his chair. "Sir, you must excuse me; I became absorbed in thought. I was, so it appears, oblivious to all else. In any case, you now have my full attention; how can I help you? But first—please be seated! Remove the cloak of angel feathers from yonder chair, and use it properly; then we shall see to your business."

Moncrief followed the instructions, then introduced himself. "I am Marcel Moncrief, master of the Mouse-rider troupe. We have been scheduled into a slot on the day after tomorrow; Overman Zank has advised me to consult you at once in regard to such stage properties as I may require."

"Yes; just so. What is the nature of your program?"

"We shall present a medley of three sequences, each different from the others. I hope that this will not tax your resources."

Skame smiled and shook his head, setting the wide brim of his hat into flexible motion. "That is unlikely. At the Trevanian, we can provide almost any scenic effect, interior or exterior. For certain extravagant effects, such as naval battles, or the destruction of grand cities, or struggles between grotesque monsters of stupendous size, or astronomical spectacles such as collisions between black holes, sunspots, or other galactic convulsions, we use holographic projection. In short, we can produce whatever stage set you can stipulate in a very short time."

Moncrief spoke in awe: "That is most impressive!"

Skame laughed, almost waggishly. "So it must seem—still, our basic system is quite simple. If you like, I will explain it to you."

"I am indeed interested!"

Skame straightened in his chair. "The Trevanian stage is oblate, with a wall across the central diameter. While the half facing the audience is in use, the stagehands arrange the concealed half, using any of the thousands of components in our warehouses. At the end of the scene, the curtain falls and the stage rotates, so that when the curtain rises again, a new setting is revealed. Now, if you will supply me information regarding

your troupe and your sequences, also the sets you have in mind,
I will put the processes into motion."

Moncrief did as requested. When he had finished, Skame
ruminated for a time, then said, "The sequences, for the most
part, are ingenious. The contrast of mood between the first and
second sequences is effective. The first exerts a strange force;
events move with the ponderous momentum of fate itself."

"I am pleased to hear your favorable opinion," said Moncrief modestly.

Skame inclined his head, causing his hat to undulate. "The
second sequence uses a different mood, as gay and happy as a
frolic among white and yellow flowers! The concept of the three
girls each trying to bring life to the marble statue, with its erotic
intimations, is fascinating. The final scene, where the girls dance
off across the glade, and the statue—at last aroused—struggles to
follow, but can only totter and fall among the reeds, while the
girls dance away, will pull at many a heartstring."

Moncrief gave a shrug of deprecation. "I am fortunate in
the quality of my troupe."

Skame pursed his lips judiciously. "No doubt! In regard
to the final sequence, I confess to puzzlement. This piece, for
all its graceful attributes, seems a bit avant-garde for a Blenk
audience."

Moncrief laughed indulgently. "Absurd! It is intended as a
coda, to unify the entire program."

Skame was dubious. "A 'coda'? Few Blenks will recognize
the word, much less your intent—even should astonishment allow them to think."

"No great matter," replied Moncrief. "The effect will be the
same; after a blink or two, happy laughter will be heard, along
with shouts of applause."

Skame brooded a moment, then gave a slight shrug. "Possibly so. I suspect that in any event no great harm will be done, except perhaps a premature birth or two. But the Blenks would
certainly prefer a trained animal actor, or an erotic little farce."

"Not possible! My animals, and the girls, are intensely puri-
tanical. They would never show so much as their bare bottoms,
unless they were jumping from a window to escape a fire in
their bedroom. As for our other concerns, I hope that everything is within your competence?"

"For the first two sequences, there is no great problem. Each has a few difficulties, which our technicians can solve without trouble. As for the third sequence, we have problems of another kind, but again they are all soluble. We shall bring out paraphernalia from our medieval warfare collections. The equipment is both massive and impressive."

"Excellent!" said Moncrief. "Now then, what of costumerie?"

"It shall be as you specify. You may inspect my folios, if you like. You will find an adequate range of choices."

After a pleasant half hour of exploration among Skame's folios, Moncrief settled upon costumes which he considered optimum for his purposes.

"Very good," said Skame. "You choose with a sensitive eye. If you will bring in your personnel tomorrow morning for a fitting, the costumes will be ready by early afternoon."

"I appreciate your assistance," Moncrief told him. "It has been more than invaluable. The Trevanian must be the grandest theater in the Reach, certainly within the scope of my experience!"

"Thank you," said Skame. "I value your opinions."

"One small point," said Moncrief. "For the evening's performance, the troupe and the crew of the *Glicca* will arrive at the Trevanian aboard the ship's flitter. Where can they most expeditiously land?"

Skame answered without hesitation. "There is a landing plat at the northern wall of the Trevanian, on the second level, which could not be more convenient. It is designed for those Shimerati who choose to arrive for the performance by personal air-car, but it is never fully occupied. A hall leads from the plat to a parlor of sorts, adjacent to the stage. Elevators lead to the upper balconies, but these are seldom in use. A bank of seats provides an intimate view of the stage; I recommend that the crew use this facility."

Moncrief again expressed his thanks, and took his leave.

7

The next morning, Myron crossed to the office of the Port Director. He found Rico Yail as before, lounging behind his massive desk.

Yail gave Myron a casual nod and indicated a chair. "Seat yourself, and show me the papers you are carrying so carefully."

Myron settled into the chair and slid his charts across the desk. Yail sat forward and studied the itinerary with interest. At last he looked up to Myron.

"So far as I can tell, without a calculator, the routing seems as efficient as it can be. What are these red marks here, by Glame on Sussea, and again at Croy on New Hope?"

"The explanation is a bit complicated," said Myron. "After leaving First Camp on Welters, we travel to Glame, with the next halt at Croy. But if you refer to your chart you will notice that Fluter is not too far off the route. At Coro-coro a band of pilgrims is awaiting transit to Impy's Landing on Kyril; it would be convenient for us to detour to Fluter, pick up the pilgrims, then continue to Croy—especially if you could find us a parcel of cargo for Fluter."

"That can be done, easily enough."

"After Kyril, we proceed to Ocean City on Lavendry, which is the last stop on the list. After Lavendry, we veer off toward Naharius, where we have some small private business."

"Naharius?" Yail became pensive. "I have heard rumors regarding Naharius—not necessarily credible, but certainly provocative."

Myron smiled sadly. "My aunt went to Naharius, to learn the secrets of youth and beauty. I wonder what she found."

Yail looked off through the window with a musing half-smile. "Rumors flit along the spaceways like fireflies in the deep woods. Sometimes they are fascinating. No doubt quiet tales are told even of Blenkinsop, the five cities, the Shimerati, even the outcasts of the Dark Forest."

Yail squared himself to his desk. "Now then, the rugs. You can expect a profitable transaction. I have put quiet inquiries to five important magazines in the four outer cities; the response was immediate. I received offers ranging from four hundred sols per rug to four hundred and twenty-five, subject to inspection, which I tentatively accepted. Subject to your approval, the inspector will be arriving shortly, along with a dray."

"I approve. It seems a good price."

"I think so myself. As soon as the rugs are discharged, my warehousemen will begin to load cargo. You should be buttoned up before midnight, and ready for departure in the morning."

"We will be on hand one more day," said Myron. "Moncrief and his troupe play the Trevanian tomorrow evening. We will leave the morning after next."

The telephone at Yail's elbow chimed; he picked up the unit. "Director Yail here; how can I help you?"

The response prompted Yail to change his manner to an even, impersonal formality.

"No, sir; that is not the way of it. What you suggest was far from our intent." Yail listened, then said: "I am acting as an informal adviser in the case. The principal is a young off-worlder, of good character, but unaccustomed to Blenk trade practices. He is quite willing to deal with Monomarche, all else being equal." After listening again, Yail responded: "There are forty-six rugs, of prime export quality, direct from Star Home. The asking price is five hundred sols per rug. So far, our high offer has been four hundred and twenty-five."

The conversation continued. Finally Yail said, "I will submit your offer to the principal, who is now here in my office. A moment, if you please." He turned to Myron. "Monomarche offers four hundred and thirty-five sols per rug, subject to inspection. Shall I accept?"

"By all means!" said Myron.

Yail followed Myron's instructions, then put down the handpiece. He told Myron: "The deed is done. There will be no delay; the dray and the inspector will be here within the hour."

"They will bring the money?"

"Of course! Money is the life-blood of commerce." Yail calculated. "After my commission, you will net eighteen thousand seven hundred and sixty-eight sols. Does that accord with your figures?"

"Exactly."

"It has been a profitable transaction," said Yail. "I wish for many more of such happy occurrences."

"I as well!"

"One detail remains," said Yail. "I must terminate the tentative arrangement initiated with Overman Garloc of the Parre magazine."

Yail spoke into the telephone with Overman Garloc and

made his apologies, which Garloc received with formal decorum. Yail put the telephone aside with relief.

Myron said: "As soon as the rugs are discharged, the warehousemen may start loading the cargo. With appropriate bills of lading, the *Glicca* will be ready for departure."

TEN

1

At the end of the day, close upon dusk, Schwatzendale
unshipped the flitter from its bay and flew the Mouse-
riders, along with Captain Maloof, Wingo, and Myron,
to the landing plat on the northern wall of the Trevanian.

The group entered the great hall. The Mouse-riders went to
the dressing rooms to prepare for the first scene while the crew
of the *Glicca* located the parlor recommended by Overman
Skame, where they found seats with an unobstructed view of
the stage.

The hall began to fill with early arrivals hoping to secure favorite seats. Some had stopped at the stalls which lined the main
corridor for bags of delicacies: fried clams, sweet sausages,
tripe-sticks and the like, to fortify them during the performance. Others had made purchases of another sort; dead fish,
packets of carrion, rotting fruit, and buckets of slime and ordure, which they would use to rebuke an inept performer. A
warehouse under the theater maintained an inventory of such
commodities, in volume.

Time passed. The lights flickered and dimmed; from high

speakers issued a music of brass horns, gongs, and drums, in march-time cadence. A heavy gong sounded three clangorous tones, and the music ended.

A voice spoke, filling the hall. "The Trevanian tonight presents a program of unusual excellence! First, the Silurians undertake a remarkable exercise, which they call 'Sinuosities', and which you will call 'incredible'!"

From the audience came a spatter of applause.

The voice continued: "Then, Pooder Boy explains how he copes with his conniving mother. Po-po's wits are taxed to the utmost. Is his conduct proper?"

From the audience came enthusiastic applause.

"Next we present an off-world troupe of wide reputation. Master Moncrief and the Mouse-riders will bring us three sequences from their vast repertory!"

The applause was perfunctory, and punctuated by a few dispirited yelps.

The announcer went on to list the remaining events, then added: "Owing to administrative technicalities, the Futin Putos will not appear on tonight's program, nor at any time in the near future."

A chorus of hoots and hisses greeted the announcement.

The voice continued, unheeding: "And now, the Silurians, and their astonishing 'Sinuosities'!"

The curtains drew aside, revealing a scaffold constructed of a dozen poles eight feet high, standing six feet apart in a double row and joined at the tops by bars and cross-bars.

From the left side of the stage, six round gray bundles rolled out on the stage, each halting beside a pole. Each of the bundles unrolled, to become a long shape sheathed head to foot in gray fabric. At some signal, imperceptible to the audience, the six shapes reached for the poles and slid up to the cross-bars. They formed themselves into a pattern, which persisted for ten heartbeats, then broke apart, and so the first phase of the 'Sinuosities' began.

The gray shapes moved back and forth, over and under, veering and twisting, creating patterns past comprehension, returning finally to the original stasis. They held for a time; then they separated, and the second phase began. Now they moved at a ponderous tempo, with fateful decision, as if imparting an awesome secret; then quietly the shapes returned again to stasis.

For twenty seconds the shapes remained still; then they broke into the third phase. Now the permutations were deliberate, and baffling to the onlookers; sometimes only four undulated across the bars, sometimes there seemed to be eight. Over time the patterns evolved and collapsed through unlikely resolutions, conveying emotions without name. Finally, the shapes quietly slid down the poles and rolled off the stage, and the curtains closed.

For a time the audience sat blinking, then gradually rendered a tentative applause, as if not sure what they might be applauding.

The lights brightened, permitting the audience to recover their aplomb. Time was allowed for those wishing refreshment to visit the stalls; then the lights once more were extinguished.

From the high speakers came the announcer's voice. "The Silurians are gone, leaving us with our eyes pointed different directions. But no matter, somewhere nearby is Po-po the Pooder Boy, who always has his tragic woe, and an occasional triumph— as when he was asked to bring a gift of pooders to his dying grandfather! More often, his tales are tragic. Pooder is near at hand—listen!"

The audience went silent, straining for the first inkling of Po-po the Pooder Boy. An area of soft illumination remained at the center of the stage. Something appeared through the crack where the curtains came together—a nubbin so small that it escaped notice. The object thrust farther out over the stage, and now a faint rasping noise, like a rat gnawing at wainscoting, could be heard growing louder: "Crunch, Crunch, Crunch!"

The audience at last identified the protruding object as a nose, and gasped in delighted recognition. The curtain twitched; through the gap peered a moony face, with pink cheeks, lank snuff-brown hair, and a snub button of a nose. Po-po was gnawing on something he held to his mouth; he swallowed the last morsel. Then, with a sly smirk for the audience, he drew back, and the curtain swung shut.

"Po-po! Po-po! Po-po!" cried the audience, stamping their feet. Someone shouted: "Pooders by the score! Come for your pooders!"

The curtain parted, and out upon the stage capered Po-po, wearing a loose brown blouse and russet pantaloons flaring below the knees. He was notably plump and an inch or two shorter than ordinary. A saucy red cap constrained his hair; his eyes were round and set wide of his nose. For a moment he performed an odd little jig, then he halted, and began to chant in a reedy sing-song voice.

"Oh, I am the Pooder Boy! I eat them where I find them. They try to rob me of my precious pooders, but I sniff them out and have a feast! My pooders were in a pot, but when I lifted the lid, a rat looked up, the last of my pooders in his whiskers; my mother thought to make her feast, but I took the pooders and put the boiled rat on her plate! I ate my private dinner."

Po-po took a small pooder from his pocket and tossed it high into the air, then ran below and caught it in his mouth.

"Yesterday a black dog committed an offense; he stole my choice pooder! I tracked him through the bushes, then seized my cudgel and beat him with proper zest. At this time, another black dog walked past, holding my choice pooder in his jaws! I had been beating the wrong dog! No matter, the mistake was soon mended, and once more I owned my pooder!" Po-po performed a few steps of his eccentric jig.

"Oh, I am the Pooder Boy; I spy them out; I sniff them down from their aroma; I steal them from my avaricious mother! I spank the baby and take his pooder! Oh, I am the Pooder Boy!"

Po-po continued the saga of his woes and triumphs, singing praises of the sublime tuber, interspersing his chant with capers and jigs. He attempted a somersault, which he failed to execute; for a time, he struggled with his broad bottom in the air, pooders tumbling from his pockets. At last he completed the revolution and began a frantic search for the truant pooders. With pooders retrieved, and to full applause, he disappeared through the curtains.

The applause continued; Po-po returned to the stage and cut a caper, eliciting whistling, stamping, and howling approval, then once again was gone.

The lights came on, permitting patronage of the stalls.

The hall returned to darkness. From the high speakers came

the announcer's voice: "Po-po has left us for a time; he is anxious for his supper, which I suspect will be a fine dish of pooders—possibly furnished by his mother. No doubt he will return before too long with the latest news. But at this moment, Master Moncrief and the remarkable Mouse-riders are on hand; they bring us a program of three exotic adventures, in a wonderful land of magic and beauty! I now introduce Master Moncrief, for your approval!"

After Po-po's homely foolishness, the audience had no ready welcome for off-world interlopers and accorded the introduction only minimal enthusiasm.

Moncrief stepped out upon the stage, and his suave appearance did nothing to excite the sympathy of the audience. He wore an elegant suit of black velvet and a gray cape embroidered at the hem with a tracery of hermetic signs. Several whinnies and yelps greeted him as he smilingly surveyed the audience.

Still smiling, Moncrief inclined his head to left and right, by way of a polite salute. Then he spoke, his amplified voice sounding from the high speakers.

"Denizens of the city Cax, with its noble heights and hinterlands! I have little to tell you, except that it is a privilege to play the Trevanian—surely one of the premier theaters of the Gaean Reach! I suggest that you are about to discover a unique experience, which is to say, a presentation by the remarkable Mouse-riders! Nothing more! I will detain you no longer!" Moncrief performed a stately salute and left the stage.

The audience, a trifle mollified, gave a spatter of applause, then sat back to judge the marvels at which Moncrief had hinted.

The curtains parted to reveal a tropical jungle, with a range of purple mountains created by holographic projection looming across the background.

The sequence was played out to its macabre last moments, and the curtains closed upon the stage. The audience sat silent for a space, evidently uncertain as to how they felt about so strange a production, but finally reacted with cautious applause.

The curtains parted again, now upon an arcadian landscape. The sequence started with dancing nymphs in short white kirtles and developed along its fateful progression to the final pathos, the statue submerged in the reeds.

The curtains closed upon the desolate meadow. The applause was moderate, as if the audience were puzzled as to what should be the proper response to these unusual sequences. Once again, Moncrief stepped out on the stage in front of the curtains. He held up his hands, as if graciously calming tumultuous applause.

"We have presented two sequences for your apperception; I am pleased to find such keen awareness of our creative purposes. 'Art' is the transmission of emotion through the use of mutually recognizable symbols—clearly the Blenks of Cax are strongly receptive to the same impulses which propel our esthetic purposes!

"In appreciation of this receptivity, instead of a third sequence, which might come as an anticlimax, we will now produce what amounts to a coda to our first two pieces—by which we can best express our truest sentiments toward the Blenks and the fascinating Blenk civilization! We have visited many worlds; we have observed many distinctive cultures, but none has made quite the impression as has the culture of the Blenks!

"In sum, we are anxious to express our gratitude for your hospitality and your generous appreciation of our program. Our hope is to surprise and delight you—so now, we will finish our performance in a way you will long remember!"

Moncrief turned to look off-stage and made a signal. The entire Mouse-rider troupe appeared, now wearing ordinary clothes. "Aha!" cried Moncrief. "Here is our full complement." He spoke to the troupe. "You may take your posts, with dispatch and precision."

The six members of the troupe jumped down upon the shelf which bordered the stage. At intervals along the shelf were six pairs of massive shapes concealed under tarpaulins.

"Now then," said Moncrief. "Assume your positions." The three girls and the two Klutes each went to stand behind one of the shrouded shapes, while Moncrief stepped down to post himself behind the remaining brace of objects.

"Attention! I will count. You must act with full precision. Now, ready: One!"

All bent forward and pulled the tarpaulins loose, and dropped them to the floor. Revealed were twelve massive howitzers, their orifices covered with tinsel and rosettes of pink ribbons.

"Two!" called Moncrief. All put their hands to red buttons, left and right.

"Three!"

Twelve buttons were touched, creating twelve horrendous blasts of sound, and a great volume of stuffs spewed out over the audience. But instead of the sweetmeats, trinkets, fruit jellies, and perfumed confetti which Moncrief had installed, the audience was pelted with dead fish, ordure, shredded intestines, decaying fruit, and a dozen other stuffs. Some of the material ranged up into the second balcony, causing the Hummers to call out in surprise; only the Shimerati escaped outrage, and many congratulated themselves upon being present this remarkable evening.

For a brief period, a peculiar silence held the hall. Then a slow rumble of infinite menace arose, swelling into a wild reckless roar. The audience began to move toward the stage.

Moncrief reacted instantly. "Up!" he cried to the troupe. "Up, and out!"

The troupe needed no instruction. They jumped up from the shelf and ran to the off-stage parlor, with Moncrief close behind. Already the first wave of maddened Blenks was clambering up the shelf. In the wings at the far end of the stage, Moncrief saw several Futin Putos punching their fists into the air, showing white teeth in glee. "The revenge of the Futin Putos is pitiless," Moncrief told himself.

The troupe, Moncrief, and the crew of the *Glicca* ran out upon the plat and flung themselves aboard the flitter. Schwatzendale took the craft aloft just as the Blenks came racing out to crowd upon the landing, staring and shouting in thwarted passion after the departing craft.

Back at the spaceport, Schwatzendale and Myron hoisted the flitter into its bay, then boarded the ship, which promptly raised from the field.

Cax dwindled below. Up through the overcast rose the *Glicca*, then slanted away into the sky, leaving Blenkinsop behind.

ELEVEN

1

Departing Blenkinsop, the *Glicca* set off along an itinerary which after traversing remote regions of the Reach would eventually bring it back to Coro-coro on Fluter.

As time passed, shipboard routines were gradually resumed, but with differences. Moncrief had become morose; owing to his haste in taking leave of the Trevanian, he had neglected to collect his fee—a lapse which galled him to the quick. He spent hours planning reprisal against the Trevanian bursars, meanwhile neglecting his work with the Mouse-riders.

The Klutes had become more surly than ever and sat hunched in a corner of the saloon, glowering and muttering to each other. The girls had been altered in a more subtle fashion. The final moments at the Trevanian had intimidated them; never before had they been awed by events, and they had lost something of their careless innocence.

The first port of call was Falziel on the world Mirsten. The single habitable continent was dominated by a central mountain massif, with the lands along the littoral overgrown by forests where off-world species grew on equal terms with indigenous varieties. The population diligently exploited the resources of the forests, exporting precious wood to Cax and elsewhere.

At Falziel were the offices of the Institute; originally the Dendrological Institute, now the governing organization which exercised both executive and judicial authority over all of Mirsten.

Excerpt from *Handbook to the Planets:* Falziel

The traveler may wander far and wide across the Reach, but never will he find a city comparable in sheer bravura to Falziel.

The component structures occupy a site less than a mile on a side. The boundaries are strict, there are no annexes or subordinate communities; the city is an organic unit. The magnificent structures occupy sites along the avenues, some reaching seven stories high, others less. All are built to exactly the same specifications, differing only in size, and all show the same facade, which through some magic of proportion achieves an indefinable elegance. Each is surmounted by a dome of glossy red-brown mahogany, with a slender finial rising from the apex.

The inhabitants of Mirsten are a practical folk, but with a paradoxical dread of ghosts and other unnatural beings to be found in dark lonely places. Beliefs are most common in remote mountain villages, where on dark stormy nights the folk huddle around their firesides and impart the eerie lore to their fascinated children.

In due course, the *Glicca* descended upon the Falziel spaceport. The slanting light of late afternoon exhibited the fabulous city, with its hundreds of burnished mahogany domes, to dramatic advantage.

Immediately after arrival, Maloof and Myron crossed to the administration building to arrange for discharge of cargo. They found an office with a sign reading:

PORT DIRECTOR
ARMAN ROUFT
ENTER

The two pushed open the door and stepped into an office panelled in pale brown wood. Behind a counter stood a middle-aged man of moderate stature, inclined to a modest portliness which indicated a penchant for easy living. His face was round and cheerful, under a ruff of thick white hair. As Maloof and Myron approached, he put aside the earthenware demijohn which he had been inspecting, and spoke with a jovial lilt: "Gentlemen, if you are looking for the Port Director, you have found him. I am Arman Rouft, at your service."

Maloof introduced himself and Myron. "We are officers of the *Glicca*, which has just arrived, as you no doubt have noticed. We carry cargo for Falziel, which was put aboard at Cax. We are ready to discharge this cargo at your convenience."

"The cargo must wait for tomorrow, since the warehousemen have gone for the day."

"Quite all right," said Maloof. "We will have the opportunity to explore your remarkable city."

Rouft chuckled and shook his head. "If you are like the typical spacemen on the loose in a strange city, you may be disappointed. There are no resorts, nor any social parlors, where folk revel without restraint. We are, on the whole, a staid people."

Maloof laughed incredulously. "It was not a staid people who built this audacious city!"

"The notions do not intermesh," said Rouft. "It is probably this very trait which allowed Falziel its existence." He looked from Maloof to Myron. "You are puzzled?"

Maloof acknowledged as much. "Perhaps you will explain this paradox."

"Certainly. The tale is not overlong, but talking is dry work; luckily, a remedy is at hand."

He placed three goblets on the counter and, lifting the demijohn, poured tots of a tawny liquor into each. He slid two of the goblets across the counter to Maloof and Myron. "This is our prime plum brandy. Neophytes are warned to treat it with respect!"

Maloof and Myron took up their goblets and saw that they were carved with grace and finesse from cylinders of dense black wood.

Rouft raised his goblet and intoned a toast: "To tall trees, and fruitful women." He tossed the contents of the goblet down his throat, and swallowed at a gulp.

Maloof and Myron tested the liquor more cautiously, finding it heady, volatile, and intense. In the end, they followed the example set by Rouft and threw the tot against the back of their throats, where it exploded into pungent vapor.

Rouft asked solicitously: "Are you ready for a second tot? A man can hop only so far on one leg."

"Not just yet," said Maloof in a thick voice. "Of course, I cannot speak for Myron."

"Perhaps in a moment," said Myron.

Rouft, however, poured himself a second tot, and as before swallowed it at a gulp.

"Aha!" he said. "We can now proceed. I revert to a time six hundred years ago, when the old port city Skolpnes was destroyed in a great flood. Despite the flood, this was a time of prosperity, and the factors of the Dendrological Institute proposed to rebuild the city—but in a way to best represent the commercial consequence of Mirsten.

"An architectural genius named Riyban Trill resided then on Mirsten. Trill had worked far and wide across the Reach, achieving a remarkable reputation for superlative creativity and technical excellence, and had settled on Mirsten to live in semi-retirement. From the first, the factors were resolved that Trill should be associated with the grand new project, though he was well past his first youth, and not in the best of health.

"A formal proposal was put to Trill soliciting his creative talents. Trill considered the proposal for a week, then responded with a document specifying the conditions under which he would accept the commission. In effect, he required total control over every phase of the project, without the possibility of interference of any sort. He allowed the factors only two options: they could either accept or reject his requirements. Flexibility or compromise was not offered.

"Grudgingly, the factors accepted Trill's conditions. The contract was signed and embossed with the seal of the Dendrological Institute, and Trill immediately went to work. The site was surveyed, a grid of avenues delineated, and a pilot building erected on a site beside the central plaza. When completed, the structure stood seven stories high; it was built completely of rich, red-brown mahogany, and was surmounted by a dome of ravishing rotundity. Ultimately the building would house the offices of the Dendrological Institute.

"The building met with universal approval; even Trill's detractors were silenced. But at this precise moment, with Trill's career at its zenith, his health deserted him; he suffered a debilitating stroke which enfeebled him, curtailing most of his physical functions.

"Trill realized that he could not complete the city as he had planned, but at almost the same instant he arrived at a scheme which obviated all his difficulties; with one stroke of the pen, he ordained that every building of the city should be constructed to the same specification as the pilot building, varying only in size.

"His boldness astonished everyone. From the factors came a storm of protest—along with the opinion that, since Trill's ploy was clearly the irresponsible whim of a madman, it must be invalidated forthwith. But the idea stimulated unease in the public. I mentioned that we are a staid race; the trait includes an ingrained regard for individual responsibility, and the sanctity of a formal contract. Eventually, the factors' suggestion that Trill's contract be violated aroused such outrage that the factors abandoned their plan.

"And so the new city came into being, and almost immediately was considered a work of ultimate genius. Trill was honored as never before; he was granted a patent of nobility and made a full Fellow of the Institute, which awarded him a gold coruscation to wear on his shoulder.

"So there you have it: Falziel, a tribute both to Trill's reckless creativity, and the steadfast faith of the population." Rouft indicated the demijohn. "Shall we try another dram or two, to memorialize the occasion?"

Maloof looked toward Myron, who gave a fatalistic shrug. "Perhaps, then, just a taste."

Rouft tilted the demijohn with a loose wrist, replenishing the goblets to their former level, then proposed another toast: "To tall women, and fruitful trees!"

The goblets were dealt with as before; the ardent fluid was consumed in appropriate style.

When Maloof found his voice, he asked, somewhat haltingly:

"Can you recommend a tavern where we can sample the local ale?"

"Easily. The 'Court of King Gambrinus' instantly comes to mind; it is a place where I myself am a frequent visitor. The Darkling Stout is somewhat heavy for my taste, but the Bitter Silurian is beyond reproach. The tavern is convenient to hand; proceed along yonder boulevard to the first intersection, then turn left. Fifty yards ahead you will notice an arched portico supporting an effigy representing the demigod Atlas, carrying the globe of Old Earth on his shoulders. This effigy, by custom, marks every tavern of Falziel."

"Interesting!" said Maloof. "The information might be invaluable, if we had more time to explore the town."

Rouft sighed. "I often wish that I could drink in two taverns at the same instant. It would save much wasted energy, wandering to and fro."

Myron muttered, half to himself: "If anyone were capable of such a feat, it would be our engineer, Fay Schwatzendale."

Shortly after sunset, Captain Maloof and his crew sauntered forth from the spaceport; Moncrief and the Mouse-riders elected to remain aboard the *Glicca*. The men proceeded up the boulevard, turned at the intersection, and presently came upon the Court of King Gambrinus. Entering the tavern, the four men found themselves in a long, narrow, dimly lit chamber with a vaulted ceiling, and walls panelled with polished planks of wood the color of dark honey. Tables were scattered along the length of the chamber, with a bar flanking the wall to the right.

Business was slack. At a table far to the rear, a pair of old men sat hunched over a chessboard, with tankards at their elbows. On the wall behind them an artist of long ago had painted King Gambrinus, sitting in state on a majestic golden throne; in one hand he held a scepter, in the other a tankard of foaming brew. His expression as he surveyed the chamber was at once stern, yet benign.

Behind the bar stood a fat bartender, wearing a white smock and small white cap. He took note of the newcomers, displaying minimal interest, and spoke in a ripe, rolling baritone. "Good evening, gentlemen; you come at a late hour. Still, we will take pains to accommodate your thirst." He flourished his hand toward the tables. "You may sit where you notice your correct hermetic sign. Or if you prefer, I can advise you."

"That might be wise," said Maloof. "The signs are some-what arcane."

"True," said the bartender. He reflected a moment, then pointed. "Yonder is a congenial table. It is dependable and has supported thousands of tankards with only rare spillage. It seems to induce kindness and liberality, even among strangers. There has never been a glottal congestion at this table, nor has anyone ever failed to pay his score."

The four seated themselves at the recommended table. The bartender asked: "What can I serve you?"

"Describe our choices," said Maloof.

"Very well. Our beers and ales are excellent. We serve Dark-ling Stout, Dankwel's Special, Wyvern, Old Spiteful, Pale Gothic, and Bitter Silurian Ale."

Maloof opted for the Bitter Silurian Ale, as did his companions.

The ale was served in tankards turned from billets of a dense dark wood. Maloof studied his tankard at length, turning it this way and that. He asked the bartender: "Does this black wood have a name?"

"Of course! It is swamp-gnarl, a tree which grows half-submerged in the swamp, never more than nine feet tall and four feet wide. The tree cannot be cut in place and must be pulled up entire by a floating derrick. The trunk is trimmed, cut into baulks, and seasoned for five years; then it is sliced into billets, and turned in a special lathe to become unfinished vessels known as 'blanks.' These are boiled in a special oil for three days, then shaped, carved, and finished by hand. Now they are tankards, no two alike! They cannot be broken, and last forever."

Maloof held up the heavy black tankard. "It has an extraor-dinary appeal, and seems to complement the ale. Are they avail-able for purchase, and if so, where?"

The bartender looked at the clock upon the wall behind him, then said: "My information is both good and bad." He pointed through the window, toward a shop on the opposite side of the street with a green starburst over the door. "Yonder shop is di-rected by a true galardinet named Dame Florice. She sells cu-rios, objects of vertu, and miscellaneous oddments to tourists, spacemen, and local folk alike, making no distinction so long as they can pay. She keeps an adequate supply of tankards, which she sells at reasonable prices. That is the good news. In five minutes, she turns off the lights and closes her shop with inexorable determination—that is the bad news."

Maloof stared up at the clock. "Five minutes?"

"Ten seconds less. You have time to finish your ale, pay the score, and dash across the street, with about two minutes and thirty seconds remaining to make your purchases—if Dame Florice sympathizes with your plight. I myself close at the same instant."

The four men drained their tankards. Between gulps, Myron gestured toward the chess players, one of whom had just made a move.

"What of them?"

The bartender shrugged. "They will continue their game by candle-light, and I shall find them here in the morning."

Maloof paid the score and, departing the Court of King Gambrinus, the four men hastened across the street to the shop under the green starburst.

Dame Florice was a tall woman with a long bony nose; she eyed the last-minute customers with disfavor. "You are overly casual; the shop is about to close. Business is done for the day."

"Not quite," declared Maloof. "There is time for you to sell me six swamp-gnarl tankards."

Myron added, "While you are serving Captain Maloof, it will save time if you will bring me six tankards, as well."

Dame Florice spoke sharply: "By the time I bring your orders from the stock-room, it will be time to turn out the lights. Do you propose to pay in the dark?"

"It might be more expedient if you would extend your business hours by another minute, or perhaps a minute and a half," Maloof suggested. "But you must do as you think best."

Dame Florice turned on her heel and strode off to her stock-room.

The four men took advantage of the delay to look about the shop. Myron came upon a small effigy of Atlas on his knees, supporting Old Earth on his shoulders. The figure was about six inches tall and was carved from a dense white wood. Ever the romantic, Myron was charmed; here was an amusing souvenir of Falziel and its taverns. He added the item to his purchases. A moment later, he discovered a rack from which hung a number of delicate chains about five feet long. Looking closely, Myron saw that the chains were carved with exquisite nicety from long wands of pale wood.

By this time Dame Florice had returned from the stock-room with the tankards, and had reconciled herself to the unprecedented experience of working after the close of regulation business hours. In response to Myron's questions, she explained that the chains were carved by a coterie of old women in an isolated mountain village, and that these women were held to be witches by local folk.

"Sheer nonsense, of course," she added with a frosty smile. "The chains are carved from long shoots of mountain hazel, and the work is uncannily precise, but witchery? Bah—rank superstition!"

Myron noted that despite her words, Dame Florice made a surreptitious sign with the fingers of her left hand. He selected two of the chains, to be used as necklaces to delight a certain Tibbet at Duvray on Alcydon.

The spacemen settled their accounts and, seven minutes after the ordinary closing hour, returned to the spaceport.

The next morning, warehousemen appeared and the cargo was off-loaded.

At noon the *Glicca* lifted from the spaceport; the burnished mahogany domes dwindled below, and the *Glicca* slanted away toward the next port of call.

2

After Falziel, the next two stops were Chancelade on Avente, then Organon on Archimbal.

Despite many similarities, the populations of the two worlds differed significantly in social philosophy. The folk of Avente were tolerant, sensitive to aesthetic subtlety, and intensely aware of themselves as individuals; the people of Archimbal, while of equivalent culture, were gregarious and most comfortable when working in communal groups, guided by precepts of progressivity and comprehensive altruism.

Even before the cargo had been fully discharged, the Port

Director of Chancelade offered Myron a parcel of onward
cargo on terms so advantageous that Myron immediately agreed
to the transaction, though there would be a delay of three or
four days before the cargo could be made ready. The layover
was welcomed by everyone aboard the *Glicca*, since Chancelade
was a pleasant city of many charms; picturesque, romantic, and
casually elegant.

The city occupied a parkland at the confluence of three
rivers, which were joined by a dozen lazy canals. Along the banks
of both rivers and canals were shops, salons, cafes, restaurants,
conservatories, and music halls, rendezvous for masked harle-
quins, gamins, dryads, and nymphs, venues dedicated to the unexpected and the preposterous. East of the city rose massive
mountains with crags and gorges, upland lakes and forests, and
dozens of wilderness resorts, some rustic, others refined and luxurious.

Immediately upon arrival, the crew went off to explore the
city and test its potentialities. Moncrief went off to solicit employment for the Mouse-riders.

Time passed quickly. Early on the day of departure, the
cargo arrived at the spaceport and was loaded aboard the *Glicca*.
The crew opted for a final afternoon and evening out, visiting
their favorite haunts about the city.

During the afternoon, with the crew absent, the Mouse-
riders boarded the ship, collected their belongings, and departed,
never so much as looking back. When the crew returned to the
Glicca, Maloof discovered a note on the galley table along with a
sum of money.

Maloof read the letter aloud: " 'To the esteemed Captain
Maloof and others of the crew: by a happy circumstance, we
have been offered long-term employment among the mountain
resorts. Contracts are lucrative, and we must of necessity accept.
Our best wishes to everyone aboard the *Glicca*; you will not soon
be forgotten. I enclose funds sufficient to settle our outstanding
accounts. With best respect: Marcel Moncrief and the Mouse-
riders.' "

Maloof tossed the note down upon the galley table. "So.
They are gone." He stared down at the note. "All taken with all,
their style of departure is commendable, or so it seems to me."

Wingo spoke, his expression bleak. "The ship will seem very quiet without them."

Schwatzendale leaned back in his chair and stared up at the ceiling. "For a fact, their going was opportune, for everyone. The atmosphere aboard had gone stale; Moncrief was a derelict, his magic fading; the Klutes were like lumps of rancid meat in the shadows. And the girls were feckless creatures from a lost land—they danced their own dances and sang their own songs; they knew nothing of responsibility and distracted us all. They leave behind only bittersweet memories."

Smiling wanly, Maloof said: "That is a moving testimonial."

"It is more like an epitaph," growled Wingo.

"They leave a gap," Myron agreed. "Still, life will be simpler without them."

"Bah!" said Wingo emphatically. "What good is simplicity? Even their foolishness was an event. With the Mouse-riders, anything was possible."

Myron nodded somberly. "Including the possibility that they might never leave the *Glicca*, but remain aboard forever."

Maloof winced. "The idea is alarming."

Myron apologized, and the conversation came to an end.

Early the next morning, the *Glicca* departed Chancelade, and set off toward Archimbal. The ship seemed unnaturally quiet; the corner of the saloon where the Klutes had brooded and muttered seemed curiously naked. Wingo abruptly halted his production of novel pastries. But as time passed, memories of the Mouse-riders became less vivid, and the new reality gradually submerged the old.

3

The *Glicca* arrived at the Organon spaceport halfway through the local morning. Cargo was expeditiously discharged, and the crew set off to explore the city. If, along the way, they chanced to discover a hospitable tavern where they could test the quality of the beer, so much the better.

An omnibus conveyed the four men along a scenic boulevard to the central plaza: an immaculate area paved with slabs of polished granite. At the center, fountains played around the base of a heroic statue celebrating the legendary locator Hans van der Veeke, who had first set foot upon the world Archimbal. He was depicted wearing a black frock coat and a flat black hat; his pose was portentous, with one great arm raised on high, saluting generations of the future. Ranked around the periphery of the plaza were narrow-fronted buildings of a spare, almost gaunt architecture, generally five or six stories high. At the ground level, shops of understated elegance relieved the austerity of the structures in which they were housed. Most sold goods of discreet luxury. There were also restaurants in evidence, as well as a number of agencies and salons.

Upon alighting from the omnibus, the four off-worlders paused to take stock of their surroundings. Inhabitants of the city strolled about the plaza. Men and women alike wore garments of formal cut and excellent quality, as if it were not reputable to appear in public wearing clothes which might not be considered genteel. As they passed, they gave the spacemen quick side-glances, then immediately looked away to avoid any imputation of undignified curiosity.

The four men from the *Glicca* turned their attention to shops around the square, noting restaurants and cafes, but nowhere any establishment suggesting the presence of a tavern. Myron theorized that such premises might be relegated to the back streets, or even a separate district of the city; Wingo agreed that the theory was as plausible as any, and that the mystery in good time would be resolved.

The four men set off around the plaza and soon came to an establishment, apparently a cafe, identified by an ornamental sign as 'The Blue Urn'. Windows under three wide arches afforded a view of persons sitting at tables, taking refreshment of various sorts. At a table nearby, four middle-aged gentlemen of obvious status drank from glass tankards containing amber liquid, under a notable collar of white foam. With one accord the four spacemen entered the Blue Urn and seated themselves at a vacant table.

A tall, gray-haired waiter of stately demeanor, wearing formal garments of impeccable cut, approached the table. He bowed slightly, as if to acknowledge their status as off-worlders, thereby entitled to sympathetic understanding. He spoke in a nicely modulated voice: "Gentlemen, may I enquire your wishes?"

"You may indeed," said Maloof. "We have worked up a thirst—you may bring us your premium bitter ale, in large tankards."

The waiter smilingly shook his head. "We offer no libation of this sort, sir."

"Oh?" demanded Maloof. "What are the gentlemen yonder drinking, with such gusto?"

The waiter politely turned to look. "Of course! They are enjoying our premium Mark Twelve Special, which for a fact is my own favorite."

"In that case," said Maloof, "you may bring me a tankard of the Mark Twelve Special."

The others gave the same instruction, and the waiter departed to fill the orders. He presently returned with four tankards, deftly served them around the table, then withdrew.

Maloof took up his tankard. "For want of a better toast, I salute the ten thousand generations of brewmasters who, through their unflagging genius, have in effect made this moment possible!"

"A noble toast," cried Wingo. "Allow me to add an epilogue. At the last moments of the universe, with eternal darkness converging from all sides, surely someone will arise and cry out: 'Hold back the end for a final moment, while I pay tribute to the gallant brewmasters who have provided us a pathway of golden glory down the fading corridors of time!' And then, is it not possible that a bright gap will appear in the dark, through which the brewmasters are allowed to proceed, to build a finer universe?"

"It is as reasonable as any other conjecture," said Schwatzendale. "But now." The four saluted each other, tilted their tankards, and drank deep draughts.

At this instant Maloof felt that bewildering shock of surprise which would never vanish from his memory. He slowly raised his head and stared at the waiter, who came inquiringly forward. "Sir?"

In a low, passionless voice, Maloof asked: "What is this liquid you have served us, when we called for beer?"

The waiter spoke feelingly: "Sirs, you were served our best barley-water!"

"Barley-water?" cried Maloof huskily.

"Exactly so. I did you a kindness! Alcohol is highly toxic; its use is interdicted on Archimbal."

Schwatzendale asked in a hushed voice: "There is neither beer nor ale to be had in Organon?"

"None at all."

The spacemen glumly paid the score and returned to the spaceport. An hour later the *Glicca* departed Organon and set off for the next port of call.

4

The *Glicca* continued along its eccentric course, finally returning to Coro-coro on Fluter.

Immediately upon arrival, the pilgrims converged upon the *Glicca*. Maloof met with Perrumpter Kalash and Cooner, who had become coadjucator; he assured them that the previous commitments remained valid and that the next port of call would be Impy's Landing. Kalash and Cooner expressed satisfaction, then, citing their religious affiliation, argued for a discount from the fares previously quoted. Maloof explained that religion was known to be prevalent on certain over-populated worlds, but was conspicuously absent in space; for this reason, among others, no discounts would be allowed. Grumbling and disgruntled, the pilgrims boarded the *Glicca*, along with their chests of sanctified soil. And so the *Glicca* departed Coro-coro and set off for Impy's Landing on Kyril.

During the voyage Wingo became acquainted with a certain Efraim Cuireg, a peripatetic savant associated with the Institute of Transcendental Metaphysics, at Bantry's Bog on the world Montroy. Cuireg was a gentleman of obvious distinction. His stature was moderate, or a trifle less; his physique was trim, and his habits were fastidious. Under a cap of white hair Cuireg's features were crisp, his gaze cool, his expression austere and somewhat ironic; he carried himself with the erect posture of a patrician.

Cuireg travelled alone, and kept himself aloof from the pilgrims. The pilgrims, in turn, thought him condescending and supercilious. Nevertheless, the Perrumpter tried to include him

into the company, and invited him to join the morning colloquies; but Cuireg declined participation. Cooner had evolved
an abstruse theory postulating an infinite regression of ever
more complex godheads, each subservient to the entity looming
behind, with the Gaean race abjectly at the forefront; he de-
ployed his theory before Cuireg, only to encounter a stare so
blank and incurious that the confident smile froze on his plump
pink cheeks. Cooner recalled urgent business elsewhere.

Wingo found Cuireg's presence an enigma, which gnawed at
his curiosity. One day he invited Cuireg to a mid-afternoon collation of tea, scones, and fancy pastries. Cuireg, a dedicated epicure, readily accepted the invitation and appeared precisely
upon the appointed hour. He surveyed the delicacies gracing the
table with approval, and seated himself at Wingo's direction.

For a time the conversation was general, then at an appropriate moment Wingo put a casual question. "In all candor, I cannot
understand why a scholar of your credentials should be travelling
to Kyril, like one of the pilgrims, and presumably planning to
join the march around the continent. Can you explain?"

"Naturally," said Cuireg with a cool smile. "However, I do
not propose to do so, since you would surely find the ideas abstract, and probably beyond your comprehension."

Wingo raised his eyebrows, somewhat taken aback. A singular
remark, indeed, and not one calculated to elevate his self-esteem.
He sought for a suitable response, and finally said: "Naturally,
you have a right to your assumptions, although from my point of
view they are far too pessimistic."

Cuireg showed little interest in Wingo's opinion. "Indeed?"
He selected a lemon tart from the platter and ingested half of
it with a quick snap of small white teeth. "Ah well, no great
matter."

"Except that, as we sit here, apparently at our ease, communication has been disrupted."

"Oh?" Cuireg's attention was caught. "You have left me
behind."

"Just so!" said Wingo. "If folk want to exchange information,
clarity is essential. If they want to confuse each other, various
methods exist. They can use glossolalia, or a primitive language
of clicks and grunts, or, as a last resort, the esoteric jargon of the
Institute."

Cuireg was only mildly interested. "A pungent analysis. To what is it relevant?"

Wingo leaned back in his chair. "In regard to your visit to Kyril, you felt that your remarks would only confuse me. I suspect, however, that if you spoke in the ordinary Gaean idiom, using standard syntax, I should be able to capture the gist of your remarks."

Cuireg was sardonically amused. "Take care, Wingo! The epistemological jungle is dark and deep! There are pitfalls and strange byways, and monsters lurk in the shadows. An intrepid traveller such as yourself, however, should manage to discover at least the basic dogma, which is starkly simple, and germane to our discussion; it asserts that between individuals, exact communication is never possible." He inspected Wingo. "You doubt the proposition? You need only refer to the physical laws of uncertainty—ignoring, of course, the mischievous corollary which states that the laws themselves are laughably uncertain! The lemon tarts, incidentally, are excellent."

Wingo pondered a moment, then shrugged. "This is all very well, but it would seem that you do not concede the reality of 'Truth', at any level whatever."

" 'Truth'?" Cuireg made an indolent gesture. " 'Truth' is a refuge for weak minds—why concern yourself? It is a nonfunctional notion, like the square root of negative infinity or, if you prefer, a mare's nest. The good Baron Bodissey issued a definitive dictum: 'Truth is a barnacle on the arse of progress.' " He took the last lemon tart from the platter.

Wingo sighed and rose to his feet. He replenished the platter and resumed his place at the table. "I suggest that you try the rainberry creamcakes. The frosted eclairs are also quite good."

"Thank you," said Cuireg. "I shall do so at once. Is there still tea in the pot?"

Wingo refilled Cuireg's cup.

"Now," said Cuireg, "if you are still interested, I will tell you why I am travelling to Kyril."

"Just as you like," said Wingo, rather stiffly. "I do not care to intrude, even slightly, upon your privacy. My curiosity, such as it is, is only casual."

"In that case, I can satisfy this concern in five seconds or

less." Cuireg took a rainberry creamcake from the platter. "I
am visiting Kyril to verify the recollections of my first visit."

Wingo stared in surprise.

Cuireg went on pensively. "All this happened a long time ago,
during the romantic phase of my life. The visit to Kyril seemed a
gallant adventure, and so it was." His voice fell, and he seemed to
reflect. He said presently: "There are too many memories. They
come in a welter: images; voices, colors, faces, landscapes. Thousands of episodes; large tragedies, small triumphs." He watched
silently as Wingo refilled his teacup, then went on.

"Kyril is not a kindly world. The pilgrim's way leads across
arid wastes, dunes, bogs and moors, and rolling savannahs where
nothing grows but thorn trees and canker bush. The weather is
unpredictable; there are morning mists and afternoon thunder-
storms. At night three dim moons drift across the sky.

"There are occasional inns and shelters along the wayside,
where one may sit and watch the pilgrims pass by in never-ending
diversity: young and old, men and women, often children. Sometimes they sing as they march past; sometimes they chant mantras.
At times a madman rushes past, dancing and leaping, cursing the
sky. His cries fade into the distance, and all is as before.

"In the far west is the Holy Mountain, a dying volcano with
a crater at the summit where red-hot lava bubbles and seethes.
The way up the mountain is hard and steep; some of the pilgrims are forced to crawl to the top."

Wingo was perturbed to hear of such shocking hardships.
"What happens to these poor unfortunates?"

Cuireg shrugged, not over-interested in the topic. "They
drag themselves up to the rim, where they rest and mend themselves. Eventually they rejoin the others.

"The way around the lip of the crater is, in effect, the focus
of the pilgrimage. Halfway around, a look-out platform projects
over the void, providing a spectacular view of the crater and the
glowing magma below. Most of the pilgrims avoid the platform
for fear of vertigo. However, at times someone succumbs to an
attack of religious frenzy and runs out on the platform and
throws himself into space, plunging down to disappear into the
lava. Occasionally he seizes up his child—or someone else's
child, for that matter—and hurls it out into the void. Most often,

though, he is restrained by other pilgrims, and the child is dragged back to safety—often followed by the father, who has decided not to jump after all."

Wingo shook his head in wonder. "The pilgrimage is intense and dramatic beyond all expectations. I begin to understand the motive which urges you back to Kyril."

Cuireg, ignoring Wingo's comment, tested a frosted eclair. "In any case, the pilgrims finally return to Impy's Landing. They set off to the west, they return from the east; it is a moment of supreme exaltation! They laugh, they cry, they drop to their knees and kiss the ground; never have they known triumph so intense. The memory of this instant will be with them always."

"All this is clear, and dramatic," said Wingo. "To complete the pilgrimage is an act of personal vindication. But why do they come to Kyril in the first place?"

"There are as many reasons as there are pilgrims," said Cuireg. "Some want to appease their divinity; others want to mollify an ancestral ghost. Many are hermetics who want to mortify their flesh. Some hope to atone for forbidden acts; others want to evade an irascible spouse."

Wingo asked, half-facetiously: "And where on this list is your motive for undertaking the pilgrimage?"

Cuireg responded to the question without rancor. "There is no simple answer. Originally the pilgrimage was a challenge to my self-esteem, which I felt obliged to meet. Then, after three or four days along the way, my attitude insensibly began to change. The challenge lost its thrust, and faded from my mind. I found myself watching, and listening, and feeling with ever more intensity. I felt ever more aware of details and textures and nuances. One morning knowledge came to me in a burst of insight. I saw a black lump of rock thrusting up between bushes at the side of the road; I stopped short and said: 'Rock, I see you well enough, but you cannot see me. Why? Because I am sentient, but you are not! Why should this be? Simple enough! I am animate, and you are an inert lump.'"

"Remarkable," said Wingo. "There are inspirational elements here—although it seems rather pointless to taunt the rock."

"It did no great harm." Cuireg rose to his feet. "Thank you

for the pleasant occasion. The pastries were beyond reproach."
He nodded courteously, and left the galley.

Wingo remained at the table, drinking tea and brooding
upon what he had learned.

5

The voyage proceeded without untoward incident. The pilgrims occupied themselves with study, doctrinal discussions and
a few low-key games of Cagliostro, from which Schwatzendale
was excluded, his past successes still rankling among the defeated players. Cuireg remained as aloof as ever, avoiding the
morning colloquies and rebuffing all of Cooner's attempts to
engage him in sectarian discourse.

The crew of the *Glicca* performed their usual duties, although Wingo now spent much time thinking over what he had
learned of Kyril, and the march around the great continent. By
degrees he began to comprehend Cuireg's perception of the pilgrimage as a metaphor for an event of far larger significance. All
very well, thought Wingo, but what of the pilgrims themselves?
What compulsion induced them to undertake the hardships of
the great march? The motives which Cuireg had facetiously
suggested could not be taken seriously; what then? After deep
reflection, Wingo thought to comprehend the impulse which
prompted the pilgrims to undertake their great adventure—an
urge superficially like that which sent the lemmings of Old
Earth swarming out to sea. This, of course, was not the essential reason, thought Wingo; rather it was a real—if perhaps
subconscious—assertion of vitality, and a rather desperate test
of personal fortitude, physical and spiritual alike.

Wingo's preoccupation affected his ordinary conduct more
than he realized. His cheerful ebullience became muted; his lo-
quacity dwindled to absent-minded mutters. The change at-
tracted the attention of his shipmates, and finally Schwatzendale,
confronting him across the galley table, put an uncompromising
question. Wingo gave an evasive answer, but Schwatzendale persisted, and in the end Wingo reported his conversation with
Cuireg in full detail. He went on to say: "Despite his manner,
which is hardly engaging, he is a most complicated man: a savant

of high prestige, also an epicure, a cynic, and at the basis—almost incredibly—a romantic adventurer!"

"Peculiar!" said Schwatzendale. "He seems modest and retiring, with a rather sour disposition."

"That is an illusion," said Wingo. "He cultivates a manner of supercilious detachment to discourage excessive familiarity. The pose actually masks a keen perceptivity; when he chooses to speak, his views are most illuminating. I now understand the true nature of Kyril, and the conditions which the pilgrims encounter as they travel the great circuit. The march is not altogether sterile; there are surprises along the way—not always happy, but those who ultimately return to Impy's Landing find the triumph of their achievement an adequate requital for the hardships suffered along the way."

"Bah," growled Schwatzendale after a moment. "If this moment of relief is the only reward for so much toil, what is the point of the pilgrimage? It would seem a useless exercise, except for hermetics and flagellants."

"Not so," Wingo declared. "The pilgrimage has a subliminal purpose, which, admittedly, cannot easily be verbalized."

"I have no trouble," Schwatzendale stated. "It is an exercise in sheer futility, leading from nowhere to nowhere. It seems inexpressibly pointless."

Wingo managed a patient smile. "There are aspects to the pilgrimage which you do not understand! They are admittedly on a subliminal level, but still they are intensely important! The great march is a gauge by which a pilgrim can measure personal worth. When he returns to Impy's Landing from the east, he feels a personal vindication which must be close to exaltation!"

"Understandable," said Schwatzendale. "They are tired of walking."

Wingo, still smiling, shook his head. "Cuireg has already made the circuit. He has found imponderable aspects to the pilgrimage, which, in candor, I do not fully understand, but I am bound to take seriously."

"My dear fellow, you have been hypnotized," said Schwatzendale, rising to his feet. "I see that I must have a word with this redoubtable savant."

Wingo's smile became wry. "I wonder which of you will end up the more bewildered."

Schwatzendale said: "Despite his erudition, Cuireg still pulls on his trousers one leg at a time." He departed the galley, leaving Wingo first to sigh, then ponder.

Schwatzendale found the scholar in a relatively expansive mood. In amusement he described himself as not only a scholar, an epicure, and an adventurer, but also a creative financier who might undertake certain commercial developments at Impy's Landing. In response to Schwatzendale's questions, he provided information regarding the pilgrimage, some of which Schwatzendale found intriguing, some daunting, even macabre.

Time passed, and the voyage approached its termination. On the day that the cold white spark that was the star Rhys appeared ahead, Wingo entered the pilot-house, where Captain Maloof sat checking the entry on Kyril in *Handbook to the Planets*.

Wingo, distraught and half-desperate, came directly to the point. "Captain! After much turmoil, I have finally arrived at a decision!"

"Indeed," said Maloof, looking up and setting aside the *Handbook*. "In regard to what?"

Wingo came to stand before him. "Over the last few weeks I have taken stock of my life, and I find that it has arrived at a juncture. In one direction I continue as before, along an easy route. In the other direction there are challenges; the way is difficult and often bleak, but this route shows me to myself. After weighing both options, I have made my decision. At Impy's Landing I will resign my post aboard the *Glicca*; I will then set off to the west, like any other pilgrim. In the end I will return from the east, inflated with pure triumph much like lurulu!" Wingo held up a clenched pink fist as a peroration to his remarks. "That is the gist of it. You have heard what I came to tell you. Our friendship persists!"

"Naturally," said Maloof. "Perhaps more than ever! But a thought occurs to me. Perhaps you will lose more than you gain."

Wingo grimaced. "I know what I am losing. It is a fellowship which I cherish beyond words! My dearest wish would be that we dock the *Glicca* at Impy's Landing and all four of us march off into the west, to return at last from the east, where we would share our triumph together, in the happiest moment of our lives!"

Maloof spoke dryly: "I am sure that we would all be glad to get back." He sighed. "Even in a dream, such a fantasy would seem bizarre."

"You must open your mind!" declared Wingo. "With dedication, the vision becomes real, and the triumph lives with us forever!"

Maloof sighed again, and leaned back in his chair. "Let us call in Schwatzendale, and test his reaction to the scheme."

Wingo said dubiously: "Fay is often indecisive; we must remind him of his bent for gallant adventure."

"Ha hm," said Maloof. He spoke into a mesh.

A moment later Schwatzendale appeared. He glanced from one to the other. "What is required of me?"

"We need your counsel," said Maloof. "We are faced with an unprecedented situation. Wingo intends to leave the ship at Impy's Landing, and set off pilgrim-style on a circuit of the continent."

"Truly?" Schwatzendale turned Wingo a grave inspection.

"That is not the whole of it. He wants the entire crew to join the venture—so that, when we return to Impy's Landing from the east, we shall celebrate the triumph together. Am I right, Wingo?"

"You have stated the matter concisely," said Wingo. "I might add that the feat is guided by a set of subliminal archetypes, which will transfigure the rest of our lives with grandeur."

"It is a novel idea," Schwatzendale admitted. "Startling, preposterous, and innocent! It would never have occurred to me—especially after my conversation with Cuireg. Apparently there are negative aspects to the pilgrimage, which are never publicized. For instance, only a modest percentage of those starting out from Impy's Landing to the west ever return from the east; many abandon the venture after a day or two. The way is especially hard on folk with sensitive feet, because of sharp flints in the road."

Wingo stared down at his own delicate feet. "This makes for poor hearing," he told himself. "Still, it cannot be ignored."

Schwatzendale went on to discuss more of what he had learned from Cuireg. "Many old persons with little vitality set out from Impy's Landing and die along the way from disease, hunger, dysentery, and physical abuse. Nights are especially dangerous; thugs come to steal boots—they use cudgels to smash knees and ankles at so much as a whimper!"

"That is inhuman!" gasped Wingo. "One should only travel with trusted companions!"

"The plan is attractive, but not always practical. You must pay a large sum to join a group. They march at a quick-step, and you must keep pace, sore feet and all; otherwise you will be left behind. If you pay out all your money, you will not have enough to buy food from the roadside shelters—should you choose to do so. Squeamish persons avoid the pale pink stew at all costs, and forage on tubers and seeds. But the worst is still ahead. Where the way crosses the hills it is paved with flints which cut your feet into bloody lumps; what then?"

Wingo considered the unpleasant possibility. "I have no choice! I must continue on hands and knees until the road is better."

"All very well," said Schwatzendale, "but the road is still only a tumble of shards and flints, and in the end your knees are a clutter of broken bones; what now?"

Wingo spoke in a taut thin voice: "I have not thought that far ahead, but I suppose that if I must, I will turn about and skooch along on my backside. It will be slow and painful, but better than sitting alone in the wilderness, at night under the light of the three dim moons. It is not a happy prospect."

"Even where the way leaves the hills, another enemy awaits you. The thorn trees hang overhead and drop thorns into the way. As you skooch along, these thorns will be driven into your bottom, so that every thorn will require a halt, a search, and a withdrawal before the next gallant surge forward. I suppose that a person in this condition might complete the circuit in ten years, to gain what? Glory? Triumph? More likely, a sickening grief for the tribulations which he has suffered for nothing."

Wingo sighed. "It has become clear—starkly so!—that I am not the man to test my fortitude in this fashion. It is troubling, certainly, but I must alter my resolve, and gladly."

Maloof asked with gentle solicitude: "Then you are not leaving the *Glicca* after all?"

Wingo sighed again. "Definitely not. The pilgrimage no longer carries a romantic association."

"You have arrived at a wise decision," said Maloof. "Do you not agree, Fay?"

"Totally, and in every respect," said Schwatzendale.

TWELVE

1

In due course the *Glicca* arrived at Impy's Landing. The pilgrims disembarked with graceless haste, led by the ineffable Cooner; Cuireg followed more deliberately, ignoring the others as if they had been strangers, and took himself to the most pretentious hostelry of the town where, if his statements were to be credited, he would prepare to transact the business which had brought him to Kyril.

As soon as the chests of sanctified soil had been discharged from the cargo bay, the *Glicca* prepared to set off for Port Tanjee on the world Taubry. Myron noticed that Naharius lay not far from the direct route to Port Tanjee. Prompted by a surge of old emotion, he felt a strong impulse to visit Naharius; if nothing else, he wanted to learn what transformation the fabulous local therapies had worked upon his great-aunt, Dame Hester Lajoie.

Captain Maloof was also curious, and made no difficulty about altering the ship's course so that the *Glicca* might put into Naharius.

2

Handbook to the Planets, for whatever reason, had little to say about Naharius. After citing geo-physical statistics, the text went on to state:

> The population of Naharius, for a variety of reasons, is relatively sparse and is concentrated in the neighborhood of Trajence, a partially urbanized settlement adjacent to the spaceport.
>
> A few miles east of Trajence an extinct volcano, Mount Maldoun, rises from a line of low hills. Down the mountainside flow three streams, which, after seeping through wooded vales grown over with unique plants and mosses, become charged, according to local beliefs, with remarkable powers.
>
> Even more potent are the waters from the sacred springs appearing at the base of the mountain. These waters, when used in conjunction with the therapies provided by local practitioners, reputedly neutralize the ravages of time and are said to restore at least the superficial aspects of youth. Such reports, whether or not accurate, attract ailing and aged persons from far and wide, hoping to participate in a miracle.
>
> What is the truth regarding the therapies? Rigorous evidence is hard to come by. The *Handbook* advises caution.

3

The *Glicca* arrived at the Trajence spaceport. Other vessels were docked at the far end of the field; the *Glodwyn* was not among them.

Wingo and Schwatzendale rode an omnibus into town, while Maloof and Myron set off to learn what they could of Dame Hester Lajoie. They inquired first at the three principal clinics, then at less formal facilities.

During the afternoon of the second day they were referred to the Wayfarer's Hospice, a cheerless block of gray concrete on the

outskirts of the settlement, which provided terminal shelter
for the aged, the ailing, and the indigent. An orderly conducted
them into a cavernous chamber, dim and ill-smelling, lined along
the walls with narrow cots, at the moment only partially occupied. He indicated a cot at the far end of the chamber, then returned to his station and left them to their own devices.

Maloof and Myron approached the indicated cot. Under the
sheet a thin and fragile shape barely created an outline. A gaunt
head protruded, the skin drawn drum-taut around the contours
of the skull. Arms brittle as twigs, terminating in bird-like
claws, lay on the sheet beside the body.

Myron studied the bony wisp, controlling inner spasms of
pity and horror, with an effort. A limp straggle of maroon hair,
a long, pointed chin, and a twisted tendril of what once had been
a rapacious nose identified a version of Dame Hester Lajoie.

A slight up-and-down shift of the sheet indicated that vitality was not yet exhausted. Peering into the dull eyes, Myron
thought to see a flicker of recognition. Her lips twitched; her
throat clenched; she produced a rasping sound. Myron leaned
forward and thought to hear her say: "You have come at last."
Her voice faded; then once again she managed to whisper: "It is
very late. They took all my money, then they abused me, and
cheated my hope, and put me here to take my wonderful life
from me."

Myron could think of nothing to say.

As if driven by an obsession, gasping and wheezing, Dame
Hester contrived to tell the bitter tale of what had befallen her.
In the beginning, the practitioners, after receipt of their fees,
had seemed to fall in with her requirements. They started her
on a regimen of standard therapy, which she found overly stringent, but which they would not modify. There was arduous exercise; she was fed coarse black biscuits and a thin grassy soup.
Daily she was rubbed with a few minims of water from one of
the magic springs, and daily she ingested a gill of a secret ichor
compounded from water of the three most potent streams.

As time went on, the practitioners took more of her money,
but she discerned no significant changes in her personal attributes. The practitioners warned her against impatience and continued the regimen; but the metamorphosis into lissome new
youth was slow in coming.

She complained, but the practitioners only demanded more money. At last Dame Hester dispensed with their services and embarked upon a therapy of her own devising, and instead of one regimen, she undertook three at the same time. Instead of careful lavations with a few minims of the miraculous water, she bathed daily in one or another of the springs, and imbibed gallons of the fabulous flow of the streams.

In the end she achieved nothing, and indeed became listless and ill; finally, her constitution gave way and she collapsed. The practitioners, when they found that she had no more money, refused to help her, stating that she had brought mortifaction upon herself and must now formulate her own solution to the problem. Eventually they sent her to the hospice.

Dame Hester sighed and gasped. "It has been a dreadful time." She paused, then, clenching and unclenching her claw-like fingers, spoke on. Now, she stated, all would be mended if Myron would whisk her back to Salou Sain, where she would surely recover her health, and all would be as before.

Myron asked cautiously: "What happened to Marko Fassig?"

The frail body quivered. The rasping whisper became hectic. "He was the worst traitor of all! He stole the *Glodwyn* and took it Beyond. There was news that pirates had killed him, which I will never regret, but the *Glodwyn* is gone forever. No matter; back at Salou Sain there will be another *Glodwyn*." She fell silent; her eyelids drooped. Then she spoke in a husky whisper: "I have done you a wrong; I am now filled with remorse. Once more at Salou Sain I will make amends." The whisper faded into silence, and again the eyelids drooped. She lay still, and signs of respiration were no longer evident.

Maloof said in a sepulchral voice: "She has gone into a coma."

Myron studied the still form. "No; there is still something going on."

A moment passed. The still figure gave a convulsive jerk; the eyelids lifted. She spoke in a guttural croak: "It is folly! There is nothing more—the doom is on me. I shall never breathe the sweet air of home again. I will do now what I must." She reached a trembling arm to the table beside the cot, took up a stylus, and scrawled hasty words and sentences upon a sheet of paper. When she had finished she dropped the pencil and let her arm sag upon the cot. She closed her eyes and lay still.

Myron took up the paper and read what Dame Hester had written. "It is a will," he told Maloof. "She leaves everything she owns to me."

Maloof scrutinized the document. "It appears to be valid, and I am a reputable witness."

Myron folded the document and tucked it into his pocket. For a time the two men watched the still figure. The eyes remained closed, and there was no further rise and fall of the sheet. Maloof said at last: "I think that she is dead."

"I think so, too," said Myron.

After another few moments Maloof stirred. "There is nothing to be gained by waiting."

"No," said Myron. "Nothing at all."

The two men left the chamber. In the front office they informed the orderly that the person whom they had come to visit was dead. The orderly showed neither surprise nor concern, but appraised the two spacemen sidelong. "You are evidently blood relatives of the deceased?"

"By no means," said Maloof. "We are here only to oblige a friend, who himself is indigent."

"A pity," said the orderly. "Still, for sixty sols I can arrange a fine funeral with pyrotechnics, a priest, athletic contests, and dancing children waving colored scarves to the music of a belphorn."

Maloof said: "This sort of rite is unnecessary. The dead, during or after cremation, are indifferent to such a display; at least, this is my experience. A simple ceremony at minimum cost will suffice."

"Bah," muttered the orderly. "I can provide a simple ceremony for ten sols. There will be no dignitaries on hand, and the only music will be five recorded fanfares. For another sol, I will provide three sticks of incense."

Myron paid over ten sols. "You may omit the incense."

"As you like."

4

After a three-day layover at Port Tanjee, the *Glicca* was scheduled to continue onward to Salou Sain, where Myron now had important business to transact in connection with Dame Hester's estate. Captain Maloof agreed, however, to another detour; on this occasion, the *Glicca* would call at the city Duvray on the world Alcydon, site of the Pan-Arts Museum, and more importantly, the residence of Tibbet Garwig.

The *Glicca* landed at the Duvray spaceport. Myron gathered the parcels intended for Tibbet, departed the *Glicca*, and rode by taxicab through the elegant city into the fashionable Ranglin Heights district, to the Garwig residence: an imposing mansion at the back of a garden. Myron alighted and, after arranging for the cab to wait, set off along the path which led through the garden.

Almost immediately he was confronted by a pair of objects standing at either side of the path: statues twelve feet tall, apparently wrought by a mad genius in the avant-garde mode, as icons to represent his contempt for ordinary conventions of society. The objects were constructed of unusual materials, spars of metal, and twisted, pitted shapes contorted as if half-in half-out of another dimension. Gray-pink tubing looking unpleasantly like viscera wound in and out of the other materials. Myron stared at the objects in wonder; the Garwigs evidently were members of a clique where such demonstrations were fashionable. Odd, indeed!

He continued up the path to the front entrance, a massive door at the back of a short portico. The door lacked knob, latch, handle, or other such device; Myron looked in vain for a bell-push or knocker. Fixed to the door was a heavy demon-mask of antique copper, the features molded in high relief to express a leer of malignant triumph—or perhaps some other horrid emotion. The eyes bulged; the ears were distorted wads; a long black tongue dangled from the mouth. Myron gave his head a grim shake: here was another phase of avant-garde doctrine, where shock and novelty were accorded the highest priority. He wondered to what extent Tibbet had been infected; it was a depressing thought. He looked again for a bell-push, a toggle, or other signalling device, but as before found nothing. He pounded the door with his knuckles but produced only a muffled thump; he kicked the door with like result. Then, as a last resort, Myron pulled at the dangling tongue, and immediately from within came a peculiar fluting ululation, a quasi-musical sequence of

discords lacking all charm, but which Myron nevertheless found
intriguing; he pulled at the tongue a second time, eliciting a new,
equally random set of discords. Strange! he thought. It was not
music but the studious creation of non-music: another avant-
garde demonstration! He reached to pull at the tongue a third
time, but the door swung aside.

In the opening stood a tall woman wearing a house-maid's
uniform, bearing an expression of annoyance. She swept Myron
up and down with a severe gaze, then said: "What, sir, are your
needs?"

Myron drew together the shreds of his dignity. "I am calling
upon the Lady Tibbet. Be so good as to announce my presence."

The maid regarded him without sympathy. "That is beyond
my ability, sir. The Lady is not on the premises."

"Oh? In that case, if you expect her back within a reasonable
time, I will wait."

"That would not be practical, sir. Lady Tibbet and her husband are off-world, at the Palisades on Frantock, collecting
shards for the Museum. Do you care to leave a message?"

"Yes," said Myron. "You may mention that Peter Birdsong
called on a matter of no great importance."

"Very well, sir."

5

Myron returned to the cab and was conveyed back to the spaceport. Aboard the *Glicca*, Captain Maloof, Schwatzendale, and
Wingo were in the galley, taking a mid-morning collation of tea
and pastries. Myron went quietly to his quarters, stowed the
parcels in a locker, changed into his ordinary clothes, then stood
irresolute. At last he shrugged; there was nothing to be gained by
delay. He drew a deep breath, squared his shoulders, and
marched from his cabin, across the saloon, and into the galley.
He seated himself, poured a cup of tea, and took a lemon tart
from the tray.

His shipmates watched him with mild curiosity. Wingo at
last spoke. "You are back early. How went the affair?"

Myron made a measured response. "All in all, the 'affair', as
you put it, went smoothly, though in a negative direction." After

a moment of rumination, he added: "If anyone is interested, I will mention that there is no longer any connection between Tibbet Garwig and myself."

"We are politely interested, of course," said Maloof. "I cannot help but notice that you seem quite definite in this regard."

"I could not be more so," said Myron. He sipped moodily from his cup.

Wingo at last spoke. "If you wish to explain in greater detail, we will listen with care."

Myron slumped back in his chair. "Very well; you shall have the facts in their full regalia. I rode by cab to the Garwig mansion without so much as an inkling of doom. I arranged for the cab to wait, then set off through the garden toward the house. Almost at once I was confronted by a pair of what I shall call 'statues'; they stood twelve feet tall and were fabricated in the avant-garde style. I found them not only lacking in charm, but actively offensive. I was disturbed; the Garwigs would never have chosen such a site for their statues had they not themselves been members of an avant-garde clique."

Myron went on to describe the massive front door, the copper demon-mask with its dangling black tongue, and the wailing discords produced when the tongue was pulled. He told of his encounter with the housemaid and her information regarding Tibbet. "I disguised my emotions and, returning to the cab, was conveyed back to the *Glicca*. At this time most of the emotions have subsided, and now I feel only gratitude to whatever agency is responsible for my narrow escape—destiny, lurulu, or blind stupid luck."

"Hm," said Wingo, smiling. "Myron uses the word 'luck', which, of course, is simple fatalism. But essentially he recognizes the presence of subliminal forces working at most delicate levels." He looked to Myron. "Am I right?"

Myron shrugged. "Better to say that I am confused."

Wingo spoke seriously. "The circumstances are mysterious. 'Destiny' is what happens; 'lurulu' is far more delicate, and in Myron's case, it exerts a protective influence—which, of course, is most interesting."

"Balderdash," said Schwatzendale, tilting his head and arching his eyebrows at different angles.

Myron said: "Tibbet will certainly be confused when she tries to identify 'Peter Birdsong'."

Captain Maloof rose to his feet. "Perhaps I alone am not confused, since for the moment I have become an unalloyed fatalist. I can see, without ambiguity, that the time has come for us to continue our voyage. On the alert—seal the ports; make ready for departure."

6

The *Glicca* arrived at the world Vermazen, and settled upon the spaceport at Salou Sain. On the day after arrival, Myron visited the Municipal Conservancy, where Dame Hester's last will and testament was validated with a gratifying absence of formality. Myron found himself in possession of an unexpectedly large estate, which included the grand mansion Sarbiter House on Dingle Terrace.

Myron hired a domestic staff; then he and his shipmates took up residence among the luxurious precincts of the mansion, where they quickly developed an extremely agreeable pattern of existence. When the days were fine, they took long and languorous breakfasts in the garden. During the afternoons, they sometimes wandered into town, alone or as a group. Most often, though, they remained at the house lounging beside the pool, consuming fruit punches, and socializing with new acquaintances.

Dinners were formal, in the wood-panelled dining room, under a chandelier of a thousand glittering crystals. There were always seven, eight, or even nine courses, enhanced by dusty bottles brought up from the cellars.

After dinner, the four usually moved into the dim old library, where a fire burned in the stone fireplace, and chairs upholstered in soft leather awaited their coming. Decanters charged with spirits, essences, and distillations of notable marks were ready to hand. Conversation touched upon many topics and often continued into the late hours. Persons of recent acquaintance were discussed and their attributes analyzed; or the talk might wander to remote ports of call and the odd folk who dwelt in far places. Profundities sometimes entered the conversation, usually in response to Wingo's predilection for abstruse philosophy. Occasionally the word 'lurulu' was mentioned, and it developed that each of the four invested the word with a different significance.

During such discussions Maloof had little to say, and Myron even less, but Schwatzendale enlivened the discourse with fanciful conjectures, which Wingo felt compelled to qualify or refute before resuming his own remarks.

"If you recall, we were speaking of lurulu. At the risk of banality, I will point out that 'fate', 'destiny', and 'lurulu' are not synonymous. 'Fate' is dark and ponderous; 'destiny' is more like a beautiful sunset. In speaking of 'lurulu', however, language of this kind is not useful. Lurulu is personal; it is like hope, or a wistful longing, more real than a dream."

"Bah," grumbled Schwatzendale. "Wingo has become a poet; he decorates the air with verbal finery, in the same way that he frosts his pastry with fine icing."

Wingo sighed. "My purposes are not ignoble; I believe the cosmos to be a thing of many complexities, most of which have no linkage with the words of our language, and can only be addressed through the use of allusion."

"Bah!" said Schwatzendale again. "Balderdash, of the purest stripe! The language serves us very well; why turn it inside-out to describe something which isn't there in the first place?"

Maloof poured wine from the decanter into his goblet. "Your motives are not under attack, but abstract language is not necessary to discuss lurulu, when sitting next to you, not a yard away, is the real thing—I refer to Myron, naturally. He is strong, personable, sound of wind; he has an easy disposition and a full head of hair. He lives in a palace; he has more wealth than he can count, and he wants for nothing. The girls find him appealing, and they cluster around him in a nimbus of charming vitality. If Myron needs someone to peel him a grape, or to scratch an inconvenient itch, he need only cock an eyebrow and the task is accomplished; Myron is the very embodiment of lurulu!"

Myron leaned back in his chair. "I don't know. If I look in the mirror, I see someone quite ordinary, only lucky enough to have Dame Hester Lajoie for an aunt."

Schwatzendale amended the statement: "Better to say, for a dead aunt."

Myron nodded. "Just so. In any case, it is not so easy as you might think. Half the time I feel guilty, as if I had been caught with my hand in the cookie jar." Myron looked from face to face. "You are laughing at me."

"Such qualms are hardly surprising," said Maloof. "I shouldn't worry about them overmuch."

Myron agreed. "But sometimes another mood comes on me. I feel nervous, or restless, and I have a dim intuition as to the cause." Myron leaned forward and stared into the fire. "I would feel more secure if the three of you were always to share this lurulu with me."

For a time the four sat in silence, gazing into the fire. Then Maloof said quietly: "Your intuition is correct. Transience cannot be altered. Your program, for all its idyllic qualities, never has been feasible. I am not a natural sybarite, content to live in an enchanted dream; I am restless, and possibly Wingo and Schwatzendale as well. The *Glicca* has been totally overhauled— it gleams with fresh enamel and new metal; the galley flaunts some splendid new equipment. At the moment it sits at the side of the yard like an abandoned waif." Maloof laughed. "Could the *Glicca* be lonely? It is a point I must take up with Wingo— although I can see by his face that he has doubts."

"Not necessarily," declared Wingo. "It is a tantalizing thought."

Schwatzendale yawned and rose to his feet. "At this moment I still enjoy decadence, and I am trying to break several records in the field. The life of a full-fledged epicurean, dancing with flowers and smelling beautiful ladies, requires more strength of character than I can deploy at this time! I am off to bed—good night, all." He departed the library and was presently followed by Maloof and Wingo, and finally Myron, leaving the fire to flicker to a smoulder in the silent library.

7

On several occasions Myron visited his father and mother at the family home in Lilling. The visits were never wholly

comfortable, since his parents had never abandoned the hope
that Myron might be induced to remain at Lilling and take up a
position at the Exchange, where he could work in association
with his father. Such a step could be the basis for a most cred-
itable career, and would certainly enhance Myron's reputation.
Myron politely rejected these proposals, citing his commitments at Salou Sain.

Once Myron urged his parents to spend some time with him
at Salou Sain. The invitation was accepted, and in due course the
parents travelled to Salou Sain, to spend two days at Sarbiter
House. During this time the elderly Tanys used the utmost propriety, and irreproachable good manners, but were secretly perturbed by the casual conduct of Myron and his companions.
They thankfully returned to Lilling, convinced that Myron's
friends were vagabonds, intent upon infecting him with their
own deplorable standards.

Weeks passed, and departure from Salou Sain began to be
openly discussed. Finally, during one dreary dinner a definite
date was fixed upon, a date a week and a half hence.

The days now took on a different character, each with its distinctive identity. Captain Maloof, Wingo, and Schwatzendale
visited the *Glicca* and were occasionally joined by Myron, but
more often Myron remained alone at Sarbiter House, thinking
dismal thoughts.

A day and a half before departure, Myron was galvanized by
a sudden impulse. He visited his bank and his legal representative, made arrangements with an estate agent, dismissed the domestic staff, hired caretakers, and packed his personal gear. On
the appointed day, at the specified hour, the *Glicca* departed the
Salou Sain spaceport. Aboard were Captain Maloof, Schwatzendale, Wingo, and, to no one's surprise, Myron Tany.